AUTOBIOGRAPHY

OF THE

LOWER EAST SIDE

A Novel in Short Stories by

RASHIDAH ISMAILI

Northampton House Press

Cover design by Naia Poyer from photographs by Daoud Abubakr and Shawn Walker, with thanks.

Northampton House e-edition, 2014

Northampton House Press trade paper edition, 2014, ISBN 978-1-937997-39-7.

10 9 8 7 6 5 4 3 2.

Acknowledgments

For this book, I would like to thank all those whose lives have touched mine on the Lower East Side. It is a testimony to the things we shared that most of us are still friends and in touch fifty years later. I thank those who read the work and for their honest critiques. Most of all, I want to remember Tom Feelings, who introduced me to Umbra and artists of African descent living there during the early 60s. These wonderful creative people have both inspired me and comforted me all these years. I don't want to list all the names for fear of forgetting someone, but must mention David Henderson, Steve Cannon, Tom Dent, Valerie Maynard, Askia Toure, Archie Shepp, Calvin Herton, Joe Johnson, Dorothy White, Amiri Baraka, Ishmael Reed, and Diane di Prima. It was a heady time and I am a better human being as the result of that experience.

AUTOBIOGRAPHY
OF THE LOWER
EAST SIDE

Stories

IN THE BEGINNING, NUSA

It's late August 1959 on the Lower East Side. Nusa and her small son are in the back of a taxi carrying them from the Westside to the east. When the cab turns onto East 10th Street, the driver curses and quickly raises the windows. Nusa is temporarily distracted from her sad thoughts as, outside, the streets are bombarded by a gushing fire hydrant. The driver's honking only adds to the sport. Children squeal in delight, running from side to side of the narrow street, clad in a variety of swimwear: panties, boxer shorts, bathing suits, skirts, blouses, trousers, whatever they were wearing when the valve was opened. Cars slow to a stop behind them. More honking as water pummels the taxi.

"Jesus! Where are the parents? Don't they know this is dangerous?" the driver asks, but he gets no response from Nusa. It's two weeks before school is to start, and the streets radiate under the late New York summer sun. From a distance a siren wails. Cars halt, then inch slowly eastward. A police car comes up from East 10th Street, headed west, right toward them. A big, red-faced cop gets out. Most of the laughing children ignore him. The policeman opens the trunk of the cruiser and takes out a familiar tool, the big wrench that shuts off the water.

"Boo, boo!" All the children, soaked and dripping head to toe, yell at the policeman. He does not look over, just twirls and twirls the iron tool until their water is reduced to a gush, a trickle, and then no more. Some of the smaller kids sit in the puddles. Others grab towels and wrap them around their bodies.

The unairconditioned taxi is so hot Nusa's glad when the driver opens the windows. Water slides down the panes. The top of the hood glistens. At last they arrive at 404 East 10th Street. A woman she met at dance class had told her about this building. That the apartments were small, but one was available on the upper floor.

So Nusa went to see the owner. He also owns a furniture store on the corner of Avenue C and East 10th. The man asked a lot of questions, and only one or two had to do with her ability to pay the rent. "Are you on welfare? If so, I'll only take you if you give me a letter with the social worker's name and telephone."

She opened her mouth to assure him she wasn't on welfare, but he kept talking.

"Oh yeah, also that form that says the monthly rent checks will be mailed directly to me. I've had my experiences with you people. So sign over the rights so the money comes directly to me, or I won't give you a lease."

After being assured she was employed and a full-time student at a prominent university, and prepared to give him two months security and first month's rent, he stopped the monologue.

Some of the next questions he'd asked were too personal and she'd refused to answer them. "I'm looking for safe housing for myself and my son. Not a therapist."

He drew back then. Her friend had told her he was having a hard time getting a reliable tenant so she knew he was testing her. They'd finally settled and now, here she is, ready to inhabit the small space that's to be home for at least three years.

Now, sitting in the taxi, she looks again at the building. It is dull brick, at least seventy-five years old. These tenements sheltered weary nineteenth-century immigrants. Now, at the end of the nineteen -fifties, Nusa is joining the new retinue of migrants to this part of town.

Two old people sitting on milk crates are watching. The super and his wife. Actually it's the diminutive old woman who does most of the work. Nusa's friend says everyone calls her "The Gnome" because of her size, and her supernaturally-sudden appearances from the stairwells. The former super died a decade ago. At first his widow took care of the building. But as she got older, the husband of her friend The Gnome said he could do the work. He was really looking for a chance to get an apartment for free. So now he's called the super, and The Gnome struggles with the bucket and dirty mop. Pulling and pushing both mop and broom, lifting those long skirts that get trapped under the heavy pail. But now, they both sit silently, giving Nusa a long, bone-through stare, double pairs of eyes assessing her.

She shakes herself from these musings and opens her purse to pay. The taxi driver takes her money. When she hands over a significant tip, as if to make up for his apparent earlier misgivings about accepting her as a passenger, he mutters, "Thanks."

She gets out and begins unloading boxes, carrying them inside the cool dark hallways of the building. Her boy tumbles out of the back seat clutching a wooden truck, standing gazing up at the building that's to be his new home, facing the two impassive guards at its entrance.

A few of the boxes are heavy but Nusa's young and strong. She braces her legs and firmly grips two. The driver gets out, takes the bigger one from her, and carries it inside the doorway. "Gotta be careful these days. Junkies can snatch up your stuff quicker'n you can lay it down."

Junkies. It's a new word; she isn't sure what it means or who they might be. But she stores it in her head on a growing list to remember.

Finally her things are all inside. During the unloading the married pair never said a word, never moved or made an effort to help. Their pasty faces remain expressionless, eyes averted, focused on some spot across the street. She ignores them, only intent on getting things inside the dark hall and up the flight of stairs before them.

"Come Moussa, up the stairs to our apartment," she directs, carrying a box. "Up, up, up we go."

He sings as his sturdy, almost five-year-old legs climb the creaking stairs.

"Next floor," she instructs. "Ah. Here we are." A sharp turn left, and there's the door to their new dwelling. She sets the box down, finds her keys, and unlocks it. "Come along," she says, urging the boy inside.

The first room is bare and white. In the afternoon light from two windows at the right side of the apartment and a limited brightness from a small kitchen window, it all looks open and fresh.

She sets the box on a long counter near the sink. The little room to the left is to be the boy's bedroom. There's a small kitchen that separates his room from the largest one. It will serve a dual purpose, her bedroom and a parlor.

She rubs her arms, which ache from the weight of so many boxes. She opens windows in the living room and looks out at wild trees growing in the backyard space between buildings. There's a good deal of debris down there: discarded toys; ragged clothes; lots of empty, broken bottles. She pulls her head back inside and lowers the windows at the bottom, then opens them at the top. It seems safer.

In the kitchen a little window faces the next building, which looks equally dim, opaque with grime just as many decades old. Moussa's room has one small window with a rusty screen. She goes to the sink, finds a cleaning cloth, and wipes away dust so the boy doesn't breathe it in. Later, she promises herself, I'll do a thorough cleaning.

She needs to get back downstairs to bring up more things. She searches her big bag and finds an apple and another of his Vermont wooden toys. She washes it and sits him in the doorway between his room and the kitchen. Says sternly, "Moussa, I must bring up some more things. You are not to touch anything or go out the door." He looks up and nods.

With her keys in her pocket she runs down to the first floor. She carries up the smallest ones first, to lessen time between the intervals of checking on him and grabbing a rest before she starts back up. Nusa makes about six trips, always staying a few moments with him. The apple's almost eaten. He's lined up the toys and is playing with them. Finally, exhausted, she hides the largest boxes under the stairwell for later and goes upstairs.

She selects a bag where her cleaning things, soap and steel wool, are packed. A brief wipe of the white stove yields little dirt. The oven is clear of creatures. Con Edison had come the day before to connect gas and lights. With the summer days so bright and long, Nusa thinks she won't need to use much electricity.

"Mama, I need to write something," Moussa calls out. His little dark-cocoa face lifts up to her. The look, so familiar, brings momentary pain.

"Yes, Papis. Let me find it." She mostly addresses him this way, in the house or privately: *Little father*.

She turns from one box to another, searching, but they're all the same size. Reading the labels, she realizes his assortment of crayons, a professional paint set given him by one of her former classmates last year for his fourth birthday, and all his puzzles and games are in one of the large boxes still downstairs.

"Oh, I remember. They're in the box I left for Baba to bring up when he comes."

A frown. "But Mama, I need it now."

"Fine. You'll have to come with me, then, and help bring it up here."

The frown disappears. "I can do it. I'm a big boy. And the apple gives me strength. Look at this." He spreads his arms and stands taller, flexing miniature muscles for her to feel.

Nusa obliges, touching one and squeezing the other. "Oh, my! I am impressed. Good, now let's get the keys and go search for your paper and pen. This is a serious mission. Are you prepared to accept it?"

He stands soldierly, arms rigid, pinned to his sides. "Ready, *madame.*"

"Then follow me."

They march down the creaking stairs to the first floor. Nusa locates the big box and they take out a checkerboard and a wooden paint box.

Moussa says, "I can carry that." He puts the board under one arm and picks up a box that looks like a little suitcase.

"Just a moment, we need to find—oh, here it is." She pulls out a package of typing paper and a big brown portfolio with drawing paper from beneath the tin that holds a bag of farm toys and his play men.

"Mama! I need those."

So she searches for a bag to put the smaller items in and packs a few other things to take up to his room. His father will be coming later in a friend's truck with furniture for Moussa's room. School will begin in about two weeks. She needs to have the place in order before then.

She carries the bag of toys to the little room and then turns to him. "Papis, this is your bedroom. Set your things up here. Baba's coming later. Then we can put it together just the way you want." He stands in the middle of the floor with his wooden truck hanging from one hand, gazing around. "My room?"

"Yes darling, all yours."

"Hurrah!" he shouts, jumping up and down, running around the small space.

Nusa feels a pang of guilt because the apartment is so small. They'd been living in a big loft a little northwest of East 10th Street. But times are changing. Her husband's about to leave them. It's supposed to be a short separation; his old professor has gotten him a position in the Music Department at USC. There he can take courses towards his doctorate in Ethnomusicology. He'll also teach two classes and, in addition, be a graduate assistant to Dr. Katz.

But that's not all. Nusa is not convinced a separation will bring them back together. Maybe if they'd gone back home to their parents or her aunt, she could've explained the feelings that curled up in her stomach and settled under her heart. But the quivers stay there, unseen and unheard. With this move, and the actual date of his departure set, the movements have accelerated. Now, in addition, her left eyelid twitches. The first time she felt it Nusa ran to a mirror to see what was wrong. Peering in, she stared until the tiny movement happened again. She has a word for it now: spasm. It's not too strong a description. Or perhaps: tic. Yes, that's what it is. A tic.

Well, Nusa thinks, and sighs as she begins to take dishes from a box and put them on shelves over the little sink. We didn't go home. Perhaps it was all for the good. That money allowed us to move and get a few things for Moussa and pay for my last semester.

Completing her master's thesis is a major hurdle confronting her, along with the boy's first class in preschool. She turns now to look at him, pride and love swelling in her chest. He looks so much like his father. The same long slim fingers, his skin an even flow of dark brown over slender limbs.

Well, on with it. She reaches for another dish.

"Mama, where's our bathroom?" Moussa looks puzzled.

Nusa smiles. "Let's have another adventure."

"Yes, yes!"

They further explore the small apartment. There are double doors just inside the back room, where she will sleep. She walks over and knocks on one, then softly calls, "Are you the bathroom?"

Moussa covers his mouth, stifling a giggle.

She puts her ear to the door. "Hmm. I don't hear anyone. Do you?" She steps back.

He presses an ear to the door too, and then takes a step back. "Hello! Anyone in there?" He turns to her, in a very serious pose. "What if we try opening the door and having a look about?"

As she tries the doorknob Moussa claps and jumps up and down. But a fresh layer of paint has caked the little white knobs and apparently stuck the doors together. She pulls harder and finally one of the doors opens. But the space is only an empty closet. She stands staring into it. "Oh. No bathroom."

"But Mama, I need a toilet." He shifts from one foot to the other.

Now she remembers her friend had said most of the toilets were outside in the hall. She opens her door and they go to look. There, across from them, to the right of the apartment facing theirs, is a door with a small padlock. Stepping closer, she sees two little keys are dangling from the lock. This handle does turn when she tries it; a small toilet with a tiny window over it looks back at them. In the tight space there's a little sink basin. Over it a towel bar and, on the floor some worn, torn lino. Still, the fresh white walls make it appear pleasant.

"There. We found it." She leaves him to do his business and rushes back inside to get a roll of toilet paper and a little cup. She returns as he is finishing. The water runs a bit rusty at first. She fills the cup and hands it to him. "Here, Papis. Clean yourself."

Moussa takes the cup, pours the water on his privates and then wipes with the toilet paper.

"Good. Now your hands."

He lets the water run over his hands and she gives him a wad of toilet paper to dry them. "We must get a towel in here later."

They close and lock their toilet, and go back inside the apartment. Walking around her new living space, she organizes it in her head. Books sit under the windows for now, but she will need a few bookcases. She decides to keep those against the walls and under the windows in order to have more free space. There's an opening with two shelves like a window between the kitchen and bedroom. This is where I'll place some of my pottery or maybe a plant, she tells herself. Turning back to the window, she wonders how to brighten up that corner.

"Moussa, I need to clean this window. Why don't you go do your writing and drawing until I'm finished? Then I'll get supper ready so when Baba comes we can eat."

He nods, but looks anxious. "Where will we sit?"

She smiles at him. "Oh, maybe we'll pretend it's a picnic and eat on the floor."

"Oh yes, let's have a picnic." Satisfied, he goes to his room to play.

Soon the window sheds its dusty coat and the transparent glass reveals the wall of a building very close to theirs. But the screen's so badly corroded, when she attempts to pry it out of the grooves it crumbles. She shuts the window again, thinking, Never mind. A bright curtain and a plant will take care of this gloomy spot.

She sets out to find pots, pans, and something to cook. In one of the boxes she put rice, oil, and a few spices, but she needs more for a meal. When Moussa's father comes he'll want to eat. "Come, Papis. Let's go shopping. We need fresh vegetables for supper."

"Just a moment," he calls back.

She checks her purse. There's enough until she can get to the bank tomorrow.

Out on the streets, sidewalks glimmer. The couple, still out front like guards, stops talking as she and her son leave the building. Neither says anything.

Nusa heads to the corner of Avenue C and East 10th Street, and turns south. Here there are lots of pushcarts, the Eastern European vendors all chatting with each other. Nusa looks at some pale, wilted lettuce and keeps going. On East 8th Street there's a big tree and under it one lone cart. She wonders why no others are taking advantage of the shade it offers.

When she stops in front of the cart she sees another reason why the old woman tending it must prefer this spot: a steady flow of water coming from a hydrant up the street. The woman has taken off her shoes and is standing in the flow. Her long skirt ripples along the top of the current. She smiles at Nusa. "You like?"

Nusa does indeed. These fruits and vegetables are not hot and wilted. She selects two bags full. The boy carries the fruits, grapes and three oranges. The bulging shopping bag in her left hand is like a moving still-life painting. Deep purple aubergines separated from verdant spinach by shocking orange carrots, leafy green bottoms up. She keeps a lighter load in her right hand to have it free in case the boy should fall. Or for any kind of emergency, and of course for crossings. The streets are overflowing and people here do not obey any decent etiquette, going forward on the left and passing on the right. Nusa always walks so the shops and office buildings and apartments are to the right of the boy.

Often when she wears full African dress people stare and give them a wide berth. Today she has on a loose flowing top. The pants actually belong to her husband. She cut them off to her own height when Hamid stopped wearing them. She's noticed he no longer wears any of his African clothes, except the woven outfit his parents sent him along with a matching set for Moussa, and an up-and-down for her. They wore these garments to his graduation concert. All his friends gave many compliments. Some asked about buying similar outfits for themselves. But of course that's not possible. This is his family's pattern, encoded with the symbols of his lineage. So now she wears his old pants of red, yellow, and orange print with a star shadowed in black. Her top she got from an old woman at the mosque who was selling them one Friday after *jumah.*

"Mama, am I allowed one of those?" Moussa points to a woman scraping at a fast-melting block of ice on a to-go cart. Bottles of colored liquid sit in a row, at hand. Children and grown-ups alike are clamoring, shouting their preferences.

"No, darling. That's just colored sugar. But when we get upstairs, I will make you the best dessert you've ever had."

Moussa nods, but with little enthusiasm. He looks over one shoulder longingly. "What kind?"

"Oh, that's the best part. My special top secret. No spying until it's all done."

They head east on 10th Street and are soon at their building again. Out of the sun, the halls look cooler but really it's just dusty air coming in the open, dirty windows. While the hot building blocks much of the stifling summer breeze, Nusa thinks the air feels too humid. It might be going to rain. When they reach their door, she puts the bags down and gets out her keys. Moussa again has to run to the toilet. She unloads the bags inside and stands in the doorway waiting for the boy to finish and wash properly.

"Now, it's my turn." She uses the toilet and locks it behind her. It's probably not a good idea to leave it unlocked while they're out. Although it's very small, there is not much space for anyone to hide. This little room cannot contain two people at the same time without serious maneuvering.

Their shoes sit neatly lined up next to the front door on a clean piece of newspaper. She'll get a real mat later. She makes a game of washing and putting away vegetables and fruits. An empty milk crate she found downstairs has become a stool, and Moussa stands on it dropping grapes into the sink. He washes and sets them on the towel she places atop the covered bathtub. When everything is clean Nusa puts most of the produce in the small white refrigerator. Moussa returns to his room to play and she cooks supper. The window by the stove is open and she imagines the good cooking smells wafting outside to perfume the stagnant air.

She shuts off the gas and lets the pots simmer, cracking the door open so cross-ventilation can cool the stifling little apartment. When a fly slips in she chases him out with the flick of a dish towel and shuts the door. In the other room, the sun is beginning to darken. An orange wash dims the dull bricks into a mottled chiaroscuro.

"Papis, look. The sun is leaving us."

He comes running. "But where will it go?"

"Oh, west, as usual. The sun sets in the west, and we are now on the East Side. Maybe tomorrow we'll walk over to the East River."

"Yes," he agrees, nodding sagely. "We are on the east side." He stands looking at the tall wild trees out in the backyard area between their building and the next. "I have a paint just like that." He points out at the changing colors.

The sound of voices, the thump of footsteps out in the hall distracts him. "Mama, Baba is home!" He runs to the door.

Nusa follows, listening for her husband's voice. She opens the door and he comes in with two other men, strangers. Kisses her lightly on the lips and then bends to kiss Moussa. "*Salaam alaiykum*, Mous-Mous."

He slips out of his shoes. The men in the hall push bed parts through the open door. Nusa pulls Moussa out of the way. They gradually finish and come in to set up the boy's room. She offers them supper but they both decline, saying they have to get home.

Hamid goes outside and settles up with them. She hears the door of the toilet shut.

Nusa spreads a cloth on the floor and, after washing their hands, they eat. Moussa always loves it when they have African dishes.

"Mama, where is it?" he asks, in the middle of the meal.

"Where is what?"

"You know. The best dessert in the world."

"Ah, yes. Well, as soon as we finish and then—we'll have it."

"Look, I ate already all my food. See, Baba."

He has indeed eaten well. "Tell you what, I'll clear things away. Baba will bathe you, and then we'll all have our treat."

Hamid takes Moussa to the toilet. She clears the tub and replaces the cover. Then she goes to the refrigerator, gets out the freshly made sorbet, and scoops it into glass goblets. She puts a wafer on the side of each dish.

Moussa runs to sit on the mat again. "Oh, look. Baba," he says, licking the spoon. "This is good. Eat yours, too." Hamid isn't much of a sweets person, though.

Nusa leaves them to enjoy these moments together. She makes up the boy's bed. After washing, a second trip to the toilet, and remembering to clean his teeth, Moussa settles under the covers, head in his father's lap as he listens to a story. Nusa stands in the doorway and worries. How will it be when Baba's not here anymore and bedtime comes? Will Moussa be upset? She reads to him often, of course, but now she wonders.

Tic. Her left eye flickers. She knows, in spite of what Hamid says, that this is the end of their marriage.

In the few nights remaining, until he takes a midnight flight to Los Angeles, she must garner as much lovemaking as possible. Lying next to him as he sleeps soundly Nusa watches his chest rise and fall. The tears that trickle onto her cheeks she quickly wipes away lest they fall on Hamid and wake him. She props her head on one hand and breathes in his male scent, slowly letting sleep overtake her.

Finally, Friday night comes. Soon, around eight-thirty, Hamid's friend will come to take him to Idlewild Airport. The suitcases are packed and sit next to his shoes by the door. Nusa tries to dislodge the hard lump in her throat. Moussa is in the bath, squealing with joy as his father pours water over his head. She has let them have almost the entire day together, without her. Hamid took him for a long walk along the East River while Nusa sat in the little apartment and prayed she would not break down, especially in front of the boy.

Now the telephone rings. Hamid's hand stops in midair. The cascade of water ceases. Moussa looks from his father's face to hers. Nusa goes over to the little stand and picks it up. "Hello, hello, yes? Oh, of course. He's ready. Fine, fifteen minutes. He'll be out front. Thank you. Good night."

She turns to face Hamid. For the first time, it seems to her that he shows a bit of concern for the consequences of his actions. But Moussa is tugging at his arm, demanding attention. Hamid takes up a towel, lifts his son out of the water and carries him to the little room. As Nusa washes out the tub, his voice rises over the din of unshed tears beating inside her heart. "I am leaving now for California. Remember, you are the man of the house now, so take care of your mother and listen to her. Be good in school."

When Moussa replies, words muffled, all she can make out is the sadness in his voice.

Hamid comes out and begins gathering up papers, tickets, passport, his wallet. "You need some money?"

She shakes her head. There was enough food now, and she stopped by the bank earlier. Hamid takes the biggest suitcase down first. She stands silently by the door, holding it open. Saying nothing for fear of screaming and clinging to him. His footsteps slow. He reaches in and pulls her to the door. Then they just hold each other. At last, gently, he releases her and takes her face in both hands. She lets his lips take possession of hers once more. Even manages to hold the tears and pain back, with great effort.

She stands at the door listening to footsteps recede as he descends, moving away from them. She imagines his feet on the street below as he and his friend maneuver his two suitcases into a small car. She conjures up the car moving eastward on 10th Street, then up Avenue D until 14th Street, and finally turning onto The Drive.

"Mama, I need a story." Moussa's voice is a gentle prick in her heart. She closes the door and locks them both inside. "Yes, Papis." And she goes to his room.

Hamid has left almost nothing. Only one picture on the bureau facing the child's bed. "Now," Nusa says, wiping her face, putting on a big smile. "What shall I read?"

"Baba got me a new book today. I want to hear that one."

She sees a brown-paper-wrapped book and brings it to the bed. "Here, you should open this. It is your gift."

His fingers make quick work of it and soon the book is uncovered: *The Red Balloon*. Colorful pictures stare at her. Nusa is surprised because they've always made it a point to search for authors and stories that have children or families who are African or black. She feels a tremor in her stomach. "*Astagfrulahi,*" she says.

Moussa loves it. When she finishes reading she pulls the light coverlet up to his chin.

He looks up at her. "Mama, I need a toilet."

She helps him out of bed. His little pajama-clad body stumbles into the hall. "Mama, Baba went to the airport?"

She unlocks the door and puts on the light. "Yes, darling."

"He's going to Los Angeles?"

"Yes, Papis." She doesn't trust her composure beyond very limited responses.

"That's in California, right?"

"Yes. Tomorrow we'll take out the map and find it. Now here, wash yourself." She hands him the little pitcher bought from a nearby thrift shop. All washed, door locked, they head back to their three rooms.

Nusa sits in the unlit living room, on the floor. Lights from the buildings across streak the floors and walls, highlight the bare white sheets. She moves to the bed. Breezes flow in and cool her dark-skinned legs and arms. His scent rises from the sheet and she sinks down enveloping herself in the linen that covered them last night. A pillow receives her sobs as she cries herself to sleep.

She awakens before Moussa, moving quietly in daybreak light and slips on a long robe to go to the toilet. Her mouth is dry, her throat granular. But after making *wudu*, a glass of water eases it. Their place is quiet; there are no sounds indicating Moussa is awake and ready for the day. Nusa goes to a basket where she stores personal items and lifts out her prayer rug. She lays it down, covers her head and says *Fajr*.

During *zikker*, she becomes aware of a soft warmth nearby. For a moment she imagines Hamid has come back. Opening her eyes she sees her son. He's sitting next to her, hands cupped to his face, eyes shut, mouth moving. Nusa finishes her beads and greets him. "*Salaam*, Papis."

"*Salaam,* Mama."

She accepts his first kiss of the day and holds the small firm body in her arms. "Are you ready to breakfast?"

The boy yawns. Then his serious thinking face turns on. "Well, I am hungry for pancakes."

She caresses his cheek. "Then pancakes it shall be. Do you want to stay here on my sleeping mat until I cook them?"

"Yes." And he climbs up into her bed, puts his head on the pillow, and snuggles under the sheet.

Despite her sadness time passes quickly. Soon there's only one more week left and Nusa has to get their lives organized. One morning as they're about to leave the building, at the curb she sees a mattress on a broken bedstead. "Oh, come Papis, let's take a look."

Closer up she sees it's in good condition. "I'm going to take this in and then I shall have a bed like you. Can you hold the door, please?"

He pushes the door back and flattens himself against the wall as Nusa tilts and rolls the heavy, unbending bed into the hall. It's too unyielding to manage alone on the stairs, so she stands it up under them until she can get some grown-up help.

Later in the evening when her floormates come home she asks them to bring up the mattress. "Oh, thank you so much. I will cook you the best African dinner ever, on Friday." James, a former school teacher and Hollis, a filmmaker, smile and accept her promise.

Both her classes and Moussa's kindergarten start off smoothly. They soon slip into a routine. Three days a week he goes with her to the university. There he plays with the children of other students and faculty. His vocabulary expands. He's already fluent in French and her home language. With Hamid in California now, she speaks with her son in French at home and English outside. On Fridays she takes him to *jumah* held in a brownstone house at West 72nd Street and Riverside Drive. Then, on Saturdays, they return for children's classes, which are also for new Muslims. These children look very different from his regular classmates. It always hurts when she sees other little boys run to their fathers at the end of class. *Yah Allah.*

In his last letter Hamid reports it is difficult to find work to fit his schedule. He shares a small apartment with another graduate student because he couldn't bear the university dorm. Professor Katz has been able to get him a teaching assistantship. The salary is small, but he should be able to send her one hundred dollars a month. This is good news. Nusa calculates that she'll then be able to pay her rent and get special foods from Brooklyn, Germantown, and a health food store on West 8th Street. The white man who owns the store always wears a white uniform. It makes him look antiseptic. That and his smile encourage trust in his medical advice. Nusa buys vitamins the man tells her will build stamina and resistance to colds and other infections. This is important, because the two of them are very sensitive to cold weather. One shelf in her kitchen is reserved for the vitamins and other supplements. Moussa is very good about taking the fish oils. Especially when the man tells him, "Soon you'll be strong enough to protect your mother. And smarter than the other boys in your class!"

She finds two part-time jobs. One is baby-sitting for a pretty white woman who is married to a black musician. They have two boys; the oldest is the same age as her son. She brings Moussa along to their apartment and the children enjoy their time together. On weekends she waits tables at a little Haitian restaurant on the Westside in the Village proper. Her former employer wants her to come back badly; he asks and asks. Nusa tells him no; really he only wants to try to get her to go to bed with him. Still, he was generous when she worked for him, giving her most of the furniture now in the boy's room. His wife was constantly changing décor and their children outgrew their beds, clothes and other things very often. So Nusa called him finally when she had all her jobs and class schedules in place.

"I really appreciate your kindness to me. My son is very happy with the bed. But with my schedule, it won't be possible for me to return for full time work."

She pauses to listen to more entreaties.

"I would set you up in a nice apartment. Never make unreasonable demands. It isn't easy for me to get away from home. Maybe once during the week and weekends." He goes on and on: if things had been different perhaps they might have been able to have a real relationship.

She suppresses a sigh. "I'm sure you're a kind person, making a great effort to help me. And yet...we are both married."

"But your marriage cannot be compared to mine. I am still in the home. Hamid has left you."

Nusa assures him she means only that they are each bound by similar constraints. That she feels herself to be married even if her husband has gone away to California. They finally end the phone call with him promising to call in a month or so to see if she's changed her mind.

Nusa sets the telephone down. She will never consent to an affair with him.

The babysitting goes well. Her friend works part-time for a publishing company and must be in the office only one day a week, staying for ten hours. She brings work home and drops it off there later. It's the other job that is difficult. La Belle Creole is a new restaurant and business a bit slow, but on busy nights she makes good tips.

The man who runs it is only part owner but he fancies himself a restaurateur. He is about the same height as Nusa, and just as slim. She observes he doesn't like not being able to tower over people. She's around five-five in stocking feet, but wearing a little heel she stands eye to eye with him. His name is Monsieur Louis, but the Haitians in the kitchen refer to him as "Petit LouLou."

His tastes in women run from big to bosomy and blonde. Sometimes she feels sad for Monsieur Louis when his countrymen mock his size and his choice of female companions. They also mock his affectations, his mode of dress. He loves to wear hats tilted to one side, with paisley print cravats. She recognizes one of his favorite assemblages from the old record cover of a French singer whose name she can't remember. But what she dislikes most is his attempts to belittle her and cheat her of wages. He always insists she count out her nightly earnings in front of him before going home, saying, "You will soon be able to open your own place with all the money you are making."

Nusa never responds when he makes these kinds of comments. On slow nights she barely makes five dollars. Monsieur Louis only shrugs it off then, and makes no reference to her salary. He maintains a table by the window for his friends, extending free food and drinks to them. Nusa is required to serve them as well as the paying customers. The women are loud and crass; she doesn't like waiting on them.

One particular night it's very busy and she feels a strain in her arms from the heavy trays she carries food in on, and the empty plates out.

Without warning on this night the Big Man stops by. Monsieur Louis is at his table with a larger than usual collection of freeloaders. Nusa doesn't see the Big Man at first because she's gone to fill a diner's request and to seat a couple who've just come in out of curiosity. She puts the tray down on an empty table and serves the woman, then the man. She's making sure their order is correct when blonde number two raises her voice, demanding her food. Nusa excuses herself, saying to the couple, "*Bon appetite.*"

She lifts the tray and goes to the table where Monsieur Louis is holding court. The cigarette holder is propped in his tobacco-stained fingers, live ash dangerously near dropping onto the wood floor. Intent on quickly serving and retreating to the back, near the kitchen where she can observe all the diners, Nusa sets two platters on the table, trying to avoid touching the chunks of pork piled high atop some stewed vegetables.

She becomes aware of the abrupt halt in their shrill chatter before learning why. Standing with an empty tray, she notices Monsieur Louis' face. Mouth ajar, words trickling from the other side of his lips. The cigarette holder left to its own devices. Following his stunned stare, Nusa turns and comes face to face with a very dark-skinned man. Tall, elegantly dressed, his stern face focused on his partner.

"*Bon soir, monsieur,*" she says, and quickly retreats.

From her position by the kitchen door in the back, she can still see her employer. In the kitchen voices are suddenly hushed; eyes peer through the small glass window the cook and helpers use to monitor how business is doing. She continues to serve tables and collect money. She takes change back to each person and, as soon as they leave, immediately clears the dirty dishes, changes tablecloths, and sets up for the next customers.

At each table she checks on the meal and refills water glasses. Finally, unable to avoid it any longer, she approaches his table. "*Monsieur.* May I serve you?"

"No, *mademoiselle,* I am fine." He pauses, looks around the small room as if noting it's a full house, and compliments her. "You are a good worker."

"*Merci, monsieur.*" She picks up the empty platters quickly and takes them to the kitchen. Returns with a wine and dessert menu, then rushes back to bring coffee in demitasse cups with a sliver of citron on the side.

No one speaks while she's serving the table. She starts away but the Big Man says, "*Mademoiselle?* Please bring the check."

"Yes, *monsieur.*" Nusa returns to her little table in the back to tally up the bill, in a quandary because Monsieur Louis' guests are never charged. He always makes out a check and then, at the table, with a grand flourish, signs his name and gives it back to her.

One of the men at another table gets up and heads to the men's room. A couple stands and says, "Well, good night. Thanks, lovely as usual."

By the time Nusa gets back with the Big Man's check only three of the ten guests remain. She hands it to Monsieur Louis, as is usual. Instead of waiting for him to sign she leaves, making herself very busy clearing two empty tables. After that she finishes the next day's set-ups, then sits at the little back table again and chances a look at her watch. Almost closing time. As she lowers her head to go over the receipts in the book, she feels a presence. The Big Man is standing near.

"Oh. Yes, *monsieur?*" She rises.

He gestures for her to remain seated. "You've done a fine job tonight all by yourself. Where is the other person, Jean-Jean?"

Nusa is at a loss for words then, because the waiter named Jean-Jean was fired more than two months earlier. For insubordination, according to Monsieur Louis. Jean-Jean had not given a special cut of meat to one guest at his table. After a loud quarrel which almost led to a fist fight, Jean-Jean was ordered out. Monsieur Louis had told Nusa, "We don't need him. You can handle the room alone." He'd smiled and added, "Just think of all the money you'll make." Well, the first month had not been so good but the second was better. Nusa found it hard work, though, and felt they really could use another person.

But now, standing between the two men, she is silent, looking at Monsieur Louis. He makes a great production of clearing his throat and says something in Creole so she won't understand. But Nusa knows things are serious because normally he always speaks French proper.

The Big Man picks up her receipt book and the two men go to the little office in back. The dishwasher comes out and helps her stack clean glasses. He's looking at Monsieur Louis most of the time, though. Someone has turned on the record player. "Panama Tombe" spreads across the room. Nusa loves the soft drums that hold the Haitian music together. She's almost finished setting up for the next day, though Monsieur Louis' table is still occupied by his perhaps-forgotten three guests.

"Will there be anything more?" she asks them. "The kitchen is closing."

The nasty blonde stands and looks down on her. "No. That will be all. Now tell Louis we are waiting for him."

Nusa smiles and agrees to do so, though in fact she has no intention of going near the back room. She continues to remove soiled glasses, plates, and silverware. Finally the sitters get up. Quickly she takes off their table cloth. By the time she comes out of the kitchen, lays a fresh cloth, and prepares to leave, she hears loud voices rising from behind the door of the little office. The cook comes out and jabs his sous-chef in the ribs. He says something in Creole and they both laugh.

Nusa goes to the restroom and washes face and hands. She is so tired; she only wants to go home. She pulls on her coat. *"Bon soir! See you next week."*

Just as she reaches the door a noise that sounds like the thud of a body falling breaks the silence. A moment later the Big Man saunters out of the back room. *"Madamoiselle,"* he calls to her. "Your night's wages."

The shock of his words lands somewhere between her stomach and thighs. *Tic.* Her left eyelid quivers. She hopes the spasms are not returning with the foreboding they bring.

"Merci, monsieur." She takes the envelope from his outstretched hand and starts towards the kitchen, to share. His words stop her at the door.

"No, it is for you."

She sees the faces of the men inside staring out and knows they have heard, too. She changes direction. The dish washer hurries past and disappears noiselessly behind the swinging door.

Monsieur Louis comes to the door and, with as much dignity as possible, emerges from the back room, hat cocked at its usual rakish angle. He pauses at the door to fluff his gold and blue cravat. Then, with an exaggerated flourish, swings a camel-hair coat over his shoulders. Odd, his ever-present cigarette holder is no longer affixed to his lips. There is something a bit off here. Or perhaps it's only her imagination? The swollen lip, the somewhat-crooked nose. Just then he takes one of those famous white handkerchiefs and holds it to his face, so she isn't certain if that was indeed a trickle of blood on his chin.

He slides past, back rigid, feet carrying him swiftly to the door. One hand flips a cocky adieu.

Nusa is mesmerized for a moment at the audacity of the little man. "Good night again, *monsieur,*" she says to the Big Man. "Thank you for your kindness. See you next week."

He looks at her gravely. *"Mademoiselle,* please call first. We may no longer be open by next Friday. Our finances are in a most serious condition."

Nusa glances over at the back of Monsieur Louis, who's being comforted by his big, bosomy blonde. "Very well, *monsieur.*" She leaves quickly, without a second glance at the kitchen workers, the room, or the Big Man.

Nusa bundles up against the rush of cold air winding around Barrow Street and walks up 7th Avenue to West 10th Street. If she spots a cab before the crosstown bus she'll take it. With twice the money she would normally have, because she didn't share her tips tonight, she can afford a ride. Her watch shows that the hourly bus is due any moment, though, so she decides to wait.

After ten minutes a city bus rolls towards her. The driver pulls to a stop and then waits a moment before opening the doors. She climbs aboard and pays her fare, thirty-five cents. Rumor has it that an increase is coming in the next year. As she starts to make her way to a seat, the driver lurches forward, causing her to stumble, but her reflexes are good. She catches herself, takes a seat and smiles, knowing he was being deliberately rude.

She's so tired; her back feels sore. The prospect of the loss of this income weighs heavily on her. "*Yah Allah!*" she sighs. But Allah gave this job to her when she had not been looking for it. Another will soon be provided.

She looks out into the dark nighttime streets as the bus heads east on 8th Street. Here and there are groups of young people on their way home or to another party walk, wrapped in heavy coats and warm caps. They appear to be her age, but she has responsibilities. For them parties, for her Moussa. He needs me to be with him, to provide for him, she tells herself. And I shall, she vows.

At 5th Avenue four young white men and two women get on the bus. They are noisy, laughing and joking. Two of the men stumble to a seat where they flop down. Cigarette smoke and stale, yeasty beer smells float in with them. One of the young women laughs in a high-pitched voice, almost uncontrollably, after one of the men whispers something in her ear. The other woman has thick, heavy red hair. She looks back at Nusa and then says something to the others. One of them turns around and laughs in her direction. Then he leans over and says something to the woman. Her answer apparently does not please him; he pushes her violently and she lands hard in the aisle.

Between 3rd and 2nd avenues, the driver pulls to a full stop. "Is there a problem back there?"

"Yeah, the problem's you," growls the man, as the woman he pushed crawls back into her seat. "You don't stop a bus in the middle of the street."

Nusa feels uneasy now. She really doesn't want to walk from here all the way home. It's cold, and East 10th Street on the B to C block is not pleasant for a woman alone, not at this time of night. After about five minutes of arguing, the passengers telling the driver what his duties are versus their rights as paying customers, they all seem to decide it's too late at night, or maybe too early in the morning, for so much aggravation. Each side backs down.

Nusa releases a held breath, grateful when the troublemakers all pile off at Avenue A and East 8th Street. She watches as they stumble across the street. It's very dark by the time the bus turns right on East 10th. Few cars are passing by. She looks out but sees no one approaching Avenue C. Nusa rings for her stop and leaves by the rear door.

"Alhamdulahi," she sighs, entering the little apartment. She eases her feet out of the laced-up work shoes but does not put the light on. Moussa is at the babysitter's house so she can bathe without worry of waking him. She sinks into the warm bath and soaps her body, then lets the smells and ugliness of the restaurant flow down the drain. After saying prayers she curls up on the couch with an extra cover and a book but is soon asleep.

She must adjust her schedule due to the loss of the waitressing job, but then Allah does open a new source of income. Hollis, a floormate, needs his scripts typed and corrected. He pays more than she was making at La Belle Creole. She's very happy because she can work at night, while Moussa sleeps.

She organizes special activities after *Jumah* on Fridays for the two of them. Sometimes it's treats at Schraft's. The waitresses are all older Irish and German women who pay lots of attention to Moussa, slipping an extra scoop of ice cream onto his apple pie whenever they eat there. Now and then they take a bus ride across the bridge to Queens. Most of the drivers take them back and forth without charging a second fare.

At least twice a month Hollis or James, the two male residents on her floor, eat dinner with them. Neither is married, although Hollis is in a serious relationship with a girlfriend. A big woman, as tall as he, with pale yellow hair. She's a painter who sometimes joins them when she stays overnight. Every time she comes over she brings a gift for Moussa. None of them has children so he becomes their son, too. He's shared among all three, whom he refers to as Uncle Hollis and Uncle James and Auntie Priscilla.

There is also the not-so-nice young man who lives upstairs on the top floor and always crashes their dinners. Nusa specifically never invites him because he's too argumentative, criticizing everything and everyone. One night Hollis asked about African culture, about what it was like to grow up as a Muslim woman. Nusa was happy to explain; she started to speak about her mother, and especially her grandparents. To tell them about Ramadan and the preparations for the Holy Month. But in the middle of her story Jake, the uninvited, wiped his mouth after consuming two full helpings. He threw the napkin onto his plate, into the remnants of sauce. "Religion. You people are so superstitious!"

Hollis turned and gave him a sharp look.

But Jake had been undeterred. "You know, if you people'd spent as much time and energy kicking the British and French out as you put into Ramadan, you'd have had independence long ago."

So it is with some annoyance now, at another night's dinner, that Nusa lets him in. She hopes he won't eat too much. Or worse, drink too much. Perhaps he has a problem because neither Hollis nor James act the way he does, even when they've had more than one or two glasses of wine. She prays he won't use Israel as a positive example again, or some tired "Religion as an opiate of the masses" argument. But no, tonight, it's an attempt to explain the civil rights phenomena occurring down South. He's very critical of the sit-ins.

"Well then, what do you recommend?" asks Hollis.

Caught in the middle of his diatribe, Jake has to pause to take a breath.

"Mama, I need a toilet." Moussa is squirming beside her chair.

Thank goodness! Nusa sighs. She excuses herself and takes the boy out to the hall. By the time she comes back, an awkward silence prevails. Jake gets up shortly, saying he has to go finish his studies. He's completing his doctorate in history. No one else says anything.

At the door he turns, as if about to say something else, but then just closes it behind him.

Later, during dessert, James tells Nusa, "While you were gone, well, we just told him we were tired of him and his loud mouth. That we're all college graduates, including you. So he needed to stop talking to you as if he has to explain every little thing. We suggested he didn't actually know everything about everything."

Hollis adds, "I told him if he was so upset about our collective stupidity then he shouldn't invite himself to dinner anymore."

When Nusa grins, James and Hollis laugh. Clearly Jake was offended by their intimations. Moussa laughs, too, although it isn't clear if he knows what's so funny.

Slowly winter passes and the semester approaches its end. Nusa's professors accept her thesis and she's recommended for the post-doctoral program in literature. She wants to teach and write on the oral literature in her area of West Africa. Also perhaps Black writings from America and the Caribbean. At some point she'd like to do comparative studies looking at African retentions in language and syntax and stories.

Moussa has passed his pre-reading readiness tests with flying colors. He's doing well with math. Hollis has been helping him using a Chinese counting board. Every night the boy says prayers for his Baba to come home and see him. These are difficult moments for Nusa, though she's become more accustomed to the empty bed. Trying to be a good Muslim woman, she prays often, especially when her physical needs coincide with emotional desires. A full day of studying, escorting Moussa to and from school, shopping, cooking, cleaning and working keeps her from focusing too much on herself.

The phone calls that used to come weekly, then every other week, have all but ceased. Nusa never calls California. Not after a woman answered once, and demanded to know who she was and why she was calling. When Hamid called back about a week later, she did not mention the woman. Nor did he.

Her friend who lives downstairs is moving away because someone got into their apartment one night while the family was sleeping. He came through the small window in their baby's room. After knocking over a few toys, causing a racket, the would-be burglar made a hasty retreat back out the window.

Nusa is not so fortunate. When she left the window open one day someone came in and stole her radio and toaster. After that Hollis fixed the window so it won't open so high and now, with the screens, Nusa feels safer. The people in the neighborhood all say it's just what junkies do. Nusa now knows that a junkie is a thief.

The building is still as dirty as when she moved in. Occasionally she changes the bulbs in the entrance so it won't be so dark, and washes the hall window so it's a bit lighter on her floor. The little apartment is comfortable, cheered by plants at all the windows. In May, she plants tomatoes, cucumbers, aubergines, and morning glory seeds in buckets and pots on the fire escape.

The streets begin to pulsate with pent-up bodies thirsting to take in the warmth of summer. The old Ukrainian ladies smile at her when she buys vegetables. She continues to baby-sit for her friend. One of the professors has gotten her a summer job at a 'progressive' cultural center about two hours from the city. She and Moussa will be able to stay out in the country for eight weeks. Hollis has a friend who wants to stay a month in the city because he's preparing for a one-man photography show. In exchange for a place to stay he'll water her plants, keep the place clean and has promised to take off his shoes once inside the apartment.

About a week before they are to leave for the country Nusa comes down the stairs with Moussa. They're going for a walk along the river. An ambulance and a police car are parked in front of the building. The building superintendent is standing up against the wall muttering. Two men in uniform come out wheeling a stretcher. It's covered by a white sheet held in with grey straps. "Stupid," The super says. "I say, take bucket. Not lot of water. Mop. Too much water too heavy. Look now, she dead. Who cook?" Their dog stands nearby looking from the men to the super. He sniffs the covered form on the stretcher and whines.

Nusa looks from the man to the stretcher to the dog. Poor old woman. The bundle lying there looks small as a doll or a child.

"Come, Moussa," she murmurs. "It's a lovely day. Let's take our walk."

She feels peaceful once his little hand is safely, softly in hers. Eastward they walk on 10th Street, across to and then past the housing projects, down the steps, and over the walkway. Then, when they are on the other side, she lets the boy run about, just a bit ahead.

She hopes his father will come back home to see them soon. She misses him.

BILL

"Do not be persuaded by the current times," Bill says from center stage. "Africa will not always be as you find it today. As you left it. Be confident of your status now and take comfort temporarily. Yet surely, as day follows night, my children will meet yours as equals. Where, is up to you." He pauses, takes a deep breath, and walks off into the wings. The curtain comes down, lights out and then up. All the while there's applause. He leads the cast of five back on. They bow a choreographed one, two, three, five in all. Bill turns away first, and the rest follow him off-stage.

After about five minutes of quiet, he begins to calm down. He needs to shower and dress. His tall body rises from an old armchair in the dressing room. Listening, he hears no feet scurrying back and forth. He cracks the door but there's no one outside. Quickly gathering towel and toilet kit, robe hanging loosely over broad shoulders, he dashes to the toilet. Although the water pressure is low, he soaps up and rinses well. His thick German-bought robe belted at the waist holds in moisture and the clean smell of soap.

Experience with fast changes between scenes over the years allows him to dress swiftly. Looking over the private dressing room he sees his costume under the damp towel. He hangs the towel on a nail, and then the robe. He leaves his Nigerian shirt and pants for the wardrobe woman. One of her tasks is to see that the cast's clothes are freshly laundered and ironed, ready and waiting for them at each performance. He shakes his head in admiration; she does these tasks well.

Closing the door, he starts out of the theater, a huge space on the second floor, and heads for the stairs. Members of the staff and crew pass, packing up gear, calling out, "Great show tonight," and,

"Good work, man." He appreciates their comments. Everyone's worked hard to get the rhythm and understand the nuances of traditional phrasing. The theater got a grant to put on this African series. He's been cast for three plays: one from a South African playwright, one from a Ghanaian, and one from a Nigerian. Two from the French-speaking writers are being done at a new repertory theater attached to the French Consulate in an old mercantile house on West 21st Street, though, and his French is almost non-existent.

It's only early evening. One of the great things about Sunday matinees is, you're finished before seven at night. Bill is a very physical and commanding presence on stage, acting punctuated by heavy sweating and total immersion in a role. So now he's ravenous, ready for a big meal. He turns the corner of 2nd Avenue onto St. Marks' Place, going west. He prefers to eat at O'Henry's, Ye Olde Waverly Inn, or Horn of Plenty. There's also a smaller spot he frequents, Mother Hubbard's.

Long legs carry him swiftly through Washington Square Park. It's an exceptional evening minus the infamous humidity of New York City. Lots of young people are sitting on the grass and benches. Children play in the round circle of a fountain with water spurting and spraying everyone around. He continues on the paved path bordered by benches, dotted with statues of some white men whose names he doesn't know.

Crossing Sixth Avenue, he sees through the big glass windows all the diners crowding O'Henry's. That isn't the ambiance he wants. So he stays on West 4th and makes a left on 7th Avenue. Yes, to Mother Hubbard's, small and intimate. A couple of actors he met in past shows told him about it. They work there sometimes, in between jobs. He's been a regular since, and now as he enters his eyes search the back of the room. There in the corner is his table, up against the wall and out of the flow of traffic. But most of all, less smoky.

Bill sits and puts his bag on the empty extra chair. With a sense of achievement he looks over the wine list. He can afford a nice glass of good burgundy with his meal. Steady work over the past year has brought some financial comforts.

He sips it while waiting for a steak, medium-well. His pad and pen are on the table and he scribbles some notes. His old teacher back in North Carolina used to say, "An artist is always thinking, doing his work. Have a piece of paper or pad and pencil, something to write with ready. Keep your thoughts. Put them down on. You never know what those little snippets of unformed ideas might turn out to be." He has an idea for a one-man play, probably a one-act. An every-black-man piece. The Nigerian playwright suggested this after listening to his story of how he'd gotten started in theater in the first place.

As Bill satisfies his hunger and is mellowed by the wine, he thinks back to North Carolina, almost two decades earlier. "Bill-and-Liza," that's how most people in the small town addressed them; always using both names. They were inseparable as teenagers attending the same high school for colored students. Each highly competitive. Liza excelled in math, he in English and history. Everybody said they were bound for college. She was going to be the first Negro woman scientist or teacher or, maybe, the unheard of, a doctor. Bill would be a writer or a college professor. Eventually, they'd get married.

They were crazy, fun-loving young people. He eighteen, she sixteen. But all the joy came to an abrupt halt when their experiments at acting adult led to her becoming pregnant. Although everyone always said they'd get married, no one, least of all them, was prepared for it. But both coming from God-fearing, church-going families, they were forced into a quick marriage. To their credit, both sides made an effort to help. Both sets of in-laws gave them a house in between the two farms. Of course much smaller, both house and yard. His mother volunteered to watch the baby so Liza could finish school. Bill was to work the farm with his father and attend college nearby, instead of going out of state as he'd dreamed.

But gradually Liza had refused to continue. She began to shun her old friends and stayed home. She'd wanted Bill to do the same.

He pushes the pad away now, frowning.

The waiter hurries over. "Is everything all right?"

"Yes, yes. Just fine, thank you."

Satisfied, the waiter turns away and gives his attention to another customer. Bill finishes the last morsel of steak, chewing the tender meat slowly, swallowing it with a healthy sip of wine. He wonders how he might portray those drastic changes in Liza without condemning her. This is both his literary and personal dilemma.

He makes a note to come back to this topic, black male-female relationships, later. He tops off the meal with coffee and apple pie, pays his check, then heads back across town to his apartment.

On a late Sunday night, early summer has its own feel. Lovers ease their pace because it's still early enough to spend more time together. Workers make their way home to prepare for the next day of labor. All seem unhurried in the before-midnight streets. He walks, loving the sights. Past Club Bohemia on Barrow Street. Decides to pass it up, not because he doesn't want to hear the music but because of a greater need for solitude. So he keeps on, eastward.

He adjusts his bag to the left shoulder. At the first bench inside Washington Square Park he raises his right foot, reties the shoe, then the left, looking around while doing so. Standing straighter, to his full six two and a half, he breathes deeply and slips a hand into his right pocket to feel the Swiss knife there. Yes, it's 1962 and this is The Village, but there are little gangs of white toughs who love to hide in bushes and behind trees, lying in wait for a black man to jump. If the man is escorting a white woman it's especially tempting. Bill throws back his shoulders, feeling height and size afford certain advantages. He waits but no one emerges and he's glad, because it's too perfect a night to be marred by a fight.

He walks past the fountain. A few young people in multicolored shirts and skirts are cavorting under a mixed glow of moon and park lights. At first glance it's hard to distinguish boys from girls because many males are wearing longer hair. Next to Garibaldi's statue, a thin white boy sits on a bench playing a guitar to which he's attached a harmonica. The youth's voice is nasal and high pitched. Bill stands for a few minutes, listening. The singer stares off into the night, words swallowed in the air and night sounds. Before Bill moves on, his hand finds some folded bills. He pulls out five dollars and drops it next to the musician.

The young man's voice rings out in the night, "Thanks, brother."

Bill waves but keeps on walking. He changes his heavy bag to the right shoulder as he waits for the light to turn green, crosses East 8th Street and 3rd Avenue and then onto St. Mark's Place. An interracial couple approaching him is heading west, the woman with the glow some in the early stages of a desired pregnancy exude. Her dark face is framed by a circular braid wound close to the head. There's something familiar about them.

"Hello, Bill!" The man calls out.

"Oh Jim, how are you?"

"We're fine." The woman—Mariama, that's her name—smiles. Her features and body shape remind him of Liza. Not her glow of happiness, of course, but the eyes and facial planes. After a few pleasantries and a promise to come see the play, they go their separate ways.

For a while the image of Jim and Mariama floods his mind and forms a backdrop for his thoughts. What really went wrong between Liza and him, and when?

A big mound of feces causes him to misstep. He curses all dogs, making no distinction with regard to their form, two or four legged.

His street gleams grey; ahead his dull building is a dark hulk. He climbs to the top floor, to his three rooms, his refuge. From here he can isolate himself from the outside world. But he's not ready to sleep. Taking out a writing pad, he sits on the couch and reads over some notes.

Relations between black men and black women are very tenuous. Distrust and criticism chafes at the possibilities of unity.

Bill remembers the high clear sound of Liza's laughter. How they'd enjoyed racing between their houses. When she told him she was pregnant he hadn't known what to do. At first he'd gone to his brother, who'd made mothers of many girls in the area. His brother told him about Aunt Maggie, who was first a mid-wife but also had saved many an unwise couple from embarrassment and forced marriage. When Bill met Liza again he told her what his brother had suggested. She'd shrieked, "One sin to cover another? No!"

Two weeks later they were summoned to a meeting with both sets of parents. He recalls they sat together on a couch facing the wrath and pain of both disappointed families. Remembers his father saying, "Everybody knew you'd marry. Just nobody knew when. Depending on when you two finished college."

He shakes his head at the retrieved image; the rage stamped on Liza's face and in her narrowed eyes when she looked at him. "College! Won't be no college. You got to get a job now. Take care of this baby and me." Then she'd cried, and he still didn't know if it had been because of her disappointment at the abrupt end of her education plans, or their predicament.

Groaning, he stretches his long fingers, cramped from writing for so long. Funny, he reflects. At around age four, before learning to write, he'd thought the words on a page were just squiggles. That was his name for the things readers pronounced when they read. The squiggles became dancing figures and play-actors before he'd comprehended word formulation. Only after he'd acquired vocabulary did they take on horizontal and vertical slants. And then the additional marks over and through letters; a short horizontal line almost at the top of a vertical made a T. Dots over a shorter vertical became an i or a combined short slant with a lower vertical was a J. There were quotations, apostrophes, punctuation marks. With all these ingredients he became the alchemist—a diviner, deciphering magical codes and secrets. So fascinated he'd been that whenever he entered that special place, the page, and began to sink into the world of words, he lost all consciousness of time and place.

All the while his brother had taunted, daring him to come out and play some game. He had his own vocabulary. But his brother's words had been deliberately hurtful: *sissy, non-boy*, other terms meant to shame him into putting aside his writing pads and books. The more his brother had tried to diminish Bill's obsession for all things literary, the more his passion had grown. Over the decades since, it has not abated. Success at commanding a thought and shaping it into a word or a phrase or knowing that his body is able to inhabit a character and space reinforces his desire to know more. He wants to be even better at what he's now doing. "And by God I shall," he promises himself and the universe.

For some reason tonight he can't shake his memories of those times. He was never able to understand the change in her. Liza started going to church about two or three months before the baby was born. At first he was glad to see her get out of the house, at least beyond the yard or to her parents' place. She seldom went to see his family.

It started with the Sunday service at eleven A.M., then grew to all day. Next it was Wednesday evening Bible study. She'd sent away for some religious magazines and waited for them every week. If they were slow in coming, she'd pore over the old ones. He'd made a little corner for himself, a desk with writing pads and books neatly stacked around and under the desk. So he'd read his books and she, her magazines. Sometimes she'd interrupt to read a particularly gruesome passage describing in detail the horrors of God's wrath flung at sinners. Those evenings had been tense, but still bearable.

Thinking of it now, Bill nods. Yes, that's when things started to get bad. The turning point had been shortly after Amanda's first birthday. With some help from his father he'd made his daughter a rocking-horse chair. He would put her in it and gently rock her. It brings a smile just remembering the way her eyes sparkled as she'd clung to a thick braided rope he'd strung through a hole where the nose of the horse was. One night, for some reason, Liza seemed annoyed. She'd hardly spoken. Later, without a word, she'd scooped up the child and taken her off to bed. He'd said nothing, then.

Now that he put the timing together, that night was around a week after he'd finished a job on his former teacher's kitchen. He'd stayed in touch with a small bunch of students, friends from high school, and they'd formed a little theater group. They'd read a play and then put it on at the old school. His teacher had asked him to be part of it and, when he'd said yes, further suggested he read novels and then turn them into plays to be performed. Mostly local people attended; his mother came once or twice, but Liza had refused.

He'd just sat down at his desk when he heard her reading very loud to Amanda from her magazine; one of the stories for children. He knew she intended for him to hear. He was puzzling over how to arrange his work schedule so he could take more classes at UNC. His father had told him he'd help out. It meant an hour's drive each way so he'd have to work Saturdays to make up the time he'd miss during the week. Bill figured he could take four classes, two days a week. Liza had been silent when he'd told her this. So he'd gone to college and she to church.

It had been a struggle but graduation was in sight. Amanda at almost four was showing signs of being very bright. Liza was teaching her by using religious books and, of course, the Bible and Sunday school. But that night she'd really gotten the Holy Spirit. Had made Amanda kneel and pray for her father, to ask Lord-Jesus-God to release Satan's hold on him. She prayed for her own salvation too, asking for forgiveness for having been led astray and ruining her life. She'd finally stopped and, looking exhausted, came out to sit on the couch. He could hear her heaving, getting a second wind. Then she'd laced into him.

Unable to keep writing, he'd turned to face her. At first she seemed almost unrecognizable, hatred distorting her face.

"What's wrong?"

"Wrong!" Her voice so shrill he'd winced. "Every night you got something to do. You don't spend time with us like a family man should. If you'd go to church the way you go to school, and read the Scriptures the way you read those devil books, things would be a whole lot better around here."

He'd repeated his mother's offer to take care of Amanda so she could return to college. It only fueled the fire. She ran from the room, crying, "It's too late. Too late."

An uneasy stalemate settled in; he continued with school and the theater group. By taking summer classes he'd managed to graduate in three years. Liza added an extra night of church-going, and a few hours of prayer at home as well. He let himself believe all was fine because weren't they doing what they wanted, even if separately? Usually she allowed him to have sex with her once or twice a week. Her duty as a good wife was to submit to his wishes, she said. He threw all his energy into working in his father's carpentry shop; into classes and the theater, and made fewer demands of her body.

Bill rubs his forehead now, but the next picture is indelible. On that fateful night, he returned from a long rehearsal to find all the lights out. He thought she was still at church and that he'd have a bit of quiet before she came home. When he turned on the lights and saw his orderly little corner in disarray, it took the wind out of him. Books thrown face down on the floor. Cut-up papers covering his desk. A chair seat full of broken pencils.

It still hurt to remember that night, the violence of her rage.

He was sifting through the remains of a manuscript when Liza opened the door. She pulled Amanda, who looked groggy with sleep, leading the child inside. They said nothing to each other. Focused on piecing together the bits and pieces of scattered pages was his primary goal. Blood pounded in his ears. Through it all he'd remembered his father's oft-repeated advice on marriage. "If you can't live together without cussing and fighting, one of you got to go. A real man don't beat on a woman." So he tried hard to be a real man.

She'd walked around him, deliberately stepping on a page, taunting him to strike out. Banging on things to get a rise. Finally she shrieked, "You're going straight to hell. You and all your heathen friends will be reading those books in the eternal fire. Now that's a theater you won't be able to pull down a curtain on and exit." Then she'd stomped from the room, slamming the bedroom door. A short while later came the sounds of furniture being dragged around.

He'd applied himself to organizing as much as possible. Most of the books were intact. The manuscript was missing two pages but he could reconstruct them later, away from the house.

Liza came out early the next morning and began preparing breakfast. When he walked out of the back room to the bedroom they didn't speak. Or rather, he was silent as she spoke to him through their daughter. "Say, Good morning, Daddy. Tell him, I prayed for you last night. God's going to save your soul cause me and Mama asked the saints to pray, too."

Not trusting himself to remain the obedient son of his father much longer, he'd gotten his suitcases from the closet in their room. Packed his clothes and took out the first one to his old car. In silence he kept moving. First the boxes of books, then the torn ones, and the scripts. When he'd come back for the last things, and to kiss his daughter, Liza had run to the door and blocked his way. So he'd just turned and left out the back.

"What're you doing? Where are you going?" she'd screamed, leaving poor Amanda at the table. The child got down and stood in the doorway watching, listening. Liza took no notice. She'd run back and forth, at one point getting down on her knees at the front stoop, calling on God and the angels, begging Jesus to save his soul. Hurling accusations: he was fornicating with his former teacher, with the women in the theater group, an old classmate. He decided not to stop loading the car, to not offer any encouragement to her wild claims. To simply concentrate on getting out. To leave quickly was the only way to save both of them.

"Bill, you better come on in this house! Eat your breakfast so you can go to work. You're already late. Staying out all time of the night with those no-good sinners!"

In his head he repeated his father's words. *If you can't live together without fussing and fighting, one of you got to go . . .*

She ran around and jumped into the front seat.

Amanda started to cry, "Mama, Mama."

Liza looked from the child to him. Voice almost gone, hoarse from screaming, she'd stumbled out of the car.

Perhaps it was the finality in his voice that had made her understand she'd gone too far. "Goodbye, Liza." His lasting memory is of a twenty-year-old woman standing outside in her nightgown, sobbing, pounding her head, clutching at her heart and rasping, "Come back, Bill. I'm sorry! Don't leave me. Don't leave us. Come back."

But he hadn't. That had been over fifteen years ago.

He stares now at his trembling hands. The power of that scene so long ago still unsettles him. His mother, bemoaning his single status now, blamed it all on the shotgun marriage and its bitter divorce. "You shouldn't let that ruin your chances of another marriage, of happiness," she often said.

"Well," he sighs now, shutting off the lights, "enough of the past."

Monday morning he's up to do his daily stretches and add an extra five minutes of push-ups to compensate for the thick steak on Sunday night. After a light breakfast he organizes his day: carry shirts to the Chinese laundry, two pairs of pants to the cleaners, take out the garbage. The apartment is small, so he tries to keep everything in its place. So far he's had no major problems with roaches or mice. For a while he had a cat, but her last heat had been so intense she'd sneaked out. He'd been locking the window when the telephone rang. In the short span of his brief conversation the cat had torn the screen and slipped out, running down the fire escape. He never saw her again. It isn't that he's overly fastidious but still it was good not to have to contend with cat feeding and litter-box cleaning any more.

At the door he surveys his compact kingdom. All is in order. Keys, money, clothes on his arm. He always secures his bike under the stairwell with a heavy chain locked to the radiator. So now he puts out the garbage, tucks his clothes under a rack attached to the back fender, then unlocks the bike and rides off to do errands.

Later in the week, on Friday, he walks back over to Mother Hubbard's for dinner. It's been a full day of rehearsing for a new play and scene changes for the current show, so he rewards himself. Takes his usual seat and sits jotting down thoughts before he forgets them. He sips wine as he waits for roast chicken and spinach. Looks out the window and watches people pass by. Suddenly he sees a familiar face. He's seen the woman and the boy near his street before, so he assumes she lives on the lower East Side. She's wearing an African dress that clearly wasn't bought from Khadijah, the resident seller of premade African garb. He knocks on the window but she doesn't seem to hear. He gets up and goes to the door. Not sure of her name, he calls out, "Sister! Sister!"

The woman turns and stares for a moment, then relaxes as she apparently recognizes his face. Bill invites them to join him. It's Friday; the boy doesn't have school the next day, so that can't be an excuse not to come in.

Bill asks the waiter for one more chair and takes his bag from the other. When they sit down he asks, "Please, tell me your name?"

"It's Nusa. And this is my son, Moussa."

"How are you, Moussa?"

The boy looks at him a few seconds before he says, "Fine, thank you."

"What would you like?"

Moussa looks at his mother before answering.

She nods. "We've eaten just a while ago."

"Won't you have some dessert? Maybe tea or coffee or apple pie? It's all very nice. I always have the pie when I come here."

She orders tea. Moussa, apple pie with vanilla ice cream.

It's pleasant having them for company. "Do you come over this way often?"

"Yes, I'm in graduate school. Moussa attends school nearby. P.S. 41."

"It's a nice place. I like coming here because you can get a great meal and they've got a brother cooking in the kitchen."

Nusa says she thinks eating out all the time must be expensive.

"Well, I'm a terrible cook. So it's either this or starvation."

She laughs. "As soon as I finish my orals, I'll invite you over for a real African dinner."

"Make sure you do." He nudges Moussa. "You hear that, Little Man? Your mother made a promise. You are my witness." The child's smile stirs something in him, a warm feeling.

Bill pays the check and manages to get a cab for them all just outside the restaurant. On the way home Nusa tells him she hopes to be moving within the next few months. "A friend from school is heading to the West coast. I'm going to take his place. It will be more convenient because the university is on West 12th Street and Moussa's school is on West 11th."

Bill listens to her voice as he would a song, enjoying the melody of pitch and rhythm. Too soon they are at her building. "I'll take care of the fare. You just remember my real African dinner."

"Thank you. I will remember, in two weeks. Goodnight." She puts a hand on the door and says to the boy, "Say thank you and goodnight, Moussa."

Bill glimpses a mischievous mix of resistance and obedience in the child's dark brown eyes, as he repeats, "Thank you and goodnight."

Bill watches them enter the building and then rides the two blocks to his place.

Monday he heads up East 10th Street on his way to the theater, to meet one of the actors and go over a scene at the end of the second act. A tricky transition; the young man doesn't understand the nuance required. On this foggy day moisture collects on his poncho and hat. Humidity and heat rise together, warning New Yorkers of the approaching summer. He takes long strides through Tompkins Square Park to East 8th Street, crosses and goes on to 2nd

Avenue. Taking the steps two at a time, feeling proud of his physical condition. Thinking, Not bad for a man approaching forty. He chuckles, recalling how he used to believe forty ancient. Now here it is, staring him boldly in the face.

Maggie, the theater's feline in residence, saunters over and stops to give a long, insolent look. Then flicks her tail and goes off to find something soft to curl up on. Marty, coming out of a little sewing room set up for costume repairs, almost bumps into Bill. He bows and lets her pass. O.T. has not yet arrived. Bill checks his watch; it's a bit early. He takes off his poncho and drapes it on a nearby chair to dry. Dropping the hat onto the seat, he opens his leather bag. Tim, a black guy who crafts sandals, belts, and wallets made it for him. It's perfect for scripts because pages lie flat without wrinkling.

He walks across stage, blocking out the scene. The theater's darkness is broken by a single row of brights casting a glow that warms him. He's in it, the village where the action takes place. He can hear voices, even the fussy clucking of chickens. Yes, this is where O.T should walk past him. He should simply be there, not entering in a way to call attention to himself. Bill sighs, because O.T. is tall and handsome, his youth in full bloom. He hasn't learned how to harness that energy yet. How to be subtle. The power of his entrance is dependent on such control. The director and writer had a long meeting with him about this already. Although very gifted, O.T. is still unable to become fully part of the ensemble. His need to be focal point still drives him. Bill predicts this may be a major hindrance in future roles.

O.T bounces in just then, interrupting his musing. That boyish grin disarms Bill, so he concentrates on having the young man understand the scene and motivation. O.T. is big on terminologies, in the throes of the new acting vocabulary coming out of studios now. Discreetly obvious is his tattered copy of Stanislavsky's book, the bible of acting to many. Bill decides to say nothing about it. During the rehearsal he finds the right analogy and gets O.T. to comprehend how ensemble is a character in and of itself. This village a communal space where it's vital for each member to participate in collective activities. It seems to get through.

They leave after an hour or so of rehearsing because there's a cast party at Bill's place. He stops to get cheddar and Swiss on

East 9th, at a small place which reminds him of shops in Munich where, compliments of Uncle Sam, he was introduced to fine cheeses and olives, good bread and wine. He's not much of a cook; the cupboard's a bit bare most of the time. Soon his bag is bulging with the cheeses and two lovely bottles of wine. Rearranging some things to better distribute the weight, he turns homeward.

Around six-thirty the doorbell rings. Instead of buzzing them in he goes to the window and yells down, "Hang on, coming!" Then runs from the top floor to let his guests in. Folks in the building have become edgy because someone left the door ajar and a dope fiend got in and broke into an apartment on the second floor. Alerted by the noise, a woman on the third floor called the police, and let her dog out while waiting for the cops to arrive. The poor guy was so hopped up he fled, leaving the bag piled with stolen goods. Oh well, his run down is good exercise. With the play and constant rehearsals, he isn't biking along the East river every morning.

By seven almost everyone has arrived. Esther carries a dish of fried chicken. Bertie lays out a platter of fish and corn. A whole feast assembles in less than an hour. David, who's discovering wine but not discriminating taste, has brought some cheap French sauterne. However, the smokes he carries in a cedar cigar box are far superior to his wine choices.

"Great idea to have a party during the week. You theater people have such weird schedules, Thursday to Sunday!" Marty whoops her deep New Orleans laugh, while her Jewish husband looks on adoringly.

The bell rings again. Bill goes down wondering who it could be, because he thought he'd counted everyone invited. Local word of mouth spreads news of a dinner party, though, and there are always freeloaders and gate crashers.

The door opens to Nusa, wrapped in a long shawl over a yellow and red print dress. She extends a package.

"Hello! I didn't think you were coming."

She makes a wry face. "Sorry to be so late. I had a meeting with my thesis advisor and it lasted longer than planned."

"Well, you're here. That's what's important."

Noise flows out the door as Bill guides her in and sets her dish on the crowded table. "Hey everybody, here's a sister from the Motherland."

The actors crowd around. Esther, having recently denounced the straightening comb, and sporting a new short-cropped Afro, embraces her. "Welcome, sister." Shepherding her through the crowd in the tight space is almost an acrobatic feat. The curious want to see the food she's prepared; to know what it is and how it's made. She seems pleased rather than flustered. "This is one of the ways we cooked rice, in the north. It has onions and vegetables in it. This is fish soup—oh, and this is okra soup with chicken."

Bill puts his plate out and Nusa serves him. When he takes a forkful the sharp sting of pepper sauce causes his eyes to smart. His throat burns and he coughs. "Some water?"

Nusa shakes her head. "No, you eat rice. It will absorb the pepper." She watches as he follows her instructions.

The cough stops. "Hey, it works."

By the time all of her contributions have gone around Nusa says, "I'm sorry, I must leave soon."

Mel and Sue say they can drop her off, if she can wait a little longer. "I only live two blocks away," she protests.

Bill intervenes. "I'll see you home. It's not a good idea to go by yourself this late. First, come with me. I want to show you something."

He takes her up to the roof. He and his floormates have fixed it up. Green paint on the tarpaper creates a grassy impression. A few blankets and pillows lie strewn around.

She clasps her hands in front of her. "This is so nice!"

He stands looking around at the lights of buildings and, to the east, latticed patterns formed by barges and lights along the far side where Brooklyn borders the river. "I come up here to see the sky and be away from the street."

She nods. "I really must go now, though. My floormate has to do some work in his studio, and I promised to be back before eleven. It's ten-fifteen now."

Sighing, Bill nods. "Okay. I'll walk you home."

Back in the apartment some couples are dancing. Others stand in groups talking about a role they'd like to play or a great part they almost got. Gathering up dishes, putting them in her bag,

Nusa calls, "Goodnight everyone. I really enjoyed myself. Maybe I'll have a few of you over sometime soon."

Bill asks Esther, "See to things for me? I won't be long."

"Sure, brother."

At the entrance to her building, he stands aside as Nusa goes up to the door. It opens suddenly and a stocky man who might be Puerto Rican blocks the way, glowering out. Bill feels negative energy emanating from him, and lets his well-toned body make its own statement. The man backs off. It happens very fast. Sensing something amiss now, he decides to go on up to her door behind her. On the way upstairs he hears a door slam below.

Nusa opens her door, puts the dishes on a table and removes her shoes before she enters the cheery apartment. Her floormate smiles and stands. He sets down the book in his hands and Nusa introduces them. "Hollis, this is Bill. Bill, Hollis."

Bill shakes his hand. They're almost the same height. Hollis is also without shoes, so before he steps across the threshold, he bends and removes his.

Hollis says, "Well, better head out. See you sometime tomorrow. I'll probably stay over at Priscilla's."

Nusa asks about her boy while Bill looks at the books neatly arranged under windows and around the room. I could've built her some shelves, he thinks, but she seems to have solved the space problem in a very creative way. His eyes are drawn to the colorful batik pillows, and the couch he suspects doubles as her bed.

"Goodnight," Hollis says at the door, then turns away and leaves.

"Thank you for seeing me to my door," Nusa tells Bill. "The man you saw is the super for the building. He is…not very pleasant."

Bill smiles at her diplomacy. Those aren't the words he would've used. "How do you manage when there's no one about?"

"Oh, I make noise and speak loud so others can hear me."

Bill doesn't like it. His father's words echo in his mind.

"Once or twice I've had to get my floormates involved. I've reported it, but the owner refuses to speak with him. He says it's hard to get a reliable super."

"Look, I have to get back to my place, but…are you sure you'll be okay?"

"Oh, yes. He'll probably stay away since he's seen you come up."

"I'll stop by again to check on you two. Call if you need me, anytime. Promise?"

A slight hesitation. "I promise. Goodnight. Thank you."

"And I thank you. For the food, and your company." He stoops, puts on his shoes, and listens outside the door until she locks up.

Just as he reaches the second floor landing, Bill encounters the super again. He lets the man pass, then stays put, listening to that heavy tread ascending the creaky stairs. At a banging, Bill races back up and finds him at Nusa's door. The super seems almost unaware of his presence. Maybe he's high on something. As they face off again, Bill explains in graphic detail how many different ways he will throw him down if he comes near Nusa and the boy ever again. "I will mop these dirty halls and the streets outside with your fat, unwashed carcass."

The super is apparently so elevated on whatever he's taken it overrides any sense of self-preservation. "She's a tease," he mumbles. "Little goody-goody, walking around with nothing on under those tent-things. She…" He trails off, gaping at Bill, having at last found enough common sense finally to close his mouth.

Bill points at the stairs, indicating he should leave, then steps aside. The man stumbles back down the four flights muttering in Spanish, followed closely by Bill. At one point the super's legs threaten to collapse. Bill grabs the back of his shirt and he manages to make it to the first floor. The man pushes himself into the little back room between stairwell and cellar door. Bill goes out then, hurrying back to his own building. He decides to ride by in the morning. Also to ask Esther if she'll come by so this fool will know Nusa and the boy aren't alone in the world. It's a good thing there are two men on her floor, but they're probably not around all the time.

The party-goers are still enjoying his hospitality; he wonders whether they've even noticed his brief departure. He checks the roof, where five people having a serious conversation about The War. He overhears one observe, "If the draft is unprejudiced, how come so many brothers are at the front?" A discussion he doesn't want to engage in. His military experiences were all positive, maybe because during the Korean War his time was spent in Germany.

In his living room a cluster of actors are bemoaning the fact that there are no black plays and films for them. A new film is mentioned, one he's seen. He comments that it was well written and acted. They agree but the point still remains: it's the "white boy" who writes the scripts. "Why can't they let us tell our own story our way, in our words?"

"Hah. Might be too strong for them."

"Look, all I'm saying is, I know those cats who wrote it. Children of parents and grandparents who escaped the Nazis. I think Germany or Poland. So they feel they know all about oppression and stuff because they're Jewish."

"I know what you mean," says Richard, a rich, handsome newcomer from a well-off family in Washington. "An actor friend helped me get a spot in a T.V. movie. It's not a big deal, you know. I play a wrongfully-accused black man to his white-lawyer role. Background framing his just position. Anyway, I asked if he'd ever played in a piece by a black playwright. Or ever done a white man saved by a black lawyer. Know what that fool said? 'Would that be realistic?'" A wonderful mimic, Richard adapts a bewildered stance, evokes the man's persona.

Bill smiles. It's all too painfully familiar. "Did you tell him your father is a lawyer and a professor?"

Richard snorts. "No, I just let him be. He probably wouldn't have believed me."

"I understand there are points of universalism. But they don't always apply to us when there are racial issues," Marty adds sadly. Although she fell in love with a white man, she has her own acting battles against 'maid' and other servile roles. She's a fine clothing designer with a good living as a costume maker and designer for many Off-Broadway shows. Her husband came to a show once, saw her onstage, and has never left her side. He owns a small engineering company; they have three young children. An older cousin helps take care of them.

"Listen, I tried to school him but he put up stiff resistance. Finally I said, Nix it. Just pay me for my work and I'll get my black self out of your face. To hell with you and your family." A couple of onlookers shake their heads, pat his back. He shrugs. "Well, speaking of that, I best be getting my black self out of your faces. Got an early call in the morning. I need at least four hours of sleep."

This causes others to notice the time. It's been almost five hours since the fun started. By one o'clock the last couple says good night. Esther and a few other sisters clean and then go home together. Maude has a car, so she gives them a lift on the way up to her Harlem apartment. O.T. helps Bill clean up the roof, saying, "I really enjoyed myself. You know, when we first met I was just, I don't know—jealous, I guess. Trying to show off and stuff. But I appreciate what you've been teaching me."

To defuse the awkwardness of the confession, Bill says, "Listen, I'm envious of you. At your age, I had nowhere near the information and technique you've acquired. Just stay focused. You'll be fine."

Later he sits up in bed, reflecting on O.T and Nusa. He glances at the clock, then plans his agenda for the next day. First, bike ride. Back, shower, then phone calls: his agent. Also his aunt, to confirm Amanda's visit. His old professor now heads the drama department at some fancy college in New Hampshire; he wants him to come up to direct a work by a young black male playwright. Bill's thoughts run helter-skelter as he half-dozes. He thinks he hears Liza saying, "*Amanda's not coming. She is saved. I won't let you and your friends take her soul to hell.*"

He jerks awake, thinking, I pray my daughter will never become a fanatic like you. The superimposition of Nusa's sad smile and her calm demeanor finally overpowers Liza, and he drifts into a deep, calm sleep.

Up with a later start than he wanted, at nine-thirty he's rushing into jeans and tee shirt, then racing downstairs. Unlocking it, he rolls the German-made bicycle out the door and heads towards East 10th and Avenue C. Smells of fresh fruit, baking bread, and over-ripe garbage from the dented gray cans lining the sidewalks assail his sensitive nose. He rides past the old Czech woman who always gives him an extra loaf, because, "In Old Country, me, my husband and friends, we make theater. Hard work! Need good food. Bread good food. I make myself. *Eat.*" Smiling, he waves to her and turns onto East10[th].

The street has a middle-of-the-week, kids-in-school quiet. He slows and jumps off the bike, securing his prize possession to a lamp post a few feet away from her building. The door is propped open. The super, pushing a bucket to the curb, looks hard at him. Bill glares back and continues inside. Neither says anything to acknowledge the existence of the other. Once when Bill was having difficulty getting into a character he couldn't understand why the writer hadn't just had the two men duke it out rather than play unnecessary games. His teacher had said, "You're right. It is a game, a male game. Like the way two male dogs approach each other when a female is near. One circles the other, sniffing, pulling back, observing, looking for weak spots, wary of strengths. Once convinced he's safe, a male is emboldened to get closer. All the while keeping his eyes on the other dog, alert for a challenge. It's a dance. The choreography of life."

Bill shakes his head at the thought of it. He cannot imagine what might make this slob, this wreck of a man, think himself in some sort of relationship with Nusa. It therefore must be the need for dominance, to compensate for his misery. Power in intimidation is all he has.

"Well, that all ends with me," he mutters, then smiles at his own bravado. "My, how noble you are, Mr. William Britton." In Paris, they'd called him Brittany, or Breton.

He reaches her landing and looks down to see the super is below looking up. The man rushes off when he sees he's been caught staring.

At her door Bill knocks, calling out, "Hello, Nusa? It's Bill."

"Mama, Mama someone's at the door," a child shouts from inside. "He says his name is Bill."

He hears footsteps and then the latch snaps open. She stands in the doorway with a look of surprise. "Good morning."

Moussa peeks out from behind her. "Good morning, Mr. Bill."

Bill reaches down and tickles his chin. The child's face is soft; his skin firm and healthy. "How are you, Little Man?"

"Today's our no-school day so we do homework and housecleaning."

"I'm off for my morning exercise. Just popped by to check on you and Moussa."

"All is well, thank you. It's a kindness of you to do so. We have so few visitors."

As he starts back down the stairs she calls out, inviting him for dinner Friday night.

"Sorry, I have something to do then. But very, very soon."

He runs back down the dimly-lit stairs. Brighter lights and clean windows would help. Somehow he cannot see this super washing windows, using clean water on the grimy floors, fixing lights in the halls. Next time he'll bring some bulbs, shed some light on the subject.

He unlocks his bicycle, rides over to the river, across Avenue D and down a path wandering through the large housing projects. Pigeons fly up in a V formation. Gulls and barges dot the river. Bill walks across Franklin Delano Roosevelt Drive and mounts his bike again. No one else is out; he has the long path all to himself. "*A man must be man of his land.*" Words from the play roll over in his head. His lips mouth them. The rhythmic rise and fall of his strong legs punctuate each sentence, frame each scene. Noises from the tennis court are only a minor distraction. Laughter in the wake of a successful serve floats in the air and settles on his ears. Bill is happy with his decision not to move away. This is one of the great pleasures in the city, even though it's dirty and sometimes smelly. The East River, at this point separating Manhattan from Brooklyn and southward emptying into the Hudson, suffers in shimmering silence, the waste of years and people sullying its waters. Bill thinks of the Single in Amsterdam and Utrecht; the little cafe where he used to meet friends sipping strong black coffee and eating buttercake and apple tarts. Maybe this is why it holds such appeal for him, this Alphabet City.

His legs are vibrating from vigorous pedaling over the last haul of the ride. He chains his bike and goes upstairs at a respectable pace but definitely not running. A hot then cool shower, a brisk toweling and a few stretches. He selects brown trousers and a white-and-brown-checked cotton shirt. The clothes lie waiting on the bed as he sits in his undergarments, making calls. He catches his aunt before she heads off to her many missionary tasks in her little community. They end their brief conversation with her usual entreaty to make peace with the mother of his child, his former wife. "I will continue to pray for your soul, and the Lord's protection for you."

Bill thanks her for her prayers and the news, then hangs up.

He takes out bread and cheese, spreads butter lavishly, and takes it to his simple, round table of heavy wood and iron, which someone cast off curbside for probably a lesser but flashier one. Freshly brewed coffee scents the rooms. A cool breeze enters through windows in the kitchen and living rooms on cross ventilation, stirring and deepening the aroma. Checking his watch, he sees he has an hour to get to the theater for a read-through. He slowly chews his bread, enjoying the sharp tang of Swiss cheese.

Bill washes dishes, puts them away and goes to dress. First trousers, next shirt, neatly tucked in with a new belt from Tim, and he feels, as his mother would say, "Presentable for public eyes." Tying his laces he recalls the row of shoes Nusa lined her doorway with. That's something I might try, he thinks. God knows what I'm stepping in out there, half the time.

Using his extensive carpentry skills he'd put up a closet and door with a full length mirror. His reflection is pleasing to him. His tenderly-nurtured moustache frames a full upper lip. On closer inspection he notes two white hairs amongst the black. No time for tweezing now. On second thought, they add an air of sophisticated elegance, he decides. Passing up the straw brim he slants his old Australian slouch, grabs the shoulder bag sitting next to his shoes and slings it over one shoulder. Lifts his keys from a hook by the door, and after a last look—all good— he locks the door and runs down the stairs.

The Sunday house is a more sedate crowd. Word's spread through the black communities of Harlem and Brooklyn: there's a play by a young Nigerian writer at Black New World Theatre! Now in the throes of Black Pride, they're thirsting for 'real African' images and experiences. So the audience come out en masse in finest African attire. Bill chuckles, peeking out from behind the curtain. Khadijah must've been working night and day these past two weeks. The designer owns a shop on St. Marks Place, around the corner from the theater but closer to 3rd Avenue. He frequents the store from time to time himself.

It's nearing curtain time so Bill hurries back to his 'star' dressing room, hangs up his trousers and hums, revving his voice. Standing in front of a floor-to-ceiling mirror, he poses in his briefs. Mugging is a good form of facial exercise. After breathing deeply for a few minutes he puts on the exterior of his character, the African clothes. Enveloping himself in Obi, the protagonist of the play, he starts to feel the gestures and body movements of a complex man who lives a simple life into which the order of daily events is ruptured by the presence of a vicar. The vicar's call on Obi two days earlier turned fractious, leaving a bitter taste in his mouth. The vicar demands he curtail his son Chike; see to it the young man stop spreading blasphemous statements about the mission of the church and her workers. Political talk of independence and black governments in Nigeria and indeed, all of Africa is dangerous. *"Hah, it is preposterous! Who has ever heard of such rubbish?"*

Obi, stung by the remarks, will respond, *"Before you arrived we had our own system of governance. Now most of that has been torn down by British Law."*

"For which you should be grateful."

Bill is struck by the similarities of the colonials' thinking about Africa to current American racial power structures. Just the other day on the news a white senator said, "Negroes on their own cannot function. Without the white man, there would be utter chaos and havoc," in response to the sit-ins and confrontations of black youth against segregation.

"Ten minutes!" calls the stage manager.

He begins to shuffle and slope, allowing the character Obi to enter his body. Reaching and stretching and folding into a once-proud, now-tired man, Bill recalls his earlier problems with the script; the difficult first reading of African words. But syntax and terminologies became clear as the playwright and director gave many corrections. Slowly his grasp of this man and the people of the village, his humor and intelligent turns of phrase, blossomed into a full character. Bill's knowledge of African writers was once woefully limited, but now he has tickets to a reading by two men from Ghana and Nigeria. Maybe Nusa would come along.

"Three minutes!"

Bill gives a final check. All props at the ready. He opens his dressing-room door. The theater darkens; buzzing voices lower to silence as a record plays Nigerian music. Bill walks slowly to the wings and, in the dimmed light, makes his entrance.

Applause, five curtain calls, and two solo bows later, he's back in the dressing room, willing his body to re-enter the present. Sweaty-faced, clothes damp, eyes smarting from the salt of perspiration. He sits and lowers his head between his knees, breathing deeply several times, then slowly raises his body. Still sitting he does a few twists: to the right, to the left, arms above head, then down with hands on the floor. Slowly he stands, feeling satisfied that he fully occupied the personage of Obi. He gathers his things for a quick shower, dresses, and then off to the cast party. One of the partners is hosting it at his place, and also to say farewell to the writer and director.

Bill lets the momentum of long legs carry him down the steep steps and onto 2nd Avenue. People are gathering in little groups, walking towards Beau and Lynn's spacious apartment. Beau's an actor and a fine director. His wife is an excellent administrator. She handles the books and keeps the bills and salaries paid on time.

It's turned into a lovely afternoon. The streets are filled with people who don't believe it will rain: despite the predictions, few carry umbrellas. Bill loves this kind of weather. Coming from the South, where it's very hot, he's in his element. Winter is not a time he enjoys. The cold wind in his face, the freezing rain that always manages to seep through wool coats and scarves and heavy clothes.

Laughter and lively music rushes out the open door to greet newcomers. Kwaku and Oke warmly embrace Bill. Beau beams and Lynn comes out to greet him. She's a beautiful white woman with flawless skin and long blonde hair. "Bill, your performance this afternoon was perfection."

"Thanks, Lynn. Glad you think so."

She continues to set out dishes on the table. One of the couple's sons runs between her and Bill. The child goes over to his father and whispers in his ear. Bill looks on, envying Beau's proximity to his children. He hopes the upcoming week with Amanda will go well. The separation has been hard for him.

The dining room opens into a comfortable living room, where Bill shakes hands with the cast and other staff members. He looks for a space near a window so as not to be boxed in when people start smoking. An empty chair by a screened window beckons. He sits, putting his bag behind it. A small group of actors, some sitting on the floor, encircle a man next to him. The new Caribbean playwright, tall and light skinned. He's explaining that all the people from his island of St. Kitts are a mixture of African, European, and indigenous Indian. Bill loved his script, the rich language, but this man is so full of himself. Well maybe that's okay, because he really is a wonderful writer.

The place is packed full of laughing, talking people but Bill is hungry. Just as he casts a longing eye towards the table Lynn comes in and announces, "Okay, everyone, please help yourselves!" Bill gets up, goes over and looks at the spread. Trying to be cool he lets two female staff fill their plates first.

Lynn sees him hovering there, and laughs. "Now, in case you're thinking about hiring me out in-between shows to do catering, I must confess, all this I did not do. A friend of Kwaku and Oke did the cooking."

Before all the empty plates are loaded up Kwaku comes forward. "Please, you know we Africans have many rituals and traditions. At a gathering such as this where food and drink are being shared, we must offer thanksgiving." He silences the crowd with the melody of Fante, his language. He bows to Lynn and then to Beau, indicating he is asking blessings on them.

Oke comes forward with a bottle and one of Lynn's plants. He pours libation. "I ask that all goodness be ours. That our hearts be cleansed of envy, hatred and fear. That our minds be filled with intelligence and wisdom. That we be kind and generous to each other. May we never know hunger. May we never know thirst." He pours gin and water three times on the soil of a potted plant.

A huge cheer and scattered applause. The group turns back to fill their plates. Bill sits and begins to eat. At that moment Nusa of all people emerges from the kitchen, carrying another dish, and he almost drops his plate in his lap.

She sees him gaping, smiles, and walks over. "Hello, Bill."

"Hey Nusa. I should've known no one else can do fish like you. But I am surprised to see you here."

"I know Oke and Kwaku. We all met in college. My mother's family is actually from the land now known as Ghana. When she was a baby her family moved east . My father's from Nigeria."

"Oh, I see. Why don't you get something to eat and join me?"

She shakes her head. "I'm fine. I must check on Moussa. He's in the back with the other children. I shall return."

He takes a bite, watching her weave in and out of clusters of cast members, until she disappears down a short hall into a bedroom.

Beau taps his wine glass to get everyone's attention. His deep basso profundo quiets the room. "Fellow thespians, I want to acknowledge our distinguish writer and director. To thank them on your behalf for giving us the joy of their tremendous talents." He pauses as the room bursts into applause. "And to inform you an invitation has been extended to bring our repertoire to Ghana and Nigeria. This will require a lot of money, of course, but we'll pursue all possibilities to raise the funds. And now, our guests would like to say something."

Kwaku comes forward carrying a big box. "A small token, from us to you, for inviting us here and presenting our work with such a magnificent cast." He shifts the box to applaud them, then says to Beau, "You must receive this for all."

Beau opens it and takes out a mask finely carved in rich mahogany. Oke unwraps another package and takes out a huge piece of fabric. "This is akwete cloth named after the city in eastern Nigeria where the weavers who make these designs live. This pattern honors those who hear the words of the ancestors. This is what we believe writers do. By extension, you the actors, all those who create the theatrical experience—you are the bearers of those words. And so we thank you. Until we meet again, may there be rain to cool you and water your crops, sun to warm you, and all goodness be yours."

He bows and hands the cloth to Beau, who says, "I promise these gifts will be displayed in the theater this week for all to see and appreciate."

Kwaku laughs. "And we brought some records from West Africa. All of you must join us in dance."

Some cast members set their plates on the table and get up. A few know steps because they're taking dance classes at a studio run by two African drummers in Harlem. Bill finishes his food as he watches. Kwaku goes to the kitchen and brings Nusa out while Oke changes the record. Bill notices the fluid movements: Kwaku calling and Nusa's subtle answers. Now bold, now teasing, now soft, but always vibrating on the beat to the drums and other percussive instruments.

From the circle of dancers Esther says, "Whew, sister can move!"

He watches her lithe, swaying body and nods. Indeed she can.

When the record ends another is quickly placed on the turntable and again the dancers are caught up in rhythms. This time Oke comes to the circle and Nusa responds. The movements are different now. She twirls and stops in front of Esther, who's now partner to Oke. Nusa and Kwaku go around the room encouraging everyone to join in. Bill unfolds himself from the chair and manages to get his tall body to move not too awkwardly to the beat. Everyone's on their feet, clapping and dancing, for almost an hour.

At last, panting, Bill drops back in his chair. "Let the young people do it."

He sees Nusa slip away to the kitchen and bring out a bowl of fruit. Then, with Lynn helping, they set out fruit drinks. Obviously Nusa made these, too. She doesn't drink alcohol, observing the Muslim prohibition against it.

Bill talks with the Caribbean writer and a few actors, then looks around for Nusa but doesn't see her. He gets up and pokes his head into the kitchen.

Lynn is there, along with a friend, washing dishes. "Can I get something for you?"

"No, I was looking for Nusa. She lives near me, so we could ride home together."

"Oh, that's nice of you. But she's gone. Teaching a class in the morning, and she has some reading to do."

"Okay, thanks. By the way, great party." She smiles, and Bill goes back to his chair.

Kwaku comes over. "May I join you?"

"Please. We haven't had much time to talk."

"Yes, it's true. I want you to know how impressed I am with your acting skills. You've trained well."

"Well, I'm also older than you young people. Been doing this longer."

Kwaku sits on the floor in front of him. "No, it's more than that. You are too modest. It's the way you prepare yourself. I can actually feel the spirit of the persona take over your body. You enter already in character. I look at you and I say to myself, if only we had more exchange with each other. My company at home could benefit so much from the things you could teach them."

"We're equally indebted to you for bringing us a new way of experiencing English."

Kwaku watches him a moment. "May I ask a question?"

Bill tenses. Something in the man's voice reminds him of that evening so very long ago: Liza, him, a couch, and two sets of anxious, angry parents staring. Saying nothing, he smiles.

"It's just that Nusa is like a very dear sister to me. To us," says Kwaku. "Her situation is difficult for those who knew her back home. She always had a smile, a cheery manner. And Hamid, have you met him?"

Bill tells him no.

"Well, he's a great composer and musician. Everyone believes he will put African music on the map. We're the product of post colonialism, if indeed we are post. We're expected to do something magnificent. Nusa has changed her course. That's why she's doing literature. The divorce makes life at home almost impossible for her."

"Where is her husband?"

"Ex-husband. They've divorced now. She's not sure where he is. So she's a Muslim woman raising an African boy-child, alone in America. She defied her father, first by refusing to marry his choice, electing to marry a man of her preference and leaving home. That began the outcast process. Divorcing, refusing to send the grandson to her father...well, that led him to make the ultimate declaration. She's no longer his daughter. All her siblings are denied contact with her. One brother, with whom she's very close, manages to send money from time to time." Kwaku sighs again.

"So I am asking you to be careful. She's strong and intelligent. Yet should a divorced woman go back she will be an object of ridicule. Some would try to use her as a sexual object. Nusa says she will not return after her studies. It will be better for her to get a job here and take care of her son."

Bill hesitates, unsure what to say to all this. "I think she's a fine woman and have nothing but the highest respect for her."

After the vigorous performance at the theater, some over-eating and dancing, and the actors begin to fade. Bill gets up and finds Beau. "Listen, man. This has been great but I'm getting tired. See you at the theater tomorrow. And thanks for the party."

Beau beams with pride as they shake hands. Lynn calls, as Bill prepares to leave, "Oh, are you going?"

"Yes, time to take the old boy home. It's past my bedtime." He picks up his bag and weaves through the crowd to the door.

Outside he walks at a brisk pace. It's cool, not too humid, so he's not dripping with sweat when he reaches his building. He hopes to get a bit done before sleep. To read over the script again before rehearsal tomorrow. He drapes his clothes across a chair and pulls on pajamas. Turning back the covers, he slides between the lightweight blanket and sheets. As he falls asleep, the pages of the script slide to the floor.

With a start, Bill awakens. He rises to go through his ritual stretches, knee bends, and deep breathing. Just as he starts out for a bike ride, the phone rings.

"Hello, good morning, Bill," says Nusa. "Sorry to disturb you so early but I have a problem. It's time for me to take Moussa to his school, but…the super is in my hallway, trying to get inside. I don't want to call the police. He is a poor man with many problems."

Bill sits down, frowning. "What's his reason for being outside your door?"

She sighs. "Last night, he tried to climb in through my window. I woke, hearing noise on the fire escape. He was blinded by my flashlight and Hollis—you remember him, my floormate? He'd put up a barrier so it's not possible for the window to be opened wide.

People came to their windows when I screamed, so the super left. However, this morning, he tried to open the bathroom door when I was inside. Now he's trying to force his way into the apartment."

Bill jumps up. "Look, stay put. I'll be right over."

He rushes over, remembering all the way what his father said. Clearly, this super is not a real man. Passing the furniture store at the corner of Avenue C, he sees the owner. Cheap chairs and tables crowd the showroom floor. Bill leaves his bike inside, near the door. Alarm spreads over the man's face as Bill nears and towers over him.

He uses his most menacing tone, projecting as if on stage so the few workers dusting and moving chairs can hear. "I've just been called by one of your tenants, a young mother with a small son. She is under siege by your super who, even as we speak, is outside her door trying to force himself on her. She says she's spoken with you about the behavior of this man, yet you've done nothing to rein him in. Now I'm going upstairs. I suggest you call the police, and your lawyer." The he storms out of the store.

After locking his bike securely under the stairs Bill races up all four flights. The super, staggering, already hopped up first thing in the morning, is shouting to Nusa through the door. "Come on honey, open up. I'll treat you good. Be a father to the boy. Come on, let me in." He spins to face Bill, who touches his shoulder, then pushes him up against the wall. Without a word he punches the gaping man in the mid-section.

"Umph!" the super wheezes, going down on all fours. At that moment, from the landing, a lone white policeman, gun drawn, yells, "Freeze!"

Bill steps back and looks down on the super, who sits up cradling his big belly and groaning. "Help me. This man is trying to kill me, the fucking nigger."

The owner stumbles up now and stands gasping on the top step. "That's," he pants, pointing at Bill, "the man. Look, he's attacking my employee."

The young policeman hesitates, looking from Bill to the owner.

Nusa opens her door. "Officer?"

The policeman turns; the gun wavers slightly, now beams on her.

"Oh, I'm so happy to see you. This man," she says, pointing to the super, "has been harassing me. Last night he tried to slip into my apartment through the window. This morning he started again, first trying to force his way into the bathroom, now trying to get me to let him inside. But why? I do not want him."

Bill steps closer to her, worried the confused policeman might shoot.

"I've spoken with him, the owner, so many times," Nusa adds. "But he refuses to help."

The policeman lowers the gun and after a couple seconds, puts it back in the holster. "Can you stand?" he asks the super.

The man levers himself up slowly, moaning and groaning, a la Acting 100.

"Do you want to go to the hospital?"

The man shakes his head because, Bill surmises, he doesn't want his ruse to be discovered.

"I didn't know these things had been going on," protests the owner. Bill gives him a look and he averts his eyes.

"But I have spoken with you and sent many notes," Nusa calls down. "You never answer me."

The owner scowls. "I shouldn't have rented to you. Nothing but trouble." He turns to the officer. "You don't know how hard it is to get a reliable worker. This man keeps the building clean and is always on hand in case of emergencies, so I—"

Bill cuts in. "Officer, let your eyes be the judge. Do you see cleanliness? These windows haven't been washed in years."

The officer looks around and smiles.

Hollis comes up the steps at this moment. "Well, so finally the police got you. Now if only they can catch your junkie friends for those break-ins." He turns to the officer. "Look, he's been harassing this woman ever since he started working here. We have to protect her from him all the time."

When the owner squeaks out, "Why didn't you tell me?" Hollis huffs in exasperation.

The officer says to Nusa, "You wrote to the owner complaining of this man's behavior. Do you have copies of those letters?" She nods. "Good. Take them to Housing Court."

Bill turns to the owner. "Told you to call your lawyer."

The policeman escorts the super downstairs. The owner follows them, still denying all knowledge of events. "Avoid all contact with this lady," the officer tells the super sternly. "Inside and outside the building."

The owner tells the policeman he will offer Nusa another apartment if she wants to move.

"I think he'll leave you alone now," says Bill. "Got to get going. I'll check on you later. I'm in rehearsal all day but I'll come by this evening."

"Thank you," she says. "I have to take Moussa to school by taxi because he's late. Then come back and type two chapters and see my thesis advisor this afternoon." As he starts down the stairs, she calls out, "*Salaam*, Bill. May Allah reward you for your help."

From behind her Moussa pokes his head out. "*Salaam*, Bill!"

"*Salaam*, Little Man. Take care of your mother."

Unlocking his bike, he sees the super standing nearby. Bill stands up with the chain in his hands, not speaking, just staring him down. The super backs into the doorway. Bill mounts and pedals off.

The ride calms him. A group of girls are walking along Avenue D, just ahead, giggling and gossiping. Bill tries to imagine his daughter, Amanda. She should be pretty, because Liza was at her age. She had such lively, sparkling eyes before their forced marriage, just like these girls. After the marriage her gaze was two candles flickering, guttering, in the last stages of life.

He prays now, under his breath, "Please, keep that fire in Amanda's eyes. Don't let our anger spoil it." Then sighs and pedals on, inhaling the fumes of car exhaust and the dark smoke spewed by a tugboat gliding down the fetid East River.

HUSSEIN

Struggling with a battered black trunk and a portable typewriter Hussein makes his way into his building on East 6th Street and Avenue C. His apartment is on the top floor. He's recently arrived in New York; the university helped him secure this place. Standing at the threshold he surveys what he hopes will be his home for the next four or five years, while he completes his studies. The kitchen lies to the left. To the right, empty rooms yawn. Clean white walls smile at him. Setting the typewriter on the floor, Hussein decides not to pause and remove his shoes. He raises his hands. "*Bismillahi walajnaa, wa bismillahi Kharajnaa, wa'alla Rabinaa tawaakkalnaa.* In the Name of Allah we enter, in the Name of Allah we leave, and upon Our Lord we depend.

But there's no one else there to say, "*As-salaam alaykum.*"

Shrugging, he goes back down to drag his trunk up the stairs, slowly. Then sits for a few minutes and designs his new home in his head. Two and a half hours before the delivery of a few pieces of furniture. He's bought a bed and a table with four chairs.

He goes out into the hall to locate the toilet. His apartment has a shower stall in a back room. That one, he decides, will be his bedroom. The shower's just wide enough for him to enter and turn once; that's about it. Still, he's grateful. For a month he lived uptown in a dormitory, sharing the space with some very unclean men. The whites thought he should wipe up after them. They often made offensive racial jokes, but he said nothing and avoided crossing their paths. This is America. He's studied the history enough to know how they have treated his people, before and now. Oh well, he's here now, and it will be much better. He hurries out to pick up a few household supplies.

There is a small general store on the corner and he's able to get a bucket, a mop, and several kinds of cleansers and towels. The owner, a man from Puerto Rico, says to him in Spanish, "You look like one of my cousins back home."

When Hussein tells him he's from Africa, the man crosses himself.

Hussein is weary of insults. He starts putting the things back on the shelves. No, he won't stand for this kind of stuff right in his face and then actually pay for it.

The man looks sheepish; he smiles and apologizes. "Sorry, *señor*. I mean no harm. It's just, I never see a man from Africa before. Only one woman who live over on East 10th Street. She got a little son. Very nice lady, smart. Goes to university. I think she gonna marry an older man from here. He black, very nice too. Give me and my *espousa* tickets to one of his plays."

Hussein relents, pays for his things, and rushes off.

A big truck pulls up to his building just as he turns the corner. He shoulders the mop and goes in ahead of the delivery man. When they get to the top floor the man turns sour. "Hey, man, nobody said you was on the top floor with no elevator. I can't be lugging all this stuff up so many stairs."

Hussein says, "Come then, I'll help."

Together they trudge, slanting the mattress all the way up four flights to the fifth floor. His arms ache when everything's finally inside. Sitting on the trunk, Hussein looks left and right. *"Ya Allah!"* He gets up wearily and shifts the table into one corner, then pushes the chairs in around it. "Good." He is pleased.

About a month later he has his first sighting of roaches. Having developed a thirst from writing and then reading aloud the last few paragraphs of a paper due in a few days, he gets up, stretches his arms overhead, and flexes cramped hands. The long fingers open-shut, open-shut. He goes to the kitchen sink and turns on the tap, letting the water run a minute. Remembering his grandmother's caution that ice water is bad for the stomach, he does not keep a jug in the refrigerator. He turns on the overhead light and sees something dark covers the counter. A moving tablecloth of brown bugs. He freezes, and almost shouts. At first he's shocked to see all the cockroaches fleeing over white enamel tops and down the white table legs, following-the-leader across the floor and under the sink. Whoosh! They're gone.

All thoughts of thirst and water vanish. What if this army, this insect brigade should return while he's asleep? His skin crawls and puckers as if a thousand slimy bodies are crawling over him, up legs and chest. He shivers and shudders. Now they will be inching their way up his neck and chin. A smell of decay and rotting cabbage, so vivid it seems real, perfumes their steady march over his face. He imagines trying to wake up, to push them all off. His lips clamp down; saliva fills his mouth. He turns to the sink, certain he will vomit, but no. At last he washes out his mouth and splashes his face. He sets the water glass upside-down on a clean, dry towel. After that it's difficult to focus on "Kinetic Abstraction and the Discipline of Idiomatic Composition." Images of an imminent invasion more deadly than a mushroom cloud run amok in his mind. Finally Hussein pushes away his pad and books, shuts off the light, and gets up. The window beside the fire escape is open. He climbs out and sits staring at the sky. It's late October, still very warm in the City. Most of the apartments are dark, because it's late.

Even as a child he hated insects, the huge bugs that collected around their carafes. His uncle crafted an air-tight top so they were unable to creep in and pollute the water. But sometimes, when disturbed by sudden motion or light, they would fly up to escape. One time, he must've been around eight, he made the mistake of coming into the cooking area to get something. He no longer remembers what. The scratching and rustling of countless bristly legs across the wooden tabletop, and the ones that flew around his head, all made him flail his arms to shield his face and strike out wildly. One scurried under his foot. When he took a step its chitinous shell burst. The horror of the glutinous ooze beneath his bare sole froze him to the spot. When he was finally able to move, the insect flesh stuck to the curve of his arch. Hussein smiles, recalling how he'd washed his feet again and again to rid them of the slime. Now, almost twenty years later, he's plotting how to revenge himself on the bugs' American cousins. Tomorrow, first thing, he'll go back to the general store and tell the Puerto Rican shopkeeper he needs to buy the most effective, powerful bug killer there is.

Yes, he will suffocate them, and their parents and children and grandparents. Plug their breathing apparatus with deadly poison and watch them slowly die.

But then his grandmother's face swims up into the forefront of his thoughts. "*Ibnou.*" She always called him that, Little Son. "Remember, do no harm to Allah's creatures. All life has value."

Well, it has not yet been revealed to him the importance of these dirty, disgusting bugs. Their looks repel him. He prays to be forgiven.

The next morning the shop owner seems shocked to see all Hussein's purchases. His arms are filled with several cans of insecticide. Also disinfectants, sponges, and two more mops. He threw the other one away after cleaning up the mess last night.

Seeing the man's quizzical look, he says, "You see, I just moved into my apartment."

Apparently that was sufficient. "Ah. Yes, I understand." The owner smiles as he adds up the bill. "Maybe you go down to Chinatown? They got some powder you can put around after you clean. They say it stops bugs from breathing."

"Thank you." Hussein pays and takes the bags. Visions of dead bugs dance before him. He smiles at that image, himself victorious.

Walking home carrying his stuff along Avenue A, he considers whether he'll go to the Chinese section, too. Imagining slowly-asphyxiated cockroaches; well, it's a cruelty he cannot support. Maybe after some intensive scouring and spraying in crevices behind the sink and counters, around the door and in the bathroom, the disgusting creatures will be daunted and vacate the premises. Surely even bugs can sense when they are not wanted.

For some reason a new image, the bloated belly of a white man, comes to mind. Then he remembers where it's from. He'd been watching the news at a bar the previous week. On the small screen a pale man stood at the edge of a public swimming pool, sun-red flesh bulging over the top of his black swim trunks. Scampering frantically, several little black children swam to get out of the pool as a crowd of whites blocked their path. For a few seconds the crowd watched as the man poured acid from a can into the pool. Fortunately the water greatly diluted the potency of the chemicals. They were finally able to climb out with only minimal burns.

Hussein shivers, considering what he's planning to do to some of Allah's nonhuman creatures. But they spread disease and are unclean, he reasons. But already he knows. Now he won't be able to bring himself to use the ultimate weapon, even on foul creatures come to try his very humanity.

He buys some oranges and apples from the frail old woman who sits on a milk crate next to her pushcart. He still wonders how she manages to move it back and forth. Maybe someone comes in the early evening to help her. He knows she's Slavic and Muslim, because once he'd sneezed when a cloud of dust stirred up by a passing bus blocked his nose. From force of habit he'd said, "*Alhamdulillahi.*"

The woman had brightened and looked up. "*As salaamu alaykum.*" Now, whenever she sees him, she acts as if they're related.

But he's on a deadly mission and cannot be deterred, or even stop to chat. He hurries upstairs to prepare for war; his extermination of an unclean species. He enters the kitchen and says, "Prepare to move, or to meet your maker."

His declaration goes unanswered. So he sets the spray cans on the table. After reading the instructions he plots his course. First, clean the floors and counters, making sure there are no dishes or glasses left out. Next cover his bed and towels. He worries a little about the effects of this sort of poison on humans. But the recollection of those crawling hordes last night removes all hesitation.

After covering everything with large sheets of newspaper, Hussein satisfies himself with a second look around. Yes, the bed is under two layers of the *Times*, some brown wrapping paper, and a week-old *Herald Tribune*. He picks up his book bag, with a snack inside, along with his writing pad, and puts them out in the hall. Then he sets up the aerosol bomb in the middle of the kitchen floor. As the label instructs, he lays newspaper under the can as well, so it doesn't mar his beautifully-painted floor. Quickly he snaps the weapon open. It hisses with reptilian fervor, spraying an immediate mist of deadly fumes. Then, holding his breath, he rushes to the door. "Whew!" he exhales at last, shutting himself out, and the poison vapor inside.

It's a sunny fall day. School is out, and thousands of youngsters have taken to the streets. In front of his building a makeshift game with a stick, reminiscent of cricket, is under way. A slight brown boy flexes his bat, eyes fixed dead on another boy a few feet away, who's gripping a white ball. Now, this is a street where two buses traverse east and west. Although they have irregular schedules, there are also lots of cars and pedestrian traffic. However, none of this seems to bother the boys. Clearly their game, played under a clear sky out in the warm fresh air, is most important.

Pop. Stick connects with ball. With a clatter the stick drops to the street. The little boy's off, flashing towards designated spots. His fans cheer him on, while other two boys scamper down the street after the ball. Barely avoiding an old lady who yells in outrage, and a young woman pushing a baby carriage.

Hussein decides to walk over to the library on the Westside. He has four or five hours to wait for the insecticide to do its murderous work. Streets are festooned with people in bright dresses and shirts, all kinds of get-ups. The percussive rhythm of feet pattering on pavement at East 11th Street thrills him. Cars add a chorus: *beep-hee-honk*. Shapes dot an impressionistic canvas of steel gray; buildings, sidewalks, a few of the people. A lighter feeling twirls up inside from his belly: Hussein wants to dance up and around the fire hydrants and play hide-and-seek between cars, too. But he keeps his stride westward.

By the time he crosses Avenue C and 11th Street again, deepening purples are giving way to naval blues. At the corner of 11th three young men are speaking Spanish to a pretty girl sitting in a first-floor window. She smiles broadly, basking in so much male attention. Hussein makes a wide circle, careful to keep his gait but far enough away not to 'touch their shadows." As he passes their voices lower. There's a 'sizing up' pause. He keeps on, crossing on the east side of Avenue C onto 6th. Turning the corner onto his own street he lets out a held breath. One of the older tenants in the building has warned him about the local "do-nothings" who hang around all day plotting how to rob a person or break into your apartment and steal everything they can get their hands on, mostly to buy drugs. "They're junkies," the super says. "What do they care?"

Hussein climbs the stairs to the top floor. He opens his door with some caution. Fearing perhaps an armed defense; an uprising of creepy-crawlies, he waits for the onslaught. Nothing attacks, except the odious stench of shut-in gases. He opens all the windows, breathing shallowly. Then back out into the hall, where he waits about five minutes and then reenters. Gingerly he removes the empty canister. He rolls up all the paper from bed, table, chairs and sofa. The few plants he has are on the fire escape. They can stay out overnight. Wadding the paper and everything up, he stuffs it into one of the large shopping bags from a little storage bin he's put under the sink He runs with this down to the garbage cans, shoves the contaminated stuff in, and shuts the lid tight.

For now he washes just the things needed to prepare his dinner, including the stove. Using soapy water, then rinsing with diluted white vinegar, he feels cleaner as he wipes it down. Then pots, a pan, a plate, glass and cutlery. All the while he keeps the door propped open. The cool cross-breeze it pulls from the windows blows the scents of insecticide and cooking out, so his apartment smells fresh. Around midnight he writes out his plans for the next day. Tomorrow, Thursday, he will wash down the whole place so that Friday he can go to prayers at the Riverside Drive mosque, then come home and do some printing. Most of his photographs are yet to be developed. He must create a schedule for printing, studying, reading and writing. So much to do! Up early, he attacks the massive cleaning project with well-rested vigor. But shortly after he finishes mopping the kitchen a wave of nausea rolls over him. At the same time, there's a tightening in his chest. Hussein gasps for breath and struggles to the door. Once out in the hall his lungs expand more freely. An old woman, the super's wife, appears out of the gloom like a ghost. A small apparition, clutching a mop and sniffing. The dimly-lit hall makes this impression stronger. Hussein is briefly fearful that she is a *jinn*. After impassively watching him heave and gasp a few moments, the old woman goes to his door and looks around. She peers in at the bucket on his clean floor, and his cleaning agents: ammonia, bleach, cleanser. Plus a fresh spray can of death-to-bugs mist.

She steps back and waves her arms wildly. Pointing to the bucket, she shakes her head and holds up one finger. "One," she manages to make her tongue pronounce in English.

"What? What're you saying?" Hussein wheezes.

The woman goes to his living room window, but the catch is too high for her to reach. She does an animated pantomime, a sort of arm-waving jig, and he comes back in to open it. Dusty air from the shaft between too-close buildings tickles his throat, and he coughs. The woman goes into his bathroom, wets a towel and hands it to him. Hussein holds it against his face until his eyes stop tearing. Later, when he tells one of his fellow students about this scene, he says, "Whew! You could've killed yourself. Bleach and ammonia together? Man, that's, like, poisonous." Well, now he knows.

Hussein settles into a three-day-a-week class schedule, and a twenty-hours weekly teaching assistantship with an old professor who, it's whispered behind his back, will soon retire. Hussein, brought up to respect age, enjoys his talks with the older man. Professor Benton was in The War. That is, World War II. A medic because of his beliefs about not bearing arms and killing. After the war he was able to go to college under veteran benefits. "I'm the first college graduate in my family," he tells Hussein. Who nods, understanding just what that means. While he's not the first, there were many in his own family who'd wanted to continue their studies but were unable to do so. His father is a successful merchant who's managed to send many of his brothers to college. His uncle, his mother's brother, is head of the local school. He teaches all subjects, including Quranic and Arabic texts and traditions. His mother comes from an old family who pride themselves as being among the first Shahadahs. His father chose wisely.

Hussein is at an age himself when a man should wed. His youth is in full bloom and he often has an urge he recognizes with some fear. But in this new place, there is no one to negotiate a *bori* for him. His brothers and uncles have warned him about foreign women with loose morals. He does not wish to sin, but his manly needs keep asserting their wishes. It has been a long time since he's been with a woman. He imagines his mother's face, bordered by her *hejab*, admonishing him against fornication. Oh, he tried hard to obey her, but his friends explained it was unmanly to be as inexperienced as a wife on the wedding night.

So he decides now to scout around for some nice girl. There are many unattached women in New York. His mother would most certainly comment on this, were she here. He sighs and feels a swell of loneliness rise. He's been in the City by then for almost two semesters

Adding a light jacket to shirt and jeans, Hussein heads off to enjoy a free night. He walks around, passing several local characters in full costume and wishes he'd brought his camera. With no specific destination in mind he ambles over to Avenue C and continues north until he comes to a bar called Stanley's. He opens the wood and glass door. A cloud of smoke greets him, so pungent a force he almost turns away. Blinking, he enters. This is a popular place for artists to meet, with a reputation for serious talk and boozing. Truly Bohemian.

The thick glass and ornately carved door seem out of place. It's what Hussein imagines Old European cafes must look like. Behind the bar, a mirror running the width of the counter reflects short and tall, various-sized, colored bottles. A sticky white man stands before it, a white dish towel in one hand, a beer stein in the other. He's having a deep conversation with another man sitting on a bar stool. Hussein walks past to the back where the serious writers and artists hang out. From here, it looks less overcast with dark-grey tobacco clouds.

"May I join you?" he asks a table of men. At the sound of his deep voice and crisp accent, ears seem to perk up. Two men push back and make space. "Sure, grab a chair." Hussein turns and sees an unoccupied one at the next table. He takes it and drapes his jacket over it, sitting with his back to the wall. Everyone introduces themselves. About nine men, mostly black, with one lone white man and an olive-skinned fellow who says he's from South America.

"My name is Hussein Ali Abdullah. I'm a graduate student at NYU. A photographer." He adds that last to qualify his presence in their midst.

"Where you from, Hussein?" a black man asks.

"I was born in Nigeria."

"Nigeria, eh. Well, that's all right with me. I'm from the South, Tennessee, to be exact."

A younger man extends a hand. "Charles-Michel Beauchamp. But everyone calls me Charlie. I'm a writer."

After introductions are complete, they order rounds. When Hussein asks for seltzer, heads turn to stare. "I don't drink alcohol. It's against my religion and culture."

Bill, older than the rest, asks, "Oh, say. Are you Muslim?"

Hussein nods.

A brash young guy smirks. "Well, that's not my situation. In fact, the more the merrier." He laughs and looks around for support but mostly gets embarrassed looks.

Jim, the white man sitting next to Bill, nods. "*As-salaam alaykum.*"

Hussein responds appropriately. One of the black men quips, voice dripping with sarcasm, "Jim—or rather Ja-mal— just married an African woman. He's converted to Islam."

Hussein salutes him, "*Alhamdulillah.*"

Bill says, "My lady's also a Nigerian Muslim. I was turned off religion so badly early on, that it's hard for me to commit to any faith. But from since being with her, I can say it has much I like."

The conversation shifts gradually, taking on a racial drift. Clearly the black men are not pleased that Jim-Jamal, a musician from Canada, has married a 'sister' and also plays jazz.

"You're stealing our identity," one says.

Tim, a painter and leather craftsman, says, "People should be free to love, be with and, marry whom they choose. But," he adds, "An artist needs to be careful when selecting a mate. Sometimes people have specific needs."

Charlie nods. "It's hard being a male artist. I mean, women are brought up to expect men to take care of them. Most of us can barely take care of ourselves. I lucked out. Emily, my white woman, helps in many ways. Types perfect copies of all my manuscripts. She understands I love her but my work comes first. That's just the way an artist is."

Another man, whose name Hussein didn't catch, says, "I was married to a sister, but had to leave her. First thing she wanted to know was when we were gonna get a house. I said I needed time to sell some paintings to afford one. I was a substitute teacher with two free days to just paint. Well, she hit the ceiling. Said I had an education better than most white men did. She expected me to get a good job so she could quit hers and start a family."

Heads nod. The men all agree black women don't see art as a real job. No way equal to a doctor, lawyer or business man's. More a hobby no one can afford.

Bill frowns. "Nusa's both a scholar and writer. She encourages and supports me. Her position in a rich white girls' college pays the bills. Now we're married, I'll even have benefits."

Tim cheers. "Man, you got it made! Better not let her escape."

Bill adds, "Well my work at the theater and a few T.V. appearances help."

Most of the rest goes over Hussein's head so he doesn't add much to the conversation at this point. Besides, he knows different. There are three women in one of his classes; one black and two white. The black woman is pretty, very sharp. She speaks up, even to the professor. Hussein heard one of the white women say the black woman is probably just there because the school's trying to prove it's progressive. "She gets a better grade because the professor feels sorry for her." But seldom does either of the white women speak up. However, his need is so great now, he feels willing to compromise on some of the qualities he would demands in a companion. It would not be a permanent situation, just some temporary relief until he can marry a good Muslim woman.

Hussein finds it interesting, for example, that black women here wear their hair uncovered, in a variety of modes; a halo around the face; very short; sometimes even shaved close. The other day he complimented a woman wearing a huge *gele*, but she smiled, saying, "Thanks, brother. But I'm from Charleston, South Carolina."

Now here he sits, thousands of miles from home, his back to the swinging doors of the kitchen. One of his professors wanted to give him an American name, "Harry" but he refused. His name reflects both grandfathers. Tradition dictates the use of the father's middle name. Abdullah is his father's and paternal grandfather's. So his name, Hussein Ali Abdullah is one he's proud of.

The smoke is getting thicker, making his eyes water. He goes to the men's room to wash his face. When he rejoins the table four more black men, two white women, and a black woman have pulled another table near. They all colonize the back of Stanley's while the din up front threatens to drown their philosophical pronouncements.

After another round of introductions, Hussein sits close to the black woman. Perhaps she will be interested in knowing more about him. She's from the Caribbean; her voice is lovely. A willowy white waitress dances over and with elaborate movements gives all the men special looks, almost ignoring the women. After taking orders she undulates off to the bar.

One man, Don, says, "I just wish I had my own name." He sighs. "This one is simply another consequence of slavery and racism."

At this moment "Dancing Diana," his name for the waitress, comes back. She sets their drinks on the tables, serving Bill first. "The manager sends this with his congratulations." She plants a kiss on his cheek.

When Bill raises his glass towards the bar to thank the manager, they all lift glasses and toast him.

Jim-called-Jamal tells Hussein, "I'm hoping for a position at a university on Long Island. They're trying to start up a modern music division. If I get it I'll begin a jazz studies program."

Hussein feels a vague ripple of some discontent run around the table, but Jamal continues, "My wife's finishing her dissertation and we're expecting our first child. I put my graduate studies on hold until I secure a teaching job. I'm a family man now. Speaking of which, we're planning a trip to Nigeria in two years then to Canada to see my family."

An uncomfortable silence falls at this news. Hussein isn't sure why.

A shabbily-dressed man comes hesitantly over. He approaches Jim and speaks to him quietly. Hussein sees Jim discreetly slip a hand in his pocket and hand the man some bills. The poor man hastily leaves, after Don and Tim turn their backs to him. One of the white women holds her nose.

Charlie shakes his head. "That's a shame. Cat used to be a fine musician. Now look at him. A damned junkie."

Hussein gazes after the man with interest. So that's what a junkie looks like.

Larry adds, "He used to play with you, didn't he, Jim?"

Jim faces them. "Yes, Fred played with us. Always dependable and on time. He just got hooked. Lots of us have fooled around with stuff. But we were more lucky."

Don looks abashed. "Well yeah, but there's a difference between fooling around, knowing when to quit, and getting strung out."

Jim gets up and goes to the men's room.

Bill shakes his head. "Don, go easy. Fred was young and naïve when he came here. Never did anything except play his horn. Word is, Chip got him started."

Don backs down, either because he respects Bill or at least the truth of the statement.

Just as Hussein gets up his nerve to engage the black woman in conversation, one of the white women says, "I've always wanted to go to Africa."

Bill asks, "Really, where? It's a big continent." He turns to Hussein. "So, what're you studying?"

Hussein answers, still looking at the black woman, "Literature but I take photography classes as well."

"I'm a dancer," says the woman, "But I studied education so I can teach when things get hard. All artists need a fall-back plan."

Melvin is in film. Susan's an actress interested in directing. "But being a woman makes it difficult. Men don't want to take direction from women."

"Maybe you'd like to come over to my apartment and see some of my photographs," says Hussein.

Courtney, the other white woman, jumps up. "That sounds great!"

All during this exchange, Naomi, the black woman says nothing.

"I can make something for you to eat." Almost everyone agrees to accompany him home. They settle the tab and leave, though Jim begs off because he has to go home to his wife. Some of the men snicker but for a moment Hussein feels a twinge of jealousy.

They stop by an all night delicatessen on 14th Street, then head south to East 6th, and Avenue C. Hussein takes out his keys and opens the downstairs door. After a series of break-ins the super put a lock on the door and insisted everyone use keys. Once again he blamed 'the junkies.' Hussein wonders if the man he saw earlier also steals.

On the top floor Hussein tells them, "I have few rules. First, no shoes inside. You may leave them here on the mat." He slips out of his and enters his bright, clean kitchen. Hears the 'oohs' and 'ahs' as they bend to remove shoes and comment on the apartment.

Naomi offers, "I'll do the food." Hussein shows her where things are and leaves her to it. As the group wanders around admiring the rooms he selects a record, leaving the door propped open to minimize the smell of smoked-infused clothing. Bill sits listening to Clifford Brown's trumpet fill the room. Melvin and Susan wrap around each other on floor pillows. The rattle of utensils from the kitchen drifts in to accompany the record. Tim and Don are talking by the window. Courtney's looking at his books on the shelves he made out of a discarded cabinet from the street.

Don is saying, "...after all, I'm a Southern boy. Just walked away from my father's farm. I miss them, but I got tired of being polite to folks just because they white, even when they nasty."

Tim nods. "To be honest, I was shocked by the racism here in New York. Yeah, it's the Lower East Side and we're all artists and thinkers. But I'm telling you, man, some of these cats act like they don't know it's 1962."

Finally Naomi calls everyone to come eat. Don offers a blessing. Hussein says his silently. They each take a plate and go back to the living room, telling stories how they ended up down here. Mel kisses Susan's neck. Don and Tim slap five. Susan asks Bill about some obscure writer who's enjoying a resurgence of performance. She's just read for a part at one of the Off-Broadway theatres on 2nd Avenue. "Oh that's wonderful news," Courtney squeaks. "I hope you get the part."

Hussein speaks up. "If you like I'll show you some photographs. Two are of my family. Three were taken in London and three in New York." He brings the portfolio from his bedroom and lays the black and white images on the floor.

"Hm, hm, hm!" Don muses. Hussein wonders what this means. "Yeah, man, this is *bad*."

Hussein draws back, hurt.

Bill quickly adds, "That means it's great. You know, comes from creating code words so our language won't be comprehended by The Boss. 'Bad' usually refers to a bodacious black man 'cause we supposed to be good little Negroes. So when somebody says bad, it means the best."

"Oh. I see." Hussein smiles and stores this away in his colloquial dictionary.

Naomi picks up a picture of the family compound.

"I took that when no one was looking," he explains, "because most of my people don't believe in photographic images. They think a camera is a soul-stealing instrument."

"This looks just like parts of Trinidad." Naomi points to his aunt's face. "And she looks like my mother."

Don snorts. "Sister, I keep tellin' you, we the same people."

Tim shrugs. "Maybe, but all these years, mixing and stuff, we got differences."

Everyone nods sagely.

"Hey, I heard in Africa a man can have more than one wife. That true?"

"Yes." Naomi asks, "What about your family?"

Hussein says simply, "I have six brothers and five sisters."

Don won't let go. "Does your father have more than one wife?"

"Yes." Bill also wants to know, "Does he have children with other wives?"

"I have two other mothers," Hussein admits. "One has ten children. The other has eight."

"Mother of God! That's thirty children," one of the women gasps.

"And there are about twenty grandchildren," he adds.

"But where do they all live?" Courtney asks.

"It's a very large compound. Each woman has her own place to accommodates her and the children," he answers quietly.

Courtney looks puzzled still. "So how do they, I mean... you know." Her voice tapers off.

Mel cuts to the heart of the matter. "Where do they go to do it?"

"Oh." Hussein's face feels warm. "My father has a schedule. Each woman has her night. We all eat together at dinner time. Sometimes he eats alone. Each wife contributes to the family meal. The children are shared. If one of the mothers is tired or unwell.

the others take on her responsibilities. My mother is the senior wife. Her special duties are to make sure the household runs smoothly and that there's food for everyone, and the children are well."

Hussein gets up and plays some African dance music and pushes back the pillows. "Maybe we talk enough and you'd like to dance." He picks up the pictures and takes them back to his room. Mel and Susan clutch at each other, unmindful of the rhythm. Naomi moves like a Nigerian and Hussein joins her. Don tries to dance with Courtney but she's constantly bumping up against Hussein, trying to get his attention.

Mel and Susan are the first to leave. Don and Bill soon follow. Larry offers to walk Courtney and Naomi home. When Courtney pulls a face it's obvious she was hoping to add Hussein to her list of black male bed partners. He feels put off, though; she is too aggressive. After they head down the stairs, though, he watches from his window and spots the tops of Mel and Susan's heads as they walk home to their place around the corner.

The small flat is his again but the lingering smells of food, the misplaced furniture, the rumpled pillows are evidence of the presence of people in his usually-solitary space. After putting things back in order, he takes a shower. He'll sleep a few hours and then get up to finish his assignment for literature class. Maybe get in an hour in the darkroom to finish a series he's mounting for a show. The super has given him the use of an old, unused hall toilet, and he's built a darkroom there. He keeps his cameras hidden in his flat, fearing they might be stolen. Under the dining table he's lifted a few floor boards and hid the cameras and a few valuables in a box between his floor and the ceiling of the apartment below. In a small safe in the back of his closet, in a metal box, he keeps his passport, student visas, and bank book. He's even managed to save some money. His father warned him to always have enough passage money at the ready to get back home.

November winds whip through his thick coat the next day as Hussein hurries into the United Nations' Building and up an escalator to the Delegate's Lounge. He's meeting an old friend for lunch. They used to be roommates, together terrorizing the head and some of the bullies at school. Each won all the competitions from their class and field. Now his friend is with the foreign service while he's still in school with at least two more years to go. He's decided to change his major to Film Studies. One of his professors has written him a recommendation to teach at the undergraduate level, two new courses in African literature that just got approved by the curriculum committee.

He's floating up on the "stairs that move without feet" as his mother once described her escalator experience in a department store in France. The only time she's gone to Europe, for his elder brother's graduation. Riding up he overhears two French men laughing about the night before, and their host's lavish party. Said host is a former colonial subject who went "all out."

"And his country's one of the ten poorest in the world," the fattest one sniggers.

They discuss how they ate and drank gluttonously and danced with African women provided for their pleasure, mocking the poor host's attempts to impress.

Hussein has no problem locating his old friend whose blue-black face, as he approaches, lights up with joy. Clearly Mahmoud is happy to see him. The smile slips a bit as Hussein removes his coat and jacket to reveal a shirt of *adire* with intricate shadings.

"Hey Bo, how body?" Hussein teases.

Mahmoud stiffens, adjusts immaculate white cuffs with tasteful but expensive gold links. "My brother, how are you?"

Hussein smiles. "Well, I am here. And it's so cold! I never imagined so many people could live, move, work and be next to each other all the time, and not go stark raving mad."

Mahmoud curls his lip. "Don't be so sure. They're all loony. Come, let's go inside and eat. You must be hungry. Remember as students how we were always hungry?"

Hussein allows him to lead the way into a large cool room. All the tables look the same, covered with white cloths topped by a glass vase holding three flowers to cheer the space. At strategic locations men in black suits and starched white shirts, with snowy linen towels draped over one arm, are stationed at the ready. Mahmoud gives a signal and one hurries over.

"This way sir." Singular, it's clear he is addressing Mahmoud. Hussein raises his eyebrows.

They're seated by a window that overlooks the East River. How different it appears from up here. Mahmoud smiles encouragingly over the tall menu. "Order whatever you like."

Hussein settles on baked salmon.

"Excellent choice, sir."

He doesn't respond because he's not sure a reply is expected.

"Hmm," muses Mahmoud. "I think I shall have the steak, medium rare, and salad. Would you like some wine? No, I suppose, since you are an observer."

Again, he does not respond. This time puzzled because Mahmoud should be 'an observer' as well. He takes advantage of Mahmoud's distraction to observe him handling the menu and giving his order to the waiter. And then acknowledging an acquaintance who waves to him. Mahmoud smiles as he stands to nod to the man. How well he is dressed, Hussein realizes now. A suit of Italian silk, such impeccable tailoring, Spanish leather shoes, discreet tie, all imply chic without being ostentatious. His new friends would call Mahmoud 'cool.'

Yes, things have changed. One friend is outwardly, successfully elegant. The other, ethnic and perhaps sophomoric.

They eat their meal sprinkled with reminiscences and safe, superficial conversation, nothing political or cultural. Once Hussein slips from the script, though.

"I'm really getting a bit of play with my photography. A small downtown gallery is exhibiting two dozen pieces for two weeks. There'll be a reception this Saturday. If you could make it, I would love that."

Mahmoud picks an invisible bit of something from his cuff. "Oh. And what time? You know, when the Assembly's in session, we're on call. What with the conflict in Hungary, we're scheduled to vote as soon as the language is hammered out."

Hussein shakes his head. "Yes, of course. It must be terribly busy for you. I'm just a little school boy, playing at being an intellectual and artist."

He pauses, looking Mahmoud right in the eye. "But I really would like it if you could attend, so you can see what I'm becoming. And to meet some people who've helped to develop my eye."

Mahmoud shrugs one shoulder. "Well…"

"I went south last year, to Tennessee and visited some churches. I met lots old black people. They were so like us! I mean, they still look like us. Sometimes I'd close my eyes and I could almost hear the inflection of Hausa or Yoruba. I took pictures of the land. Some of those are in the exhibit. The last two of a woman who was battered by a white man. He tried to snatch her in broad daylight, pull her in a car to rape her. She fought back. Nothing happened to him. Apparently she was lucky not to be charged with attacking a white person, so I—"

But now Mahmoud is looking pained, perhaps annoyed. Hussein quickly changes the subject.

Lunch winds down. His friend gives subtle hints that his time is limited, and he soon leaves.

Down the escalator Mahmoud's final advice echoes in his ear. "Hussein, be careful. This place is not as it appears. You must get a good position when you graduate. Look, I can help you get assignments for the U.N. to go abroad, photograph situations. They pay very well because often these are dangerous places and the risks grave. But if you have too strong an opinion on The War or Black people in the South, they won't hire you. Just brotherly words of caution."

Hussein sighs, wanting to believe him. Mahmoud had been closer to him than even his senior brother. It was his old friend to whom he told his secrets. The first one he told when he decided to apply to schools outside of West Africa, and the first time he went to his uncle's *bori*. Now he isn't sure if there's still a bond. Although Mahmoud promised to put together a show for him at their consulate in the near future.

Hussein did not tell him about the conversation he'd overheard on the escalator.

Saturday mornings, sidewalks are usually littered. Mounds of dog dung sit like mines in the spaces where people are supposed to walk.

This morning Hussein asks a woman if she would pull back her dog, as he needs to pass by.

She looks up in utter shock. "Why, a big strapping man like you, afraid of a little puppie-wuppie like my Baby-waby?"

Hussein shook his head. "Miss, I'm unafraid of dogs. I just don't want him to touch me."

"Why?" Incredulity seemed to push the question out of her mouth.

"Because in my culture dogs are considered unclean animals. It would require me to cleanse myself afterwards."

A rash-like redness creeps up from her collar and seems to choke off her response. She grips the leash as her body stiffens. The dog's ears swivel to zero-in on some perceived danger to his mistress.

The woman curls her lip. "Well, in my culture black men are unclean animals. After coming in contact with them we must clean ourselves." She spun on one heel. "Come on, Baby. Mommy will take you on the other side of the street so that that bad man can't see you. Unclean!" She glares back over one shoulder. "Mommy loves her Baby Boy, yes she does." She fumbles in one pocket. "Look what I have for you!" She pulls out a dog biscuit and the dog takes it, slobbering into her hand. She raises the hand to her mouth and kisses her fingers.

Hussein winces as they cross the street, shaking his head. He'd seen Baby lick a spot of some dog urine on the sidewalk just before he'd spoken to the woman. But then, he'd already deduced that New York people love dogs more than humans.

Saturday mornings he reserved to write letters home, then go to the post office to send them and to collect his mail from the box he rents. Mostly his father writes and tells him what his mother says. In the last letter she was very insistent that he send for his arranged 'wife' soon. Hussein smiles, remembering Salimatou. She's about eight or so years younger than he. At seventeen he'd felt very grown-up coming from his night with Binti. Now that he is twenty-eight, she must be nineteen or twenty.

Hussein sighs, guilty. He did not feel quite ready for a wife. Besides, this is not a good place for an African woman. She won't have her village, or a gathering of women to talk to. No local mosque to run to for daily prayers.

He's made such excuses as he occasionally bedded one of the willing women of the Lower East Side. Naomi still ignores him. But his school load and photography make more and more demands, and act as a sort of restraint, too.

At the post office he takes his packet of letters out and notices his father's neat, precise script. Two letters have a small likeness of the Queen stamped on them. One will be from his middle brother, who's studying in London, and one from his second mother's last son, who's just begun his courses. He takes them all and heads home.

One letter is from his mother. "Dear son," it begins, as usual. She tells him of all the latest happenings. This one has brought forth. That one passed his Cambridge. Baba is well. But then he spots a paragraph that stops in his tracks.

*So I am sending your wife to you. We did the marriage last Jumah. Al Hajji Latif stood in. She will arrive in shallah on the 28*th*. She is travelling on BOA and will arrive 2:00 at Idyllwild Airport. May Allah protect her and let her reach safely. Salaam.*

Hussein stops short in the hallway and nearly misses the first step, almost falling on his face. He clutches at his precious camera, instinctively choosing it over his armload of books. But quick reflexes save everything. He rushes upstairs. Then, sitting at the table, he reads the letter again. In only ten days Salimatou will arrive. Here.

"*Ya Allah*, what to do now?" he whispers.

The place is clean. He's been very careful not to bring his few women to the apartment, but still. He isn't ready for a wife. They haven't seen each other in years. Here on the Lower East Side it is easy to forget the past. And so many new things he's experienced...well, he isn't sure he can adjust. But it's too late to call home and say no. Salimatou would lose face. His family would be disgraced.

He drops the letter and groans. "*Oumi*, you have no idea what my life is like here. The life of a student and artist. There are no women for her to be with! And I must have quiet to do my studies."

Even as he argues with himself aloud, Hussein looks around at the small space, unwillingly blocking out niches for Salimatou and her things. Oh, he knows very little of her now: what she likes, how she looks. This development feels like a major obstacle right now. On the other hand, it will save him from more sinning.

Reluctantly looking on the brighter side, Hussein puts the letter away with all the others from home. He warms his dinner and plans for at least three hours of study: an hour to read, an hour to write, and one more to review the work before bed. His professor has gotten the two courses for him to teach so that will bring a little extra money. Now that he's to be a married man, with responsibilities, he must be able to take care of a family.

But there is no one around to tell. He could speak with Bill but he's out of town doing a movie. It would not be proper to call on his 'wife' while he's gone. To ask her help in shopping for his coming bride. So he goes to Orbach's alone, with only a guess as to her sizes. He buys a woman's coat, and a sweater. A wool hat and small gloves.

Two days after the semester ends, he is standing at the airport Arrivals door, in a throng of others. His is the only dark face. Apprehension knots his stomach. He simply can't call up Salimatou's face. He supposes he'll have little trouble spotting her, though. Undoubtedly she'll be the only African in the debarking crowd.

"Now arriving," intones the overhead speaker, "flight number 1417, British Overseas Airlines. At gate C20."

Yes, that's her flight. Hussein straightens and fixes his gaze on the big metal door. It opens and the slow but relentless tide of waiting relatives and friends sucks him toward it. Slowly, feet and bodies move, hesitantly at first. Then come cries of recognition and joy as mothers, fathers, aunts, lovers all spill out into the airport's fluorescent light.

He hears a few gasps and looks around. There, in the door, framed by gleaming marble floors and bright lights, his bride has paused, looking for him. She's taller than he remembered. Body still slim but not shaped like that of the skinny girl of his past. The folds of her *grande boubah,* the saucy tilt of her head tie, all make his fingers ache for the camera.

She sees him then. A slow smile warms her face. Hussein walks over with the new coat and drapes it around her shoulders. All the while she stands calmly watching him. He bends down and brushes her lips lightly. "*Salaam,* Salimatou."

She automatically bends her knees and clasps her hands in the traditional greeting of wife to husband, especially under these circumstances. "*Salaam,* husband."

People stare, perhaps because they can't understand the language. It's likely they've never seen Africans before, except on television, and of course Salimatou doesn't look anything like

Hollywood imagines. He's proud she's dressed this way, even though no one here would know the value of the fabric, the symbols of her cloth and tying of the head wrap. She unwinds and pulls the rich woven shawl from her shoulders and wraps over the brown coat with which he's covered her bridal gown.

Sali gives him her baggage ticket so he can collect her portmanteau. It's huge and heavy. Inside will be gifts from her family. He hires a burly porter with stubbly cheeks to help them carry the things to a car borrowed from Jamal. He settles her in the passenger seat and locks the door. As he slides the key into the ignition, she whispers, "*Bis mi lah.*" He repeats it.

He gives an abbreviated tour guide as they weave through traffic, onto the highway and the Midtown Tunnel. Instead of staying on the FDR, though, he heads down 2nd Avenue so Sali can see some of the City she'll be living in the next three or so years. She's quiet, gazing out to take it all in without making foolish comments.

Good, he thinks. Maybe she won't be too talkative. Her eyes sparkle; she seems impressed by the sights.

As they turn off 2nd Avenue onto East 10th, the view becomes bleaker. The buildings look pathetic in comparison. He almost wants to apologize for them, but she still says nothing.

When they reach his place she gets out and helps him struggle with the heavy bags. Finally she suggests taking out some of the things, and to make more than one trip up and down. From inside the neckline of her gown she pulls a tiny pouch hung on a silken cord, and fishes out a small key to open the lock. Hussein goes up first, carrying a much lighter bag. She stays to watch over things as he climbs back and forth. Each time he comes down she's unpacked more items until, finally, they can go up together.

At the door she stops to remove her shoes and bow her head, making a short prayer. They enter and she smiles, looking around at the cheerful, comfortable place where she'll now make her home. Hussein has stacked heaps of fabric and gift packages all over the living room floor. She looks in one and then finds his wedding clothes. He takes the marriage certificate from her hands and kisses her again. Those soft, shy lips barely respond. He goes over to the bookcase and finds an empty frame. He slips in the parchment with elaborate gold calligraphy announcing them husband and wife, and for now hangs it over the bedroom door.

"These are gifts from my family," she murmurs. "And this is the jewelry your parents gave me on your behalf." She lays his bride-price out on the table.

"We'll find a safe place to store them tomorrow." His aunt, his representative made good choices in selecting the three gold bracelets and silver *taha* Salimatou extends. He bends and she fastens it around his neck. Then he shows her the other things he's gotten for her: sweaters and gloves and boots. "It gets very cold here in the winter. You'll need to wear woolen things then, not the cottons, or you'll catch cold. I don't want your parents angry with me!"

She laughs. He likes the light, musical sound it makes in the tiny apartment. There's seldom been a woman's voice here, only the few times he's had people over.

Sali is very curious to see the rest of the place. She admires what he's done with so small a space. "It is very clean. Now I shall keep it nice for you."

Hussein notes the time. "Why don't you go inside and lie down for an hour or so? I've some studying to finish. Then we'll go out for dinner to celebrate your arrival."

Sali nods. "Thank you." She goes to the little bedroom and stretches out, still in her wedding clothes. He hangs up her new coat and goes back to the little desk. The truth is, he really wants more time to reflect. His wife has arrived. He is indeed a married man. And most of all, she really is lovely. He won't have to sin anymore!

Two hours later Sali bundles up in the coat and gloves, then wraps a shawl around her head over the head tie. The weekend on the Lower East Side is usually celebratory in some way. At the end of a work week, no school, the close of the Sabbath for Orthodox Jews. And now, for him, two whole weeks before classes resume. He takes her out to the restaurant where Isaac, the head waiter, comes over to seat them. "*Salaam*, friend." He always greets him this way.

Hussein urges her forward. "Isaac, this is my wife, Salimatou. She's just arrived from home."

Isaac's kind, expressive face looks surprised. Perhaps because Hussein has come here before with two or three different young women. But diplomatically he only says, "*Salaam*, young lady. You have a fine husband. A noble gentleman."

He leads them to the back and seats them before a window. Isaac holds the chair as Sali disengages from the coat and arranges the swirls of her *boubah*. Hussein picks up the menu and eyes the list of offerings. Vinegar and dill waft up his nose from the glass jar of pickles pierced by a wooden spoon. From the back comes Yiddish conversation. Occasionally he can pick out a word or two when it's one close to German or Hebrew. So he knows they're talking about him and his newly-acquired wife.

Sali looks up, her expression troubled. "Hussein, there are so many choices here. I hardly know what to select. I've never eaten food prepared by Jews before."

He laughs. "This place is safe because they slaughter animals according to Judaic laws. We're allowed to eat this food. Tell me what you like and I will help you choose."

She looks down at the menu again. "Well, I'd like rice and chicken, but it's late. So maybe something not so heavy."

He studies the offerings and decides on chicken soup and an order of potato latkes with applesauce for her. Isaac takes the order and leaves quickly. A few couples come in but these sit up front, so he and Sali almost have a private wing.

"How was the trip?"

Her eyes widen as she describes it. "I've flown before, a few times. My sister sent for me when she was put to bed. Her husband was in the midst of his clinics and couldn't take care of her and the baby."

Hussein is a little taken aback. "Oh. I didn't know you'd gone to England."

She nods. "The first time I stayed two months. And then again, when Rashid graduated. That time I stayed only three weeks." It seems she's experienced many things he had no knowledge of.

Their food arrives and she stops talking to investigate everything. Hussein has his usual baked potato and pastrami. "Bismilah," she murmurs, then tests the soup. She smiles and eats more soup to show approval. When she picks up a latke, she hesitates. "Is this how they eat, potatoes and apples together?"

"I think it's a European-Jewish dish," he explains. "Most of the people here are European Jews from Poland, Holland, and Germany. They make wonderful bread and something they call *babka*. You can eat it buttered for breakfast with coffee. Or for dessert."

Sali finishes her soup and eats more potato pancakes and applesauce. "Finished, *Alhamdulillah*."

Afterward she drinks hot tea. Hussein has seltzer. He enjoys the clean, crisp taste of it in his mouth after a meal. A woman who looks familiar passes by but he doesn't look up or acknowledge her. By now he's captivated by Sali. Her face glows with excitement as she observes the strangely-clad people of this new village she's come to inhabit. Occasionally other diners take a second look at the young woman with something weird wrapped around her head.

Finally Hussein waves to Isaac for the check. "Do you want anything more?"

She gestures with clasped palms that she's satisfied.

"Okay, then I need to get you home and to bed. You must be exhausted."

A little ripple of apprehension at the words "get you home" shows on her face. He smiles to reassure her.

Outside they pull the coat collars up to their ears. He can hardly see Sali beneath the yardage of shawl, the heavy wool coat. Okay wind, he thinks. She knows you're here. You needn't try to knock us over. He puts an arm around her shoulders and draws her closer. Maybe this would be a good time to get a second-hand car. He decides to put the word out so his friends can be on the lookout for a good deal. Now that he'll be teaching and coming home late, a car would be a great convenience.

They reach the building and they rush inside. Sali's teeth are chattering but she smiles at him. "It's cold, yes. But that was fun."

They head upstairs. More and more Hussein is thinking about the beautiful young body waiting for him under the folds of her garments. They put their shoes on the mat inside and then shed some of the layers that hide and separate each from the other. Hussein steals another look at her, again struck by her quiet beauty. The adult Sali is nothing like the shy, gawky child his mother introduced him to at his eighteenth birthday, saying, This is your future bride. For almost ten years he's resisted her coming. Putting the marriage off, using his studies, and the distance of America. But his mother had written a few years back to rebuke him, saying his betrothed had waited long enough. Therefore he was to send money for gifts for her family and she would begin to look for someone to be his proxy at the wedding. Tradition is tradition, she reminded him. So Hussein had begun sending money home then. Now, here's his live, in-the-flesh wife, all five feet seven or so, the beautiful, smooth blue-black skin of Salimatou Boubacar.

Hussein suddenly feels shy. He hasn't been exactly celibate and she is a properly-certified virgin. This is his first time to be with someone without experience, a real wife. If she is apprehensive now, though, she isn't revealing it. He shows her the toilet in the hall and it doesn't seem to bother her. She comes back wearing nightclothes. He'd been concerned she might be put off by the bathroom out in the hall, but she says, "I prefer it. In England the loo was inside, not too far from the kitchen."

She prepares some hot mint tea. They sit in his living room listening to music, drinking the tea she brought from home. The fresh green smell fills the room. He sits close, wondering if he should tell her he's not been as faithful to her as she's been to him.

But before he can speak, she turns to him. Her face is a palette on which is written some concern. "Husband, is there a second wife?" In a quiet but firm voice, she speaks directly to the matter. Not that it makes things easier for him. Hussein knows it's just the way of things. Of women who often are taken for granted. As he'd done with her.

"No Sali, you are my first and only wife." He explains briefly about the three or four other women, not brides, not like her. Only the mere filling of a basic male need.

"Yes, I understand." Her smile is tinged with sadness. "You know, some of my age-group used to say you would never come for me. Most have seen their husbands return with foreign women. Some do not come back at all." She pauses, drinks more tea. Face averted now, as she stares toward the window. "The truth is, I did not believe it at first when your mother came for me. I had already asked my mother to return the gifts. All the way over on the plane I prayed you would not reject me. My parents would have been so sad. And then it would have been very difficult to find another good husband." She turns to face him again, eyes brimming. "And now I am here and there is no senior wife. We will live together in the same flat."

Hussein puts his cup down and gently draws her to him. "Sali, I'm so sorry for making you wait. You're a good woman and I am grateful to Allah for giving me such a lovely wife as you. I'll do my best to be a good husband." He bends to kiss her lips and finds them parted, eager to accept his. Then he pulls her up and, with one hand holding hers he uses the other to shut off the lights. He leads her to the bedroom. She comes willingly, the way she's been trained to act as a good African wife. This bed is new, so there's no history of another woman in it.

Lying next to her as she sleeps, Hussein traces a circle around her breasts. She stirs and rolls over, her back to him. Underneath them is the wedding cloth she placed there to send to his parents. It is stained with her blood from his initial thrust, and with the overflow of his seed. She was a little tight at first, and scared. But he'd been able to relax her to the point of even some pleasure. As he'd slid inside her he'd heard her prayers that his seed should not be spent in vain.

"I hope so too, Sali," he'd paused and told her. "But not right away. Let's enjoy one another first. Get acquainted before having a child."

Having listened to the men at the artists' bar, and with Bill's cautionary words echoing in his head, he knows how important it is for there to be some kind of understanding between them. This is a strange place for her. He wants some of the old ways to be maintained in his home. He suspects, too, that keeping a small flat, doing for him, and taking care of a child may not answer all the needs of a well-educated, intelligent woman. Maybe she can take classes at the Y on East 14th Street, later.

The next two weeks are a whirlwind. Mahmoud, as promised, is organizing a reception for them at the Mission along with an exhibition of his photographs. The first two chapters of his dissertation are due. Sali has to register in order to take English and history classes in the Adult Education division. He has less time to spend with his friends since she's arrived and with the pressure of school, but they agreed to come to the reception. The super's wife is helping to get Sali settled in by taking her to shop from some of her friends who are street peddlers. Nusa took her down to Essex Street to the markets to buy yarn, so she can begin knitting winter things. Hussein bought a sewing machine and Sali has made new curtains and covers for pillows in the living room.

Bill and Larry are first to arrive at the UN Mission. They hang their coats and go to look at his latest work. "Hey man, this is bad," says Larry, who's a good painter, so Hussein is pleased with the comment.

"Where's your wife?" Bill asks as he shakes his hand. At that moment Sali comes in with food. They help her put the platters on tables covered with African fabric. Mahmoud follows her, displaying his cool elegance and diplomat's persona. Everyone shakes hands and introduces themselves. A huge crowd is soon gathered and Hussein makes his kingly public appearance in a white *grande boubou* Sali's aunt had made especially for him.

"Ladies, gentlemen, members of the diplomatic corps and His Excellency Ambassador Bello. We extend to you all our warmest welcome," Mahmoud announces, in his most mellifluous voice. "There are many reasons for tonight's events." He pauses ever so slightly, glancing at the spot where Hussein stands next to Sali, holding her hand. "We wish to say that our mission is your refuge because we are independent after centuries of slavery and colonialism. So we urge you to plan to visit us in the very near future."

There's loud applause.

"The second reason is to celebrate our brilliant artist whose works adorn these walls. And are of course for sale! The third and most important reason, though, is to announce a wedding first contracted for over twenty years ago. This marriage, through our traditional system, has now been consummated. We will ask Al Hajji to come forward to do a short prayer."

The senior diplomat slowly steps out of a circle of men gathered around a platter of food. He smiles widely. Hussein feels him to be a kind man. "Come, son, daughter." He reaches for them and Hussein leads Sali closer. They cup their hands over their mouths as Al Hajji gives thanks for their union. He prays for them as they embark on life's journey together, and offers blessings on them and their progeny. Then blessings on their studies. And finally, blessings on those gathered.

Everyone says *"Ameen."* Some of the sisters cheer loudly. Mahmoud steps forward again. "And now let us eat, dance, and enjoy."

A little band begins to play Hi Life music. People sway and tap their feet. When most of the crowd has finished eating, Hussein and Sali open the floor. She's a fine dancer. Soon a few others choose partners and join them. Hussein wonders if someone will later talk about the wasting of government money on private parties thrown by foolish former colonial subjects from poor countries.

As Melvin and Susan dance near them, Melvin says, "Brother, you Africans sure know how to throw a party."

Sali asks, "Are you having a good time?" Melvin lets loose with a wild joyful yell.

Jamal and Mariama are there too, and she's in full bloom. Sali was happy to meet her because they speak the same language. Jamal has just returned from Germany where he took part in a workshop at a major jazz festival. Don is there with Naomi, although he's living with a white woman. She looks lovely. A little earlier, when they were next to each other by the bar, she'd whispered to Hussein, "Sorry, I guess I blew it."

He'd frowned. "What do you mean?" Although really he knows, he wants to hear her admit she knew he was interested in her but never responded. "It could've been me if I hadn't been so caught up in my West Indian thing, right? You know, 'Think of the children.' Look, I really wish you and your wife all the love and luck in the world."

Hussein watches as she hurries off, back to Don. Even if something had developed between them, his mother would've never accepted any other woman as his wife. And now, looking at Sali from across the room, as she dances with Mahmoud, Hussein knows she was, and still is, the only one for him.

CHARLIE

In the late fall of 1960 Charlie first plants his feet firmly on the sidewalk of the Lower East Side. His leather suitcases broadcast quality. Onlookers watch, silent and suspicious. A couple of men shift a bit, allowing him room to enter the building. The eyes staring at him have become accustomed to the sight of black men moving in. Times have changed. The older Europeans pull back in fear: of differences, of colors, of other languages. Spanish speakers, themselves fairly new arrivals from islands across the Atlantic Ocean, look closely to determine if this one is a member of their tribe. He is not, they conclude after close scrutiny, after hearing him say a few words to the cab driver.

He is not so much big as tall; taller than the other men standing around. His body is slender yet still suggests strength. So when he hefts one suitcase easily up four flights, leaving the other sitting outside, no one makes a move to grab it and run. They just stand, looking on, as he carries the second suitcase up.

Not surprisingly, he knocks on the door of the black man who was the first to move in. Now there are three other apartments in the tenement housing blacks. All artists of some sort, so this one is presumed to be an artist as well. The door opens, and the audience looks elsewhere for diversion.

"Hey man, come on in." Jean-Pierre opens the door wider and reaches for one of the suitcases. Charlie enters the small space, noticing at once a pungent smell. "Thanks. I really appreciate this." He's grateful because he knows no one else in the City.

They leave the suitcases by the door.

"Listen, come and have some breakfast. Or is it lunch now?" Jean-Pierre checks his watch. "Hm, later than I thought. Had a full night. Too much wine. Ugh! 'Scuse me. Gotta take something to settle my stomach, clear my head."

Charlie sits on the only chair that has no clothes on it. From there he can see his host in the kitchen. His name is Jean-Pierre Rousseau. They met at a conference at Howard University last October. Charlie, then a student at Tennessee State, had come out of curiosity. His parents insisted he go to graduate school and he wanted to get away from Henderson County, so coming to Howard provides his vehicle for exiting.

Jean-Pierre is from New Orleans. The family is a part of the Creole Society; his father an important person, president of an all-black university. Although he tells everyone to call him J.P, Charlie insists on using his full name. He likes the sound of French. Though they're from similar backgrounds, Jean-Pierre is a few years ahead of him. He's living in The City, not Harlem, but the lower East Side—true Bohemia. In addition, and more important to Charlie, Jean-Pierre is a published writer with a short story in *Avante Garde* and three poems in *Daedalus*. A recent review in *The Herald Tribune*, small but significant, said Jean-Pierre is "a writer to read and watch." That his work opens doors on the lives of "ordinary Negroes." No one is certain what that means, but the most important thing remains: a reputable white press has reviewed the writings of a young black man.

At the conference they'd gotten on well. His invitation was open, and Charlie, anxious to leave home, to come to New York City, had prepared daily for this moment. And now here it is. He's to stay until he can secure a place of his own. In his letter Jean-Pierre said he'd begun to make inquiries. That when he arrived they could go look at a few possibilities he'd lined up.

Those letters had been a major point in convincing Charlie's father to let him come. Of course, support from a mother who wanted her son to have wider experiences than her husband had been allowed was essential, too. Times were indeed changing. They could now help their progeny go beyond former boundaries. So, after sending sample writings, along with his application, Charlie was accepted at Hunter College in the Master of Arts Program in Literature. His father agreed to fund it, adding, "As long as you're pursuing a graduate degree. And not getting into the sort of trouble I read about in the newspapers."

Charlie thinks now of his spacious home in Henderson County, so carefully maintained by two women, a housekeeper and a maid, plus a handyman who is also the family chauffer. All three operate under the watchful eyes of his mother, who keeps their home immaculate and orderly. He had a wing to himself. That's the best way to describe it: a big bedroom opening onto a sitting room, with a full bath and dressing room. Over the years he took full advantage of its private entrance.

The family consists of just the three of them. A very beautiful, fair-skinned mother who, although a bit heavier than when she married his father, is still considered a most attractive woman. His father is just a little darker than she, which had been a major stumbling block when they were courting. But he too is handsome. And, Charlie would add, distinguished. Yes, he's quite satisfied with this description of his parents.

Carlotta Beauchamp Tobin, his mother, was also an only child. Her father was white; her mother the man's black 'wife' or, rather, concubine. His grandmother Tobin always referred to his Beauchamp grandmother as such. Apparently a prominent white man could afford the notoriety, since he had been very open in displaying her in certain settings. Charlie wondered how his grandfather's white wife had felt about that. But then, many white men made such arrangements. Grandmother Tobin, from a different part of the South, wasn't sure she wanted a near-white New Orleans Creole to marry her favorite son. But Carlotta turned out to be a wonderful wife, an asset for her husband. She'd been educated at a snobbish school for young ladies from backgrounds like hers. Also she'd brought a huge dowry from her father. Despite the white wife, he'd come to their wedding and personally handed her over to the groom.

His father's father had worked in a mine; gradually he rose to the steel foundry where the pay was double. He saved his money and became a preacher. His grandfather was able to marry a light-skinned woman from a good family. Charlie's father looked a lot like her. His grandparents had also made sure his father got a good education. Grandfather Beauchamp also paid for his and his sister's education. He'd helped his father set up his first business because, as Grandmother Tobin used to say in a tight, mean voice, "He didn't want his baby to have to live like most of us Negroes."

He is in fact named for that grandfather, Charles-Michel.

Jean-Pierre returns after medicating himself. "Now, now I feel a bit more like a human being."

Charlie rises and takes the mug Jean-Pierre offers, not quite sure he really wants to drink it. But he doesn't want to offend his host. After a few polite sips he gathers the courage to ask. "So, were you able to speak with your landlord?"

"Uh-hunh. Says he wants to meet you. There's an apartment on the second floor, and he has another building on 5th Street near 1st Avenue. So you should be able to get your own place soon."

And yet, despite New York's reputation as one of the most liberal cities in the north, Charlie is met with slammed doors and the return of his deposit once owners and or agents who've advertised at Hunter actually see him. He's beginning to feel a little down because he needs to leave Jean-Pierre's apartment. It's too small and too unclean for his taste. Jean-Pierre is out at least three nights or more a week, and sleeping on the couch is not comfortable.

Charlie waits. And in the waiting he continues to sleep on a mat in the living room because the floor is more comfortable than the couch. He's looking forward to not doing so much longer, because of a fear of roaches crawling over him. As they do to the pile of dishes Jean-Pierre leaves unwashed in the tiny sink. Nor is he fond of hearing mice squeak around him. His parents would be horrified to see his living conditions. But Charlie feels this is just another trial all artists must go through. He plans to begin classes in February, though, so he needs to have his own place before then.

A month later he steps over the threshold of his own apartment, feeling pleased with himself and glad he's on 5th Street. This street has more trees than further east, maybe because fewer dogs are urinating on the ground here. His apartment is sandwiched between an enclave of elderly Russians above, on the fourth floor, and a mix of Puerto Ricans and whites below on the second. It's a five minute walk to the subway that brings him directly to Hunter.

By December Charlie has a new typewriter and four bookcases to house his ever-increasing collection. His furniture is comfortable. He lives more in the manner to which he's been accustomed. His parents sent money to furnish the place, and his tuition for the semester has been paid. He's working in a bookstore owned by a Jew. The man is a communist, a badge of honor in Charlie's eyes, and the owner's wide knowledge of literature and history puts the Hunter professors to shame. Due to him, Charlie is now well-read in a variety of works unknown to his classmates.

He reads for about three hours every day after writing at least two to three hours. A slow process, yes, but he needs to have a draft of his novel for the writing class come the end of February. Working at the bookstore, and in discussions with Mr. Weinstein, he learns more and more. After hearing of the habit of an author he tries to imitate, he too keeps a little black notebook into which he jots ideas and things he hears along the streets, in class, or in the stories Mr. Weinstein tells. Charlie wants to see some of the places the old man speaks of so longingly. Prague. The Berlin of his youth, not what it has become now. And, one day, Moscow and Paris. He observes his own script style and notes a tendency to make curlicues. Deciding that's too ostentatious he tempers it, holds back the sweeping strokes. Good. Simple is better, more thoughtful and above all, more creative. His down-stroke is hard. He read somewhere this connotes passion. I'm very passionate about writing, he decides. I am and I will be a writer.

Back home he socialized with lots of young women and a few older married ones. Here on the Lower East Side all social possibilities extend themselves. For about a month he dated Greta, an exchange student from Sweden. Most of the black men date white women, especially Jean-Pierre. Everyone wants to experiment. Charlie likes the way white skin looks at night under the light of street lamps. Long hair flowing over his pillows is a turn-on. Envious frowns from white men as he passes by with a luscious blonde or brunette on his arm boosts his ego.

"Be cautious around certain areas, because white people are still the same, north or south," people warn him. A few men who hang out at Jean-Pierre's have had their share of white gangs chasing them.

At Stanley's, Charlie is particularly popular. Known as a snappy dresser, quick-witted and smart. In other words, someone to watch for. A core group of artists hangs out there. In his circle there are two actors, three painters, two photographers, three musicians, and two writers. Others sit near and join in when a pause occurs or even interrupt when passion dictates.

Certain tables have reputations enhanced by those who occupy them for hours locked in serious dialogue. He sits with the writers, ears tuned to receive nearby conversations. He wants to be everywhere at once. A growing need to be a part if not the center of attention drives him further into foreign territory. Yet, even after having admitted to unbridled needs, he cannot tolerate heavy drugs. His old fears of needles, of choking on big pills, keep him out of the clutches of heroin and enticing multi-hued pills. So one table just to the right of his is off-limits. And after Stanley came upon Todd slumped on the toilet with a spike in one arm, almost dead, Charlie was glad he'd decided against trying H.

However, his introduction to marijuana is a joy, something he'll always feel appreciative to Tim and Jean-Pierre for. They schooled him first to its spiritual attributes and then to the mind alterations caused by the herb. Jean-Pierre has a connection, through one of his many girl friends, to the best cannabis. She's an airline stewardess; her regular route is Hawaii. Jean-Pierre says this variety is grown in the black ash that covers the ground around the volcano in Hilo. Charlie buys from Jean-Pierre, and keeps his stash in a double brown paper bag inside a bright-hued pillow. Charlie is not a drinker. He dislikes both the taste and the subsequent headache and nausea, and sticks to a glass or two of wine. His preference is always for Mary Jane.

After his first good critique Charlie celebrates at Stanley's. He plucks courage from half a joint and two glasses of wine in order to read after two "Writers" with caps and quotation marks. He presents two pages of the beginning chapter of his novel and is complimented by Mel, who encourages him to continue writing. And Tim, a painter who also makes leather bags, sandals, and clothes and is currently showing on East 10th Street in one of the galleries, invites him to the "real" artists table.

Bill, an actor who's a bit older than most of the rest, asks, "Ever thought of writing a play?"

Charlie thinks about it now. "No, I haven't. But that doesn't mean I won't. It's just, right now the short novel is where I feel most comfortable. Got to develop my chops before going off into something so heavy."

Cal nods. "Yeah, I can dig it. Do your dailies and you'll get there, Little Brother."

Charlie stays up almost all night trying to put down on the page the rhythm of what transpired at Stanley's. Steam-hissing radiators, at first annoying, became a part of his dialogue. He wants to be terse and use hip language, but the white chicks won't let him. That pretty redhead on East 11th Street and Avenue B says, "I really dig your drawl." When she pronounces 'drawl' her tongue flickers; the word fills her mouth. He's made a date with her for Tuesday. That's his free night. Classes follow a Tuesday-Thursday schedule but end at four. He works part-time at the bookstore all day Monday and Wednesday, and sometimes helps out on Saturdays. Mr. Weinstein has a son about his age, but the guy shows no interest in books or the store.

It's late, and his eyes are burning. His fingers cramp. They hurt when he lets go the pen and straightens them. Sighing, Charlie's content, feeling he's closer than ever to being a real writer. He wants to polish this short story and send it to *Graphology,* a new journal. He loves the sound of it. He loves words, sometimes spending hours paging through the dictionary, noting the various meanings and usages of a single word. He loves mixing metaphors—standing words on their heads, so to speak. But his eyelids are growing heavy, so he sets the notepad on his writing table. He's very proud of this piece of furniture. It obviously belonged to someone who also enjoyed writing. The dark, smooth wood feels solid under his fast-moving hand. In the back there are two slots for nibs. He fills his fountain pen from a heavy cut-glass bottle into which he's poured royal-blue ink. Yes, all the accoutrements of a writer.

And now, said writer gets up, stumbles to the toilet, washes his teeth and hands after relieving himself. No, *voids.* That's a better choice. He carefully takes off and folds his clothes, setting them on a chair near the bed. He pulls it over near the window and opens it a bit from the bottom. Stanley's is great, but he hates carrying home the thick stink of cigarette smoke and booze in the nice wool.

Charlie finishes both short story and first semester in high style. His writing professor nominates him for a prize which includes a cash prize of a thousand dollars and a two-month residence at

Cambridge. As in England, of Europe. "No, not New England. *England*, land of the British," he tells his mother during his monthly call. His parents are praying for his success in attaining the Kent Prize for Emerging Young Writers. His classmates, almost all of whom are white, seem to view him with suspicion and, in a few cases, open hostility. One has gone so far as to suggest both his nomination and perhaps winning of the prize connotes mere liberal guilt, never mind the merits of the either work or writer. Charlie is surprised when the other two black writers in the class, a young man around his age, and a younger woman, do not come to his defense. Instead, they wait until after class to say they support him but have problems with parts of his positions and conclusions.

Mr. Weinstein, sitting in his old chair, head buried in a book, looks up when Charlie enters to begin his shift.

"Well, well, my boy." Dark eyes sparkling, he focuses on Charlie's face, his tone playful. "The Call just came. Here is your message." He hands over a slip of yellow paper.

We are pleased to announce that our fellow examiners have decided. It is our honor to bestow upon you The Kent Prize for Emerging Young Writers for 1963. On behalf of our readers and Advisory Board, we congratulate and look forward to meeting you at the awards ceremony in June. Details and travel instructions to follow.

The reality of this achievement slams into Charlie, beginning at the top of his head, flowing down his face, neck, spine, and stomach to finally settle in a mushy feeling around the crotch. He drops heavily into a chair that protests with a squeal of springs. Some magazines cascade to the floor but he barely notices.

At this moment the owner's son comes down the long corridor leading to the back of the shop's warehouse. Malachi has an order form in one hand, a book in the other. Charlie tenses as he approaches.

"Well, all hail the boy wonder! I'm surprised to see you. Thought you and your little friends would be out celebrating."

His taunt hits its target. Charlie feels heat rising in his chest. He clenches the chair seat, grits his teeth, and smiles at the pallid face floating eerily in the half-light of dark walls and low-wattage bulbs in the cavernous hallway. He's reminded of one of the photographs in Pedro's current show across the street. Breathing deeply, he concentrates on the images of that exhibit; especially the one Pedro calls "Momento de la vida." This is just such a time. He's conscious of Mr. Weinstein's presence and doesn't want to offend him but needs to say something to Malachi. Or Mal, as he insists being called, standing there between him and his father. Daring him. Charlie wants to nail the jerk right in the middle of that high forehead.

They are locked in competition for respect and approval from the old man. Mal because he feels entitled as the natural son. Charlie because he sees his employer as his intellectual father, a man whose political tastes and social outlook differ so greatly from his biological father's. On the other hand, he's not 'lumpen proletariat,' as Mr. Weinstein describes his own background. So Charlie defers. "Well, enough of wasting time. I've got some re-shelving and a few orders to pull."

Just as he starts down the dark lane of books, Mal calls out, "So, when do you leave?"

Without turning, he responds, "After the end of the semester. When I receive my ticket."

He hears Mr. Weinstein chuckle as he turns right at the Black Studies section, on down to the space cleared for him.

About a week later Tim invites him to a party. Charlie agrees to go hoping to meet some new girls, because the last two or three were disappointing. One actually wanted to photograph him nude. He shakes his head, remembering her setting him up for the pose, full frontal. He'd refused the pseudo-primitive posture. He isn't a prude but her idea of his black male body ("Well, not really all that black," she had assured him) and his are definitely worlds apart. So now, as he prepares for the party, he selects casual attire befitting both a Southern gentleman and his artistic style. He takes a script along because there's to be sharing of work between the writers, musicians, and others.

Charlie heads out into the cold of East 5th Street, pushed by the wind as it swirls discarded bags down 2nd Avenue. Many people his age are out; off to parties, lovers, all kinds of assignations. A few blocks on he stops outside a bar to listen to some jazz musicians warming up. He likes this club. Whenever he reads of this or that famous horn player or pianist having just released a live recording, knowing he was there makes him feel a part of it, the real art scene. The Lower East Side, where artistic compromise is not happening.

He crosses Avenue A at East 7th Street. Tompkins Square Park is awash in snow, the trees fleshed out in white. The mood picks up, becomes festive as laughter echoes in the streets where windows are propped open to vent cigarette and cigar smoke from small, overheated spaces crammed with bodies. He pulls his scarf to his chin, loving the feel of the soft wool. One of his past flings turned him on to Orbach's on East 34th Street. He got this cashmere scarf and his kid-skin gloves there. Yes, he can take this weather in such woolen garments. Everything's covered except his ears and his face, lashed by winter's cold fingers. If those Muslim women in some country far away that he'd seen in *Life* could cover up thoroughly, then so can he.

Laughter and a mélange of good smells waft up his nose and he salivates in anticipation. Tim's voice rises and then Charlie hears others. Tim meets him at the door with a big smile. "Hey, man! Glad you could make it."

Charlie shakes his hand. He notices shoes lined up outside on a little wooden stand.

Tim's in socks only. "Hope you got your good socks on. No holes."

Charlie shrugs. He was aware Japanese and some Indians take off their shoes before entering a house, but he didn't know black people did it too. "Man, I just got these new boots."

"Sorry, that's a house rule."

A couple of white girls troop up; huffing and puffing a bit. "Ooh," the blonde squeals as she bends to slip off her ballet flats.

Charlie straightens and sets his boots closest to the door, then starts to remove his coat and scarf.

"They must be Orientals here," a redhead offers.

Harry comes to the door and welcomes them. "Greetings! Please, let me take your things."

In the first room about ten people are lounging on floor pillows and the few chairs. Harry goes off to a back room loaded down with wraps. Tim steers them inside the living room. A curtain blocks the cooking area, from behind which emanate intriguing cooking scents he is unable to identify.

"Hey, Charlie."

"Marta, nice seeing you."

There are lots of familiar faces here, and they're so...visible. Something's missing—oh yes, that's it. No one is smoking. He looks around to locate the bar and spots a loaded table. But when he walks over there are various bowls and pitchers but no wine or whiskey.

"Oh God! No booze?"

A voice at his elbow interjects, "Turns out Harry's a Muslim. His real name is Hussein."

Charlie stands by the table, eyeing the non-alcoholic drinks displayed before him, feeling awkward. He pats a pocket for his pipe, then remembers: no smoking. Pulls back and turns slowly to see what others are doing with their hands. At that moment the kitchen curtains open dramatically and a slender black woman stands framed there with a ceramic pot in both hands. His breath halts. Voices hush.

In the stillness, Harry/Hussein breaks the suspense by crossing over to her. "Everyone, this is my wife, Salimatou. Some of you have met her already. But we thought, in keeping with our traditions, we would invite friends to celebrate our marriage and welcome her to New York."

Tim raises his hands. "Welcome, Salimatou. Health and happiness to you both."

A ripple of applause. Charlie recalls the article on Muslim women and a word pops out of his mouth. "Salaam."

The woman looks surprised, but smiles and responds, "Alaiykum salaam." The melody of her voice blesses him and all there. She continues to the table with the steaming dish. Mel's girlfriend Susan follows with a heaped platter. After a few trips back and forth the little table is overflowing with food.

Harry/Hussein cracks a window from the top to cool the overheated room. "Dear friends, thank you for coming. And now," he bows his head and raises both hands.

Charlie feels a strange stirring in the pit of his stomach. He looks from Hussein to the woman, Salimatou. She too is bowing, her hands cupping her face. She closes her eyes, lips moving. Calm envelops the room; all are quiet for a few moments. Up this high the street noise is muted. Charlie feels a lump in his throat. Tears prickle and well up. He's glad everyone is looking down or has shut their eyes. He's fearful of moving, of even breathing too hard lest he interrupt. He wills body, heart, mind, and breath to slow down, to behave and betray no emotion. Blasé, blasé.

A collective sigh. The crowd circles the table, heads bowed with reverence and respect for the cook. Salimatou dishes out food as she names and explains what she's serving. "This is a tagine. A North African dish, mostly Moroccan people prepare this. And this is okra soup. A typical West African dish. We eat it with this." She points to a bowl of something resembling mashed potatoes. "We call this ebah, or fufu. It' made with cassava or mixed with plantains and eddoes." She gives each person a small portion of everything.

Marta coughs when the sting of pepper tickles her throat. Salimatou looks with concern from her to Hussein and says, "Oh, just eat some rice and vegetables. It will absorb the pepper. I hope I did not put in too much."

Tim, a veteran since he's been invited before and knows how to enjoy the food, says, "Look, just let yourself relax. Eat slowly. You'll taste all the flavors that way."

For Charlie the spices are no big deal. His father's barbecue sauce is hotter. It isn't so much the pepper as the other things; herbs he's never tasted before. So he mixes the rice and vegetables and Tim is right, he can feel all the different textures and densities of the sauces. He eats, savoring each mouthful.

Salimatou clears the table of empty bowls and platters; Susan helps her. Then they disappear behind the curtain again. Charlie notices the fabric now, hand-woven, patterned cotton. "Probably some African stuff," he says to himself.

He's shared many a party with almost everyone in the room, and knows how loud and explicit they can be in putting forth opinions on world events. He's conscious of a quieting of his own voice and spirit, and wonders: Why? What about this moment, this space, affects me this way? His head has no immediate response. He shrugs and decides, Hey, forget it. Just groove with it.

Tim announces, "Say, people, if you need to smoke before we do our stuff, you can go up on the roof." A few get coats and slip on shoes to go ease their needs. Charlie goes along because he has a few joints and wants to keep his mellow mood longer.

The cold air slaps his face. The moon, scattered lights from apartments and, off on the horizon, sparkles from the East River play hide and seek. They all breathe deep, letting the cool March air enter and flood noses, mouths, throats. To get blood flowing vigorously, throbbing in their veins. Gradually they go back down to the party.

Now the room has been transformed into another kind of world. Pillows repositioned, waiting for them. The table holds carafes of coffee, hot chocolate, and tea, surrounded by cups. In the center are glass dishes full of cake slices, and a big bowl of stewed fruits.

"Come take some sweets and a hot drink," Salimatou says, this time allowing everyone to serve themselves.

Tim calls them to order. "We are now going to share some of our latest work. This will give Salimatou an idea of what she's landed into."

"Oh my goodness, what am I drinking?" gasps Marta. "This tea, what is it?"

Salimatou looks anxious. "Is it not good?"

Marta laughs. "It's great! Never had anything like it before."

Charlie drinks hot chocolate and eats cake silently. Waves of euphoria ride him. Marta is merely feeling the effects of the joint they shared. Hunger satisfied, he searches in his portfolio and finds the first chapter of a piece he's working on, part of his thesis.

Jean-Pierre takes out a notepad and flips through, looking for an appropriate poem or two. Salimatou lays out a grass mat and Hussein sits on it. He opens the floor. "This is a section of a novel I've been working on for a while. About midway, narrated by an elder giving counsel to mothers who've come for advice."

"'Oh my daughters,'" he reads. "'Do not let your boys go to the City. It is there the *Shaytan* lives. Sometimes dressed as a beautiful woman who cooks the sweetest food. The smells water their mouths, and your sons will eat that which is *haram*. Ah, my children, in that place, eyah, they have cows that do not low, cats without tails or fur, and camels with no smells or humps.' She pauses, her eyes cloud. Rain falls on dry fields. Her wrists are spotted with salt tears. '*La illaha illaa*. Keep your boys here with you. Bring them the finest maidens whose hearts render sincere prayers. Let them run across fields and feel good soil under their feet. Wash your mouth, then say your *du'a* seven times. Wrap the holy words in fresh water and give these to drink. Do not turn them out of your house. May your heart never break like mine.'"

Charlie sits still and fantasizes as he listens. He smells the scent of lamb cooking over open fires, in big black pots in the yards. This is what great writing can do, he thinks, but says nothing. In the after-glow of the joint he listens to comments and questions.

"Is City a metaphor for the Outside, the West?" One girl asks.

Before Hussein can answer Jean-Pierre says, "You know, this sounds like something old folks at home say. My grandparents warned my father not to allow me to come to New York. They said fancy women, gambling men, and drinkers would lead me astray."

Charlie listens, still not commenting, even though he could have. His parents worry about him. He's met many hard-drinking men and fancy women. Jean-Pierre has introduced him to several drugs. Tim drinks a bit too much. Charlie enjoys pot because it let him see things clearer.

Pedro steps forward and props up three large photographs. He's from Puerto Rico and his woman is Mexican. "These are part of a series called 'Life and Death, Death and Life.' These three are called 'Futility 1, 2, and 3.'"

Hussein adjusts the light to better illuminate the display. Everyone looks at the images staring back at them. In the first a dead man is lying on the ground, garbage framing his body. Shadows of a crowd looking down on the corpse add tension. The second is a close-up of a woman's face; the crowd is now in the background. The third is a telescopic shot of the alley, a sloping street, a crowd and, walking towards the same body, a woman with a baby in arms.

Mel frowns. "Yes, but it's too violent."

"I much prefer the other ones, the portraits of Josefina," a blonde offers, looking about for support.

Charlie thinks, All of his work is great. Yes, Pedro, you've captured her beauty. A sensitive portrayal. But this Futility series brings the truth of death and pain to the forefront. It's how I feel when I hear or read about a black man killing another black man: futile. Yes, I can dig it.

One by one, people share their stuff. Tim is sketching. Salimatou sits on a pillow somewhat apart from the circle, looking from the pictures and faces to Hussein. So open in her display of love. She breathes when he does. She catches Charlie watching and drops her gaze for a moment.

Finally Charlie uncurls, takes out his pages, and says, "I'm working on a novel for my degree in literature. It's based on a poem that frames the story. I'll just read a bit of that to set it up, then a page or two of the first chapter.

"Ethiopia stretches her hand
open palm—a date, ripe
for the plucking. A breast
waiting for the sucking. A pair
of open legs—black
receive the whiteness
of a raping horde. Kush, close your doors."

He looks around quickly to assess the reaction. All is quiet; waiting. Salimatou's hands reach up as if for reassurance that her head scarf is securely fastened. Almost without moving, she is nearer Hussein's side. Charlie takes this as a sign his words are having an effect on this little audience. He resumes reading.

"'So I said, "What you mean man I can't come in here? This ain't the South. This New York! No prejudice here. No segregation. I just want to sit down and have a quiet dinner." The man, the white-face-man, the white-face-turning-red-face-man stares at the well-dressed Negro. "Told you we don't got an empty table right now. You got to wait.'

"But the man is tired. Tired of waiting. Tired of lines. Tired of white folks telling him to wait. Besides, there's an empty table in the back, near the wall. Just where he wants to sit. By the window. People passing will see his black face and maybe not want to eat in a place that serves blacks. He wants to smash the waiter's face. To beat it to a bloody pulp. Make him holler like the black man he'd seen as a child, surrounded by a group of red-faced white men brandishing tree branches and stones. His mother coming out of a store where she'd gone to buy material saw him standing, watching as the black man tried to break through the circle to run away. A stone to the head knocked him to the ground. He tried to get up but they pounced on him, beating. Beating. Beating. Cursing and cursing. The man screaming, begging them to stop. His words becoming more and more muffled under the blows. His teeth loosened by a punch. Everywhere his blood, pieces of flesh, scraps of bloodied clothes. Then a shop keeper running out, shouting, 'Hey, stop! She found the money. It fell on the floor. The nigger didn't steal it.'

"The man's mother had snatched his young self away. The crowd of white folks just looked from the helpless man on the ground to the four or five with bloody fists. One man took off his belt and lashed the black man's face. They all stopped beating him and stared; at their hands and at each other. The man with the belt threaded it back through the loops on his pants. Another, puffing and pot-bellied, spat a brown liquid on the fallen man's head. But no one came forward to help him up. His nameless face was unrecognizable. The boy's mother led him away by the hand, pulling hard, urging, 'Stop looking at that white trash.' But he managed a final look. A dog came by, sniffed and licked what was left of the black man's nose. A little white boy darted over, picked up something and ran back shouting, "Look, I got his teeth! Four of 'em.""

By the time Charlie ends the reading, silence imprisons the room.

Marta raises her hand. "Does the black man leave the restaurant? Does he hit the waiter?"

Charlie realizes he is holding his breath, and inhales, then says, "Well, you'll have to wait to read the novel."

Tim is curious about this mixing of poetry and prose.

"It's done all the time," Charlie answers, trying not to sound defensive. Mel thinks it an interesting beginning. What do those words mean, 'interesting' and 'beginning'?

"I'm employing a particular sentence structure, too. No punctuation. To give the feeling of continuous movement and dialogue," Charlie adds with some self importance. His gaze falls on Jean-Pierre, whom he really wants to impress after his scathing review of the reading at the Tompkins Square Library. Two weeks ago, Jean-Pierre called him 'pompous' and 'unoriginal'. The evening ends pleasantly, though. He gets some positive comments.

Jean-Pierre's critique seems guarded. But the prize next to him is a shy girl, Marta's friend, who's going to spend the rest of the night with him.

Charlie admits with a modicum of chagrin that it was taking longer than intended to complete the novel. In class, the professor and his classmates always seemed to find some idea not fully realized, conceptualized or scripted. Character development problematic. Plot directionless. All constant carps.

But now, thanks to Emily, his current companion, he's turned in a completed manuscript, perfectly typed by her, in her office, on a Remington. Her father's a big man at Fitch and Winthrop Press. They have a reputation for discovering and rediscovering obscure writers. He's very satisfied with himself because, not only is he graduating a semester ahead of schedule, but his novel is under contract with a second book promised. Emily even managed to get him a small advance. She's handling the marketing of the book as well.

Charlie's rave reviews push him into a peculiar limelight. An interview in *Time*, an article in *Black World*, an invitation from the Progressive Writers of Italy. It all enhances his position as the black writer of the hour. When he returns from Italy, he and Emily get engaged. But he hears nasty comments. "Her daddy keeps him on the payroll to make sure his baby won't die of starvation." And from Jean-Pierre, who, he notes with some satisfaction, has had his second manuscript rejected by three publishers. Who knows if he really did say it, but it seems Jean-Pierre said Charlie's writing was getting further from the point. That he was writing for a white audience. Charlie winces and thinks, "J.P., I just want to be read."

Shortly after the wedding Charlie suggests they take a trip to Spain. "There's a writer from New Orleans I want to meet. He's been living there for years, getting a lot of work done." Emily agrees because she's never been to Spain and because he wants to go.

In Ibiza there are many black male artists and their white women. Some married with children, others living together. It's a world he never dreamed possible. The sea, old houses, women in dark clothes and stockings, quickly passing him as if afraid. He especially loves the children who come up and ask for bubblegum.

They rent a house in the midst of a little colony of expatriates, who gather at each other's homes in the evening to drink, eat great food, and share the best grass—with stronger stuff for those so inclined. Emily shares a few puffs, but not too often. Charlie is happy for the first time he can recall. He walks openly with his woman without fear of being ambushed by white gangs or censorious blacks. He's actually thinking about renting the house they're staying in for a few years. With his advance and royalties, they could manage it. Cost of living here is pretty close to the Lower East Side. But the day before he planned to go to the rental agent, a letter reaches him.

In it his mother says Tennessee is going through some hard times. Young people are confronting the segregated system. Four stores have already opened up to serve blacks. A student group at Fisk has asked her to contact him about coming down for a reading. Also a tragedy has just occurred. A black woman walking down the street in Nashville was shot from a passing car. She leaves eleven children for her husband to care for. Students are trying to organize a fundraiser and protest.

Emily is fearful but excited by his decision to return and participate in the struggle. He wants her to remain in New York. Fortunately they've kept the old apartment. He tells the expat group he's got to go back and do what he can for The People. The women think he is brave, noble, sacrificing so much for the cause. They all envy Emily.

The men say he's crazy. But Zachary, an older writer, says, "You're young. You've got lots of work ahead. Remember, take your writing with you. Collect the stories and experiences, and write your butt off."

The trip back to New York, and then to Tennessee, exhausts him. But when they arrive at the campus where the rally is taking place, he's energized to see so many people. He ends his reading by saying, "There must evolve a system that will incorporate the old ways and also make way for the new. So that red skin-tight pants can give way to loose-fitting tweeds. So that television becomes a tool for mass re-education, and radio draws the world closer. Technology put to work becomes a servant to The People."

He pauses and looks out at a sea of young, dark faces all staring back at him. Eating up every word he utters.

"So go on out. March! Sing! Resist! Retain your dignity as proud black men and women. But carry books with you. Be prepared for the demands of the new world you are creating now. Help each other with math, and pass your history exams."

There is scattered applause. He takes a deep breath and continues.

"Graduates! Take over your own lives. Be ready to teach, to be doctors, hospital administrators, professional workers, leaders. Stand tall! Power and Peace!"

The room explodes in thunderous applause and feet stamping. His sense of achievement, of power, is intoxicating and for the first time in his life he is drunk on it. A crush of people surges forward to shake his hand. A sea-like swell of thousands of people swims dizzily before his eyes. Charlie leans on a nearby guard for support momentarily, breathing deeply, and then flashes a blinding smile. He looks out to see his parents sitting in the front row. His mother buries her head in his father's shoulder, sobbing. People come and pat her shoulder, sharing her pride. They understand the tears she sheds are not from pain or shame. Rather, she is overcome by the significance of this event. Her son has gone abroad, made a success of himself and yet has not forgotten his people.

"Yes, he's a good boy," croons one woman.

"Sister, you and your husband done good," says an elderly man.

"Sweet Jesus, that boy's got the power of the Lord in him," cries a swaying woman in a wide-brimmed hat.

These comments lift Charlie's heart. He begins to believe he is special. That he possesses fire.

He returns to the Lower East Side five days later. Some of the neighbors have seen him on their little black and white TV screens. His reception at Stanley's is an orgy of welcome. They all saw his face on the six o'clock news the day before, where he was hailed as a new militant voice, a leader advocating a shift in paradigm. Now here he is, walking through their own little bar in triumph.

Jean-Pierre's voice, however, drips with sarcasm. "All hail the conqueror." The pinpoints of his pupils announce J.P is high.

"You look good in a dashiki, man," Tim teases.

A space clears at one table for Charlie to take a seat. A new white girl is sitting between him and Bill. She leans over and reaches out to pat his buoyant 'Fro. Charlie looks around at this little crowd of men whose praise and appreciation he most wants to feel; by whom he most wants to be taken seriously.

"I heard you and Emily got married. Congratulations." Bill reaches out to shake hands.

Charlie suppresses a wince as Bill's long fingers clasp his so hard it hurts. But the pain also brings the secure feeling of being part of a protective brotherhood. "Thanks, Bill."

The older man gives a slow smile and salutes him. "Well, good seeing you. Now I got to go take this old body to bed. Early call in the morning." Bill pats his back, picks up a leather bag and leaves.

The rest hang out a few hours more. After closing time Charlie floats along the streets, heading south on Avenue B, crossing the park, then left on Avenue A, a sharp right on St. Marks to 1st Avenue and then to East 5th Street. Familiar faces dance in front of him but he glides on by. He is confirmed by his peers. For the first time, he feels a sense of artistic merit not dictated by the marketing department of Fitch and Winthrop Press.

A few years later, the novelty of Charlie as Angry Black Man has grown thin. Jean-Pierre is clean now, and writing like nobody's business. Still, Charlie has a following in Europe and the States. He and Emily spend half their time abroad. Their home in Spain is a center for expatriates now that The Old Man is gone. Zachary is too. He passed away a few months after they came back from their first trip.

Charlie begins to put on weight. It's unavoidable, really; he enjoys such a rich diet augmented by generous sips of fine wines. Emily is an excellent mother to their three children. His reputation boosts sales and so, with six novels in print and one movie script produced, Charlie approaches his peak. All around him feet are moving towards freedom—in the South, the North, in Africa and the Caribbean. Sometimes he speaks at their rallies and forums. He keeps current and knows just how to say what's needed at these occasions. Many of his peers are leaving the Lower East Side, some relocating to Harlem and Bedford-Stuyvesant.

At a new school in Harlem where the artists know him, he's invited to collaborate in a revolutionary curriculum with a heavy emphasis on art as a tool for social change. His name brings publicity to the campus, and proposals are hastily written to solicit funds for books, art materials, a dance studio. The students' energy and eagerness touch him.

Now he goes to Harlem storefront churches every Sunday. He explains to Emily, "I'm gathering material for a new book of poems." His facile explanation causes her no alarm. But he's smoking more, too. The Saturday morning family ritual of movies at the Rialto, across from Stanley's, tapers off to every other Saturday. His need for sex increases and he acts more aggressive, but Emily feels these are expressions of his deepening love and passion. She delights in sharing the details with her friends, much to their envy.

While Charlie looks for himself mirrored in others, his own eyes are shuttered, almost emotionless. He searches in the crevices of Emily for hidden parts of himself. He rereads his old manuscripts endlessly. Packages of letters between him and The Old Man sit next to notepads and sheets of neatly retyped pages Emily puts on his desk. She never changes a word, not even to correct punctuation or spelling. His very scribble must be evidence of literary genius, of an *oeuvre* destined for the canon of belles-lettres.

Shortly after their return from Ibiza and reunion with old friends at Pedro's new photography show and a book launch party for Hussein, Emily finds it harder to ignore some of these changes. She tells herself it's simply seeing Salimatou again, after a few years away. After all, Charlie always had a crush on her. The important thing is that his latest book has just been nominated for the National Book Award. Emily's father is marketing him constantly, riding this new wave of fame, getting bookings a year in advance. The children are so beautiful, so well-behaved, and always impeccably dressed.

But Charlie has his own plans. He leaves their spacious apartment on West 90th Street and comes down to his old place on the lower East Side, which he kept as a writing studio. There he pastes pages of his novel in progress on the walls. After days of moving around Emily's carefully-typed sheets, he begins to arrange the pages in an order he can tolerate. Then he sits in the darkening room, smoking a briarwood pipe filled with a custom-cut blend from Turkey, with a little hash mixed in. He buys tobacco from a small, exclusive shop on West 23rd Street and 8th Avenue. He sits watching spirals of smoke curl lazily to the ceiling. After a few moments of suspension, of visions dancing on the walls to the loveliest tune he's ever heard, Charlie gets up and goes to the window. Retying his shoes tighter, grabbing a muffler, he winds it around his neck, then sits on the sill looking out. A breeze through the open window flutters the pages. He laughs at the kaleidoscopic swirls it makes of black words on white pages. "Oh yes, I know that song."

Charlie opens the window wider. He sees Salimatou dancing out there, not far away, with her arms outstretched, urging him to come join her.

"Yes," he says, and reaches out to take her into his embrace at last.

The music holds them fast. He glides on air.

JUST OFF GRAND STREET

The steps creak under the weight of his long frame descending to the first floor. Outside, he buttons his long, heavy overcoat against the biting winds off the East River. Figures huddle deep inside jackets and shawls, covered heads obscure the faces of men, women and children. Sometimes it's difficult to say who is who, or what. "No matter," Miguel Eugenio de Mateo mutters into the wool muffler wrapped twice around his neck. He pulls it up almost to the edge of a furry Russian-style cap bought from an effeminate European guy who operates a junk store not too far from Rosa's flat. His salary, safely divided, is tucked into one sock, the rest in his wallet. A trick he learned the hard way, back home. He sighs, remembering.

He hurries out into the chill, carrying a bag of newspapers to drop off at strategic locations along the way to East 10th Street. Checking for hoodlums and police—both of whom he tries to avoid. *Avanza Popular* and *La Guarda* are hard to sell because fearmongers keep telling people there's going to be a communist take-over. Miguel snorts. As if that were really possible. Americans are too comfortable with their rich, powerful exploiters. Secretly admiring and wishing to take their places, all the while picketing against 'The Bosses' and 'Corrupt Leaders.'"

All the shops are closed. He walks as fast as the long coat flapping around his ankles and his load will allow. Headlights illuminate his path. He feels some small satisfaction each time he dumps several copies inside each a tenement hall or through mail slots in the locked doors of stores which sell cheap dresses and flimsy coats to the poor. His shoes are heavy-soled; the cold pavement doesn't penetrate. He walks with warm toes, warming up thanks to the brisk pace.

Miguel feels better once he crosses over Houston and onto Avenue C. "Ten more streets and then hot coffee," he promises himself.

Just as he nears East 2nd Street he pauses, pretending to check his shoe laces, and sees approaching just what he'd feared. A group of junkies, not high enough to be sluggish, looking hungry and obviously needing a few dollars to score. Their blue-tinged faces lurch nearer. But there's traffic on Avenue C, and a few people walking on both sides of the street. The men slow and slink closer to the buildings, trying to blend into shadows.

Miguel walks faster until some giggling young people are between him and the junkie predators. The weight of his coat is slowing him down. The teenagers veer off at East 7th, and the pack, three men, starts to gain on him. Miguel darts right into the path of an oncoming car, missing getting flattened by mere inches. A change of lights, the obstacle of two more cars, both give him the advantage.

He breaks into a run, then darts into a building on East 8th Street, hoping this evàsive maneuver is shielded by the clanging metal hulk of a sanitation truck, a day and a half late on its rounds. He hears the men curse as they turn and head back to their own street, to lie in wait for some other unlucky pedestrian. He hopes the next unsuspecting mark will be able to escape unharmed, too, as he hurries on to East 10th Street. Hurling himself into his building, breath coming in painful asthmatic whoops. Fearing a heart attack, he bends over behind the stair well, the words of his physical education teacher echoing in his head two decades later. *In, out. Breathe in through your nose, expel with slightly open lips.*

"Oh God, I'm too old for this," he wheezes, chuckling at old linguistic habits inherited centuries ago. His breathing slowly eases; the spasms subside. He wipes face and neck, noticing his own sharp acrid odor. He touches his crotch to make sure he hasn't disgraced himself. After all, he's a seasoned revolutionary. "Ah, dry. Good."

Slowly he begins the steep climb up four flights to the tiny flat he shares with Rosa, off and on.

Miguel uses his keys and opens the door. What had seemed the mere whiff of a slightly offensive odor out in the hallway now balloons into a scent that threatens to choke him. Roiling a stomach still churning after the near-miss attack, a flattening by the sanitation truck and simple hunger.

Rosa rushes over, hysterical in her joy at seeing him this early, screaming, "*Ayi me amor, mi amor.*" All but colonizing his mouth with her youthful, enthusiastic tongue.

"*Querida*, slow down. Let me take off my coat, and use the toilet." He gently pulls her hands from his cold cheeks.

Once out of the heavy coat and inside the toilet, he washes face and hands, takes a small towel and wipes under his arms, again smelling it. "Ugh!" He puts some soap on the cloth and wipes again. Maybe he can get in a bath before she drags him to bed.

He wishes.

Coming back to the little kitchen he now pays full attention to Rosa. She's in a frilly black dress of some cheap, thin material stretched too tightly. It shows the swell of young breasts as she heaps something steaming onto a plate for him. A stew that makes his eyes water from the pungent piercing of hot pepper. "Ah Rosa, I hope you remembered, not too much with the chilies. They're bad for my stomach. You know what happened a week ago."

She smiles, indulgent. "But for so big a man like you, peppers are good."

This he translates to mean, they will enhance his sex drive, and inwardly groans. It's going to be a long night. "I have to get up early to finish the article for the next issue," he warns. Clearly she's not going to let him get any work done tonight.

Poor Rosa, all dressed up, trying to look like the latest fashion model she's copying this month. Poor Rosa, playing at housewife, all of twenty-two to his forty-five years. He sighs, digging into the thick muck, a ring of fire. The sting of the first bite brings tears to his eyes. He imagines tiny blisters forming at the back of his throat. His stomach growls in protest, as if it can ward off the approach of green and red peppers studding the sauce. Fortunately the toilet's in the hall. He can only grimly imagine what it will be like when all this stuff has to come out.

It's been three years and one son since he left Argentina to come be the news editor of a Spanish-language newspaper in New York. The paper doesn't measure up to his intellectual and political standards, but it pays bi-weekly. Half the money he sends home to his wife and two children. It's augmented by his Spanish-to-

English translations for several newspapers, and so Miguel manages to survive in New York.

Rosa had been working as a receptionist—really, window-dressing for the paper. She spent most of the day polishing her nails and making sure her lips stayed shiny and red. Her choice of thick dark lipstick still revolts him. But he seemed to fascinate her and Miguel must admit, he enjoyed being the object of pursuit by a near-teenaged seductress. Her tight sweaters might inspire an advertisement: "I dreamed I stabbed my boss in my Maidenform bra." They did tend to send his thoughts right between his legs.

He breaks off a piece of bread and dips it into the steaming dish. It's too hot, but he's hungry. He chuckles. Anyhow, he needs its reviving taste after that brush with danger. Rosa brings over a bottle of beer and sets it next to his plate. She is a ripe melon; at his back Miguel feels her unsophisticated, sensual heat. The too-tight dress accentuating her lush body as she all but counts the time it takes for him to finish eating, so she can pounce.

Miguel concentrates on eating, one spoonful at a time, with a piece of bread and some rice, then a sip of beer to help put out the fire. Beads of sweat mix with the suds from his beer. At last he notices the quiet, and turns to see a strange look on her face. "Where…where's the baby? Where's my Pavel?"

She winces at the name. Her face brightens with the obvious cunning of a child. "I took him to his *abuela* so we can have a nice night alone." Looking satisfied with her accomplishments she gets up, walks over to the radio in what he imagines she's practiced as a sexy undulation, and turns up the volume.

He continues to eat, more slowly now. Rosa dances about, rolling her little curved belly, shaking shoulders and breasts, licking her lips. Miguel recalls this seductive move from a grade B movie they'd seen at the St. Marks Cinema a week ago. His mouth is numb. Even the beer is of little help. After a long final swig he gets up and grabs the young wild woman. She's full and firm still, but he knows in a few years, maybe by her thirties, she'll turn to flab. The only exercise Rosa enjoys is bouncing in bed.

But now she is ready! She sticks her tongue in his ear and with legs spread rubs herself against his crotch. Her hands pull at his shirt. "Come on, Poppi." She kisses him and starts humping. Her movements are so lacking in grace he almost shoves her away.

"Easy baby," he urges, tickling her, rubbing taut nipples with his finger tips. He unzips her dress and pale young flesh spills out, reminding him in both sight and texture of dough. His mother used to set out a bowl of dough every other night. She'd knead and whack it down on a floured surface and then cover it, so it could rise again. The pasty goo sometimes rose too high and then oozed over the sides of the bowl. That's what the flesh under her armpits and upper arms, her breasts and the growing bicycle tire around her waist are becoming. He recalculates; maybe it will be less than ten years for flab to consume the tight skin stretched already almost beyond its elasticity.

Rosa continues shimmying, making sounds she must think are tantalizing. "*Ayi Poppito,* you make me crazy."

If he goes one round hard, maybe she'll let him rest. Then he can pretend to fall into a deep sleep. So he lets her dance him towards the bed. All the while she continues pulling at his clothes. He tries to get a hand free to sneak out a rubber from his pants pocket. This girl is so fertile he's afraid to even kiss her sometimes.

Lately she's been dropping hints in her unsubtle way. "*Poppi*, Junito is getting big. He needs a little sister or brother. I don't want to be too long having another baby."

Jesus, he doesn't want another child. He hadn't wanted this one. She'd told him she was using a diaphragm so he didn't need to wear rubbers. Besides, she wanted to feel him, his skin, the real thing. Then bingo, with one of her wide-eyed smiles she'd announced, "*Mi amor*, I'm going to have your baby." So here he is with a nymphet on his hands at his age, and a whole other family to add to his first, back home. And increasingly less time to devote to The Revolution.

If only she wasn't so oversexed. If only she would read more. He'd tried at the beginning to interest her in his work but she only wanted to make love. The little group of comrades was turned off by her as much as she was by them. Once during an argument over why he could not use his education to become a lawyer or successful business man, Rosa had run and snatched his slim volume of poems by Ahkmatova, ripped it down the middle and thrown it at him. Before he knew what was what, she was screaming, "Police, murder!" and he was choking her. Mortified,

Miguel dropped his hands and picked up the book, while she stood by crying like a spoiled child in the throes of a tantrum.

You should never have come back, he scolds himself, as Rosa rolls over him. He manages to run the rubber up the flag pole just in time.

During the breakup Rosa called his office three and four times a day. His co-workers thought him a '*muy hombre*' to so besot a woman half his age. Once she'd stood on the sidewalk shouting up at the little storefront where the comrades met to discuss strategies to enhance the conditions for revolution. Begging, pleading, she'd promised to read Marx, go to meetings, anything! If he would just come back to her. It was only after she tried, almost successfully, to commit suicide by taking six sleeping pills downed with Bacardi rum, that he'd started seeing her again.

She was the essence of a make-believe, sexy housewife; overwhelming him with affection in the way she'd been schooled to: a wild and very physical romp on the bed, up against the wall, or on the floor. Once when he'd been pushed to the point of exhaustion and locked himself in the bathroom, she had pounded on the door. One of Rosa's floormates, a pretty young black African woman who lived with her small son, came out to see what was going on. I bet she's read Marx and Ahkmatova, he'd thought, slinking back to the apartment with Rosa twining around him like a hormonal octopus.

His wife in Argentina calls him at the office weekly. She's been detained twice but her father, a rich and powerful man, was able to get her released each time. She's fearful that the next time they may do her harm. One of the cops threatened to rape her. Miguel's head pounds as the chilies do their job. Rosa's scratching and writhing, groping at him so wildly he's afraid she'll tear the rubber and he isn't sure he has another one. He'd really like to get up, dress, and walk out. But then she'd probably put out a hit on him. Any of the hundreds of men down here would oblige for a fix, or maybe a week in her bed.

"God, what to do?" he murmurs. With no divine guidance forthcoming, he sticks it to her. Rosa squeals in delight, moans and grunts, grinds and bucks, demanding, "More! More *Poppi, ayi, ayi.*" Soaked in their sweat he succumbs to her demands, thinking,

"How can I be prepared for the meeting on Colonialism and Capitalism; Dual Oppression, tomorrow?"

He sighs, hoping she'll think it's because he's satisfied. "Yes," he hisses, "Oh yes, I like that." A good working title for the new paper he plans to develop into a pamphlet for *New Masses.*

Beneath him Rosa has apparently been possessed by some spirits. Her body trembles as she heads for her first orgasm. Maybe if he can hold out long enough for a second one in quick order, she'll let him sleep a while. Funny, this had never been a problem with Zoraida. They'd made love, fallen asleep, and the next day gone off to work, school, or whatever else was on the agenda. Then came home and did the same again. But this one, she never got enough.

Finally it's over. He falls off limply and lies on his side. The rubber is full and messy. "Ugh, I hate these things," he mumbles. But necessity demands precautions.

Rosa gets up and tiptoes to the toilet. He slips off the latex, runs to the garbage and stuffs it under a mess of food scraps. Just managing to get back into bed as she closes the door, he tries not to move, but only breath slowly, evenly. He feels her near but keeps his eyes closed.

She tiptoes off again, this time to the other room. She makes a call. "Mommy? Yes, it's me. No, no, everything's fine." She gives a dirty chuckle. "I just put him to sleep and when I put Miguel to sleep he's out. What? No, I'm not using that diaphragm. I told him I want another baby. What do you mean? *Ayi*, Mommy, I love making babies. No, he's not too old! Not when he can go like he did a while ago. He's a mature, honorable man. And if I have two babies, he'll never leave me. Okay, Okay, I'm gonna sleep now. How is Junito? Good. Okay, goodnight."

Miguel does finally sleep, but fitfully, dreaming he's running away from three men wearing masks. They chase him into a wooded area. Ahead he sees a light and races towards it. The more he runs the further away it gets. Suddenly Karl Marx rides by on a snorting Russian steed. Reins in before Miguel and calls out, "Ready for the revolution!" Then a big snake drops down between them. It turns into a voluptuous female. She opens her legs and he is drawn in by his huge erection.

Half-awake now, his hands creep involuntary to his crotch, only to find his little man... missing? No, but there's an obstruction.

Miguel opens his eyes with a shudder. Rosa is atop him, pumping away. He pushes her off and she laughs. "I got it all, two times. I know I'm pregnant, *mi querida*. You'll never leave me now." She rubs his loins and kisses his stomach and then with a smile, lays her head on his chest and falls fast asleep.

Miguel is too tired to move. His numb body pulls him back into a dead and dreamless pit.The next two months are very busy. He's moved into a tiny backroom in the little office headquarters. His comrades understand. On many occasions one or two of them have had to use it, as well, when unable to keep up with rent at their flats, or hiding from ex-wives and children, debt collectors, or the law.

Rosa is hounding him. "I want a real marriage, *Poppi*! Divorce that old bag in Argentina and marry me." She wants to move before the new baby comes. He's not convinced that she is actually pregnant. The best thing he's done the last few months is to stay away from East 10th Street and out of her bed.

She predictably violates their agreement, though, by showing up at the newspaper office. He takes her to the conference room where, as soon as the door closed, she tries to grab his neck and kiss him. "Look Rosa, it's over," he insists, holding her at arms' length. "I don't want you anymore. I will support the boy and try to be a father to him, but we cannot make it together. We're too different in age and politics."

She scowls. "What about the new baby?"

He shouts, "I'll pay for an abortion! I know a comrade who's a doctor."

This brings on the usual hysterics, crying and cursing and hair-pulling.

"By the way," he asks. "How far along? Have you seen a doctor? I can have my friend examine you."

"No, no, no! I will not do an abortion. It's a mortal sin."

Miguel persists about an examination, at least. Rosa pouts and shakes her head. This raises his suspicions about her status.

"I'm going to the police and report you and those so-called comrades," she threatens. "I'll tell all about your plans to destroy this country. You'll get into a lot of trouble. We don't like communists here. They go to jail."

He decides to call her bluff. "Fine, then I'll get sent home at America's expense."

Now he can see the wheels rolling in her mind, clack, clack. "Then I'll write your wife and tell her you have another family! A pretty young wife, a child, and another on the way. She won't be waiting for you then."

Miguel, in a moment of cruelty he would like to think is rare, says, "Zoraida knows all about you. She's known from the beginning. And she will be waiting for me with my two children when I arrive."

Now Rosa looks like a toddler whose prize balloon has just been whipped out of her hand by a gust of wind. That it has just been impaled on the uppermost branches of a tall tree and as she watches—*pop*! It shrivels to a wrinkled, rubbery mass, dangling without hope.

Miguel, ever mindful of his responsibility to the *lumpen*, feels sympathy. A need to guide this apolitical former mistress towards the path of enlightenment. "Look Rosa," he says gently. "You're right to be angry. I'm the wrong person for you. Too old, too set in my ways. But you, you're young. Take advantage of the opportunities this city offers. Go to the library. Check out books. Read! They have adult classes on East 14th Street where you can learn things to help you and Pavel."

Oh no. At that name, she bristles. He hurries on before she has a chance to go into detail about the crime of hanging such a name on a child, a name nobody ever heard of, a name that everyone will know is from communists. How they will know this if they don't know nor have ever heard of it before, is a mystery.

He finally gets her to leave with the promise of a visit with her social worker, to work out the details of their separation and a nice settlement of support for the child, or children. Whichever turns to be the case.

After that, in the discomfort of his current cramped living quarters, Miguel dreads Friday. Normally, since the break-up, he's gone to the institution-green office of the social worker, where he sees his boy and gives Rosa child-support money. Now, this Friday, he sits on a hard chair, coat across his lap, briefcase at his feet, the final draft of his paper (which was roundly applauded last night), waiting to be called for his visit.

A buzzer pierces even the din of crying children, the scolding of mothers too distracted, too distant, too unprepared to handle them. Over the constant ring of telephones, the clack of typewriters keys, the clicking of heels of women tackling emergencies and chasing after one or more parents who have stalked out of meetings, comes the buzzing. And then the voice of the secretary, announcing, "Miguel Eugenio de Mateo, please."

Aware that he presents a different picture of a man in this desperate setting, and trying to offer a positive example, he picks up his handsome leather briefcase. And then, his cashmere coat neatly folded across the brown tweed jacket encasing his arm, Miguel follows her directions to the meeting.

Rosa shoots him a hot look of pure hatred. Her body stiffens inside a dark blue suit he recognizes as one he bought her at the beginning of his attempts to teach her how to dress nicely. A white blouse under the jacket peeks out discreetly. He'd taken her to Orbach's for their annual fall suits and coats sale. The jaunt had almost ended in disaster, until they'd both compromised. He also let her buy a low-cut black wool sweater with shiny silver threads sparkling through it. Even now he thinks, If she would only adjust the redness of her lipstick, take away the raccoon rings around her eyes, and tame the hair so bed-tousled a la Brigitte Bardot, she could pass herself off as smart looking, almost chic.

But he sits, silently. They manage, with the extremely-practiced skill of the case worker, to agree on home visits and a few hours for him alone with the child. He will be allowed to pick up Pavel from the flat, take him out for five hours, and then return him. The first visit would be next Friday, at the flat, with the case worker present.

Sitting at the table, with the patient woman mediating, they are then encouraged to talk. Miguel looks at Rosa and thinks, What will become of her and the boy? If only she could understand the importance of political education. He sits in silence, knowing the ticket for Zoraida has already been paid for by her father. The two children are going to her sister, to attend school in Spain. The lease for a new four-room flat is in his leather briefcase, signed, along with a receipt for two months rent, a deposit and a month in advance. The savings he was able to accumulate by sleeping three months on a filthy cot and no conveniences in the little room at headquarters, plus the take from three big translation jobs, has padded his income.

Rosa sighs audibly but he pays no mind. Astoria, where they'll be staying, is almost as distant as Argentina to her. To them: Rosa and his son. The Greek landlord and his Italian wife own two restaurants and have very good politics. He met them through one of the comrades who's married to the wife's sister and also teaches at City College, one of the few Reds who hasn't been forced out. The comrade assures him Zoraida should be able to get a position at the College, too, what with her extensive experience.

The meeting ends unsatisfactorily. But the home visit the following Friday at Rosa's apartment is still on.

That Friday at Rosa's place, Miguel is roused out of a reverie by the reddening of Rosa's cheeks and her sharp, "Miguel!" She may in fact have been speaking for a while.

Pay attention, Miguel, he tells himself.

"Miguel, why you don't love me no more? I do everything for you, like a wife. But no, always the books, the books and reading. Well, I don't want to read. I hate those books and I hate my son's name. What kind of name is Pavel?" With each word her voice and coloring rise. "His new name is Miguelito Junito. Miguel Junior. I don't like that name you gave him. And I don't like those books, all your teachings. You know what the problem is? You love them and that dead woman, Ahkama... Akka...whatever you call her."

He shifts in his seat. "Ahkmatova."

She shrugs. "You love all that stuff more than me and Junito. Us, your real family! You don't see us, you don't love us." Rosa starts crying.

He tries not to wince. "Rosa, I'm sorry things turned out this way. I told you from the beginning, I'm married. With a family in Argentina. That I did not want any more children or a long-term relationship. I know it's hard raising a child alone, but I'm not in a position to do more. We live in different worlds."

She sits staring then, saying nothing. It's as if he's been speaking in a foreign language, not English or Spanish. Words that have no equivalent she can comprehend.

The case worker sits with folded hands, as if waiting for things to sort themselves out in Rosa's head.

Rosa squirms uncomfortably under all the close attention being paid her. "What? Why you look at me like that?"

He decides not to say anything.

The caseworker asks, "Rosa, Mr. de Mateo has said he accepts his responsibility to your son and will continue to support the boy. He's expressed a desire to be in the child's life by spending time with him, alone, so—"

Rosa flings up a hand. "What do you mean? This is his son! He must take care of him, always. He is his father."

The caseworker nods. "Yes, he understands and will comply. What he's saying is, the relationship between the two of you is not one he plans to continue. He wants to find a way to come and see the child, to be with him without causing a problem by intruding on your time."

Rosa's forehead creases as she struggles to parse the bureaucratic phrasing. "So he not coming here to see me? But Junito stay here with me. How he see his son, how the boy see his father, if he don't see me?"

Miguel tries to think of a way to answer without sending her off on a new tirade. He worries about the books he'd gotten for his son and read to him at night; the books he tried to read to her. A little library, that's what he's created in one corner of the boy's room.

"You know Rosa," says the case worker encouragingly. "Reading is good. Why not read to the child so he can appreciate books and learning? It will help him be successful in school."

Miguel winces.

"Don't you tell me how to raise my son! I know what to do. A baby wants to play, to have fun. Not sit around with his face in a book. He's too young." Rosa scowls, still warming up. "What about his father? The father don't do nothing. Hang around with people discussing books, pretend like they can change the world. Well." She whirls on him, "They can't. Rich people stay rich. Poor people try to get as much as they can. So if you want him to have stories, you come read to him every night." She bolts from the room wailing, headed to the toilet in the hall.

Miguel feels momentary guilt. He always read stories to his two older children at night and on the weekend. He looks at the tiny boy staring silently from the doorway of his room. Pavel sits with toys surrounding him. Miguel predicts a sad future, with a mother so resistant to learning.

She stomps back to the kitchen and sulks in her seat.

"Rosa, I'm sorry things turned out this way. I never lied. I didn't say we'd marry and be together forever. But I want the boy to have a good education."

She scowls and huffs, turning away in her chair.

"I told you I had a family in Argentina," he persists. "And didn't want more children. Because I know it's hard for a young woman to raise a child alone."

Rosa starts crying again.

The child, gazing at her, also whimpers.

She bangs on the table. "Shut up!"

The boy gapes silently, tears glazing fat cheeks. He sniffles, perhaps unsure if she's yelling at him or Miguel.

"Junito, make one more sound and I'll knock your head off."

"I don't think," begins the case worker.

The child has made no noise all through the past hour. Miguel frowns. Clearly she's hit him before, because he acts as if the threat is real. Miguel tries to intervene but the social worker shakes her head. Rosa sits glowering at them both. What she will do to the child once they leave?

She taunts him. "Listen old man. You think you the only one? There's plenty who want me. I'm young and pretty. I don't need you. Go back to your old *vaca*."

No one speaks for a moment.

"You know," she tells the social worker. "He always treat me like I'm dumb, stupid, just because I don't wanna read those communist books."

"But Rosa, *Jane Eyre* is a novel. You said you liked love stories. And Charles Dickens—" The social worker puts on her professional voice, "Rosa, I'm very concerned about your interactions with your child. You may feel over-burdened. Tell me, would you like to get him into daycare? Then you can have time for yourself. Look for work or take classes at the Alliance."

Rosa swivels to her, eyes narrowed. But then her face smoothes out, as if by magic. She hangs her head. "Yes, Yes, I need that."

Inwardly he groans. Imagines what's playing on the screen in her head.

"I went to beauty academy after high school," she adds. "I can work in a shop. Save money, open my own little place." Her gaze slides back to him. "I don't need your few little dollars. I'm not some cheap *puta* you pick up at a bar. I can take care of myself and my son. We don't need you. Now get out and don't come back!"

Miguel rises to go, unable to meet the boy's confused stare. "What about the new baby?"

Rosa still has the good grace to blush with shame.

The caseworker stops, caught midway in rising from her chair. "What new baby?"

Rosa bristles. "I...I thought I was pregnant. He wanted me to get an abortion! One of his communist friends was gonna do it. That's against the law."

The caseworker looks from Miguel to Rosa. "*Are* you pregnant?"

There, Miguel thinks, the question has been asked. Rosa knows that if she says yes, they will require a test before they increase her current allotment. But since she told him, he's been giving her extra money the past month.

The woman looks stern. "Rosa?"

She lowers her head and mumbles.

"What did you say?"

She brazens it out, staring Miguel in the eye. "No, I'm not. But not because of him. Always wanting it and not letting me use pills. Just to prove he can still make babies." She glares as if daring him to contradict her. Miguel feels so relieved he just lets the lies stand.

The caseworker nods and stands, smoothing her skirt. "Then we'll work on a plan so Mr. de Mateo can see and be with his son. You are both parents. He has rights as well as financial obligations."

Rosa sputters in English with Spanish, like a little girl crying to get her way. "No! *Mira*, I no want him. Hate his books. I hate socialism and that Russian *puta*, Anna something-or-other." She sobs. "I just want him to be me *espouso*, Junito's *papa*. But no, he always wants me to read, to go to meetings." She whirls on him. "I read what I want! You can't tell me what to say, how to think." She collapses on the table, sobbing.

Miguel forces himself not to look at his watch. There's an important meeting in two hours with three groups, organized around workers' rights in the case of a factory closing that took the jobs of two hundred workers. Two delis and a few diners depended on their lunch-hour traffic. If only Rosa would shut up. But the silence of the boy feels louder than her sobs. No, he can't think about him right now. Maybe the social worker can arrange something. Maybe...

Finally the woman moves toward the door. He follows. Rosa raises her head a few inches and looks at him. "Miguel! You need to stay with your son."

He looks imploringly at the caseworker.

"Now Rosa," she says. "You remember our agreement? The last time Mr. de Mateo stayed, you accused him of trying to force himself on you. We decided he could only be here if a chaperone is present."

Rosa stares, looking confused. "What agreement you speaking about?" He can almost see the words flying over her head. Her expression turns crafty. Miguel groans.

But the caseworker is already halfway out the door. "Well, I think this has been a productive visit. We've agreed you're overburdened. That it's best for you and the child to get him into a day care situation as soon as possible. Mr. de Mateo will continue child support and we'll work out a schedule when you get set up for courses or work. Now, it's getting late. I'm sure we all have things to do."

Rosa opens her mouth, but the caseworker is faster. "So I'll get to work on the boy's day care. Five days a week. As an at-risk mother I can get you a ten-hour day, eight to six. Now." She takes a deep breath. "There are two centers nearby. You'll be able to choose the one you prefer."

Rosa looks incredulous. "You mean eight in the morning? I'm not gonna get up every day so early. Why can't his father bring him to day care?"

This appears to be the last straw; Miguel can see the woman is actually gritting her teeth. "Rosa, you're a five-minute walk from both centers. They provide breakfast and lunch so you don't have to cook until dinnertime. All you must do is get up, wash and dress him, and then drop him off for the day."

Rosa's eyes dart back and forth. To him, to the boy and again to the caseworker. She sits back in her chair, with a look of satisfaction.

Miguel moves closer to the door. The boy is watching silently, holding a wooden truck he'd bought for the child's second birthday. Shame overwhelms him. Maybe after a while he can get Zoraida to understand, to forgive his indiscretion. Too bad Rosa's sworn off reading. She has much to learn about the relationship between family and possession. But now, with a hand on the door knob, he realizes his mistake. She knows only one way; the way she was taught. Male against female. Boys are bad and bold. Girls pretty, feminine, and good. Men work, marry the good girls, have children. Mommies stay home, cook and clean. Wait for daddies to come home, eat, then go to bed and make more babies.

The whole world needs political education!

The worker hefts her scuffed briefcase again; it bulges with pages of notes on the suffering masses. Maybe he'll invite her to the upcoming symposium, "Family and Society under a Marxist Structure." It might help with the development of an anti-capitalist system.

But now Rosa is saying something again and, of course, crying. The boy looks like he wants to cry too, but is afraid.

"I'll call you Tuesday," the caseworkers says quickly. "Hopefully we can get his intake set up for Thursday." They're out in the hall now, at the head of the stairs.

"Goodbye, Rosa. Goodbye, Pavel," calls Miguel.

"Junito! His name is Miguel de Mateo, Junior," she shrieks and bangs the door shut.

Miguel gallops down the narrow stairs that stretch dimly before him. The pseudo-Marxist who lives on the top floor is apparently not in, because this time he didn't come down to meddle. But the African lady next door must've heard all the shouting. She is an example; having a child is no excuse for not studying, but rather more reason to do so. "Look at that African lady next door. She works, goes to university and is writing her dissertation and cares for her son," he once pointed out to Rosa.

This observation had an unfortunate effect. She'd screamed and thrown things at him. "I'm no Negro!"

"But Rosa, why carry on like this? Obviously someone in your family was African. Everyone has an ancestor from that continent."

But by Rosa's account no one in her family ever had a drop of African blood.

Well, when the revolution came, class and racial distinctions would be clearer. Easier to identify and destroy. He sighs, heart fluttering in anticipation of that day. Maybe, just maybe he'll still be alive to enjoy it. To see the destruction of the old, and the construction of a new, classless society.

The social worker emerges from the building behind him. She loads her heavy briefcase into a little Volkswagen. "Need a ride? I'm heading uptown."

A sharp slap of glacial air across his face spurs an acceptance. "I appreciate your kindness." He climbs in, holding his things on his lap. He's tempted to ask if she's open to joining The Women's League of the Party. He stares out at the night, not knowing what to say. His intimate life has laid out before her, a stranger. By Rosa, the mother of his only son. She probably thinks badly of him; an old man taking advantage of a young, impressionable girl. But a girl very aggressive in pursuing him.

She's first to break the silence. "Look, Mr. de Mateo, I don't want you to think me unfair. But Rosa is my client. By the nature of our relationship, she's the one whose interests I must defend. And the child, of course. I'm his protector as well."

He nods, shifting in the cramped bucket seat. "Yes, I understand."

The light changes and she drives on. The car comes to a halt at 18th and 5th Avenue. Lights from the Barnes & Noble store draw his gaze. He wants to jump out and run to the sanctuary of crowded aisles of books.

"Please, if you can let me off at 23^{rd,} that would be perfect."

She lifts her foot from the brake. The car edges closer to his street. "I know you're an educated man," she murmurs. "And concerned about the boy's future. I'll do what I can to get him into the best daycare center. Maybe the one on East 14th Street. Rosa would have to walk four more short blocks and one long one to get him there, though."

She purses her lips, as if reckoning what a daunting task it will be to convince Rosa to walk every day, farther, even earlier in the morning.

They arrive at 23rd Street. The triangular building dramatically presents itself with the park to the east, a symbol of architectural majesty. Miguel must admit he likes this place. Bourgeois taste dies hard.

"Senorita, I thank you for your help. Please don't say anything to Rosa about the education of Pavel. She won't want him to go any place where he'll be introduced to books I admire. But I'll explain the situation to my wife. She understands a man's needs." He sneaks a hand into his bag, slides out a newspaper, and slips it onto the floor just below her seat.

"You see, I've been thinking of taking him in. Making sure he gets a good education. Zoraida and I have two daughters. They're in school in Spain. Maybe when we get settled and my wife finds work we can send for them. But the boy, I fear he'll have few opportunities. Rosa may even make his life difficult to hurt me."

The caseworker nods reluctantly. They say goodnight on this gloomy note.

Miguel stands watching the little car maneuver off through traffic. He looks up again at the building, feeling very small. But his heart tells him each person is as strong as the masses he or she is attached to. Thinking of the proletarian victories to come, all over the world, buoys his spirits. He turns and goes off to his meeting, whistling the *Internationale*.

JAMES

The streets are deadly silent. Not the quiet that comes in early fall and winter when folks rush in and out of the cold that whips so mercilessly around brick buildings and gray pavements. Chilled by the air from the East River, most cross-town streets empty early. Except for well-bundled workers returning home wearily, and children stumbling along after parents, going home from day care, babysitters, or after-school programs, Lower East Siders simply don't hang about. At this time of year, life is behind the doors and windows sheltering people trying to outlast the onset of the cold until the warmth of late spring arrives. But no—this stillness is different. It's a held-breath, afraid-to-exhale-lest-it-be-heard silence. The careful lowering of human antennae, for fear of being detected. Only a few boldly desperate men and women are out, bound together under street lamps by the need for a fix. Others huddle cautiously in doorways, whispering.

Tension spreads inside the walls of Lower East Side tenements. People knock at neighbors' doors and quietly ask if all is well. "Are the children safe inside?" On the street, hair rises on the backs of their necks. Dogs quiver, stiffly alert, while outdoors answering nature's call. Cats, those ever sensitive beings, arch their backs and hiss at unseen threats. Surely some stranger is about, up to no good.

Nusa feels it too as she gets off the bus, holding her son's hand as they cross Avenue C and East 10th Street. It's been a long, tiring day. The uneasy quiet she attributes to her own state of mind. Last Friday the imam ended her idat and granted her a divorce. She's no longer married. Before she left, he'd hastened to add, "You are young and beautiful. Pray for a good man, one willing to marry you even though you're no longer a virgin, have been married, and come with a child."

Should she consider going back home to her parents and ask their help in finding a suitable new husband? She sighs, shakes her head, and continues the short walk to her building.

The super is standing inside, between the mailboxes and stairs, making it impossible to get by without passing near him. She does not like the feelings she gets from this man. The previous super is now dead as well. Everyone knew his wife had really done all the work until she died one day with a mop in her hand. 'The Gnome,' as she was called, passed away first, about three years ago. Since his death, two men have succeeded him. P, the third, has lasted three months so far, despite one tenant accusing him of breaking into his place. Nusa has caught him lurking on her landing more than once while she was in the toilet. Now he says nothing, only stands in the way blocking her entrance.

James slips out into the dim hall and eyes the super standing in her way. "Good evening, Nusa, how are you?"

At that moment the boy runs out from behind her."Well, look who's here. Hello, young man." Moussa shakes James's hand.

The super deflates like a balloon, his breath hissing out in an exhalation of disappointment. James smiles inwardly. He's such a pacifist, he'd never raise a hand to this man. Not out of fear but due to his commitment to nonviolence. The man slopes off, trying to pass by as close to Nusa as possible. She flattens herself against the wall and he's unable to brush up against her youthful body. She and James walk upstairs, where he bids her goodnight and goes on tiredly to his flat.

Inside, he exhales tiredly and slips out of his coat. Sets his boots near the door and then just sits in the dark, silently. The flat is quiet. The only noise comes up from the street. He thinks he can still smell Josh's rancid body odor. He gets up and opens his door. The apartment across, belonging to Hollis, is unlit, so he knows no one's home. He closes the door again softly. Sighing, he checks the refrigerator and finds a covered dish Nusa gave him last week when she had him and Hollis over for dinner. He heats it up and eats slowly, enjoying every nuance of herbs, vegetables, and spices. Putting the empty plate in the little sink he washes and leaves it face-down on a dish towel. His shoulders ache; he wants to sink into a hot tub and soak away his apprehension. So he removes the top and draws a bath.

Afterward he slides one leg, then the other, into pajamas. While buttoning the top he hears Nusa out in the hall. He opens his door. The super's trying to corner her again, on the steps.

"What're you doing?" James shouts. "Get your hands off her this instant!"

Looking up, wide-eyed, mouth agape, the super backs off and trudges down the stairs. Normally, James would also call the police but right now he can't afford to bring them around. He worries that he may have to stand guard, and he's so exhausted. "Nusa, let me check your windows just in case he tries that again." Once he satisfies himself on the security of both windows and door, he returns to his place.

It's difficult to get Conscientious Objector status. Josh is a pacifist; he'd grown up on an isolated Midwestern farm. In his last year of medical school he'd tried to get an exemption. His professors and other upstanding citizens spoke in support. But the draft board refused to budge. So Josh dropped out and sneaked away. His parents, Quakers, supported his decision, and now pressure is being put on them to turn their son over. Promises of non-military placement were made but Josh wrote a statement denouncing the war. His letter states clearly that he will not, cannot participate by being in Viet Nam or nearby countries in any capacity. He refuses to raise a hand against another human being who's not threatened him. To engage in warfare is a violation of his religious views.

Thinking of it now, James smiles. "Obviously the war machine doesn't recognize the theological promise of the Ten Commandments."

As long as he can remember he's wanted to be a teacher. Or, more to the point, a college professor who also does field research. His father is a professor of Anthropology. When he turned sixteen, James accompanied him on an expedition to Peru. Growing up in a small town in Wisconsin he'd been surrounded by people who looked much like him. Everyone knew each other from school, church, or sports. His mother had stayed home to raise him and his two sisters, preparing them for two years before sending them to school. All his early social life had been spent in a small circle. So when he went to Peru and saw the lush forests, climbed the green sloping hills, shopped in open markets where the Indians gathered to sell crafts, he knew he wanted a wider, more varied world.

At the university in Madison he met students from all over the world. His mother had just completed her doctorate and was studying contemporary women's literature. During his senior year there was a big literature conference in France. She was invited to give a paper and he went along. He remembers it clearly. The hazy day they arrived his body was stiff from the long flight, the cramped cabin. He was a tall reed even at twenty, almost thirteen years ago. At the busy airport French words buzzed around them like bees as they tried to negotiate customs, baggage, and hiring a taxi. His French was inadequate, and in any case, he was too shy to speak. But his mother had switched easily to French.

With her busy all day with colleagues and paper presentations, James was left on his own. He strolled around the narrow streets. French people had a reputation for cooking great food, being smart dressers, and sophistication in general. From watching French films he'd thought the people were so happy they danced in the streets. Instead, once he'd gotten up the courage to try out his college French in a shop or café, they seemed cold, distant, not very encouraging.

One day he went with his mother to the local university. Some students at the edge of a great lawn were waving signs and chanting, "France out of Indo-Chine now! End colonialism now!"

Those days were the beginning of his political awakening. He picked up flyers and went to protest rallies instead of the cocktail parties his mother attended nightly. A bilingual student gave him a long reading list on French colonization in Asia and Africa, then took him to some second-hand book shops and stalls. When he brought back loads of books his mother was pleased. "I'm so glad you're improving your language skills," she said, ruffling his hair and smiling.

One session he wandered in on critiqued the whole notion of waging war to create peace, of killing to save lives, and the possession of nuclear weapons as a deterrent. James leans back in his chair now by the window, again seeing those faces: three men and one woman at a table. They spoke passionately of non-violent confrontations to thwart an increasingly militaristic government. A system that moved farther and farther away from a diplomatic resolution and establishing social justice. How ridiculous it was, killing in order to save lives!

Back home from France he consumed books about pacifism and participated in a couple of sit-ins in Washington and Madison. His teaching career began with an appointment at an experimental school near the university. The students were white, the sons and daughters of students and faculty, but still it was great learning children's songs in Swahili and Spanish. A visiting professor from Holland had actually been born in the Dutch Antilles; her husband from Dutch Guiana. Their three children spoke Papiamentu, Sranontonga, Dutch, and some French, Spanish and English! His friendship with those foreign students and the roiling times changed his outlook forever.

And so he came to New York, and found his way to the Lower East Side, to this four-flight walk-up flat. Here he's remained for the last five years. Originally he'd had a larger apartment on the upper West Side and an attractive girlfriend who ran an ad agency on Madison Avenue. His graduate studies were going well; his rating teaching in the high school was the highest among his peers. At least until the department made a rule that, in response to the "Red Scare," children should be trained in civil defense techniques. "When the sirens wail, walk calmly and seek a basement shelter or, if in class, crouch under your desks and wait it out." As if a flimsy schoolroom desk would deflect radiation. It was at best absurd, at worst, dishonestly dangerous.

James offered his opinion at the staff meetings. He'd once met a group of visitors from Japan, A-bomb survivors. He described the scarred faces, the unhealed bodies, the nightmares they all still suffered. Some of the teachers agreed but were afraid to speak up. When they saw him in the halls and none of the administration was around, they told him they supported his position. He was on his own.

The meetings continued and so did his opposition. Finally he was summoned to an audience with the principal, who at first condescended to youth and the era of rebellion with a mirthless "Ha-ha."

James said, "I'll do as you request. Have the children huddle under desks or hug the walls in the corridors. Even escort them to the basement shelters. But then what?"

The principal's face fell and then blotched red at the presumptuous attitude of an obvious troublemaker. He cleared his throat and clenched his hands into fists. After what appeared to be a great effort to contain his anger, he jumped to his feet and shouted, "Get out!" His finger pointed erect, implacably, to the door. A security guard ran in and stood looking from one face to the other, finally settling on the principal's, awaiting instructions.

Two weeks later James received a special-delivery letter on a Sunday, notifying him of his suspension effective the next day, Monday. Further, he was to report directly to the principal's office. When he entered the room it was clear the union representative was in agreement with the principal. The arrogance in his eyes, a man none of the teachers liked, his sallow cheeks flushed with the excitement of misplaced power. At least he seemed a bit uncomfortable, seeing James had read the situation and knew the one person who was supposed to offer support had sold him out. James didn't enjoy watching the man squirm any more than he did the ostentatious bullying by the principal.

Sighing now, he finds he can't recall the union man's name. It had been only, what? Three and a half years ago. Maybe he'd never really known it. He was always just "the union rep." In the beginning the man had said, "I understand your position. Socialism and nonviolence are the wave of the future. The war is wrong. The South's position on civil rights for col—um, Negroes—is wrong. Education will change all that, eventually." The union man said he was glad that James was taking advantage of tuition reimbursement to finish his graduate studies. He too was going to graduate school. James never found out where or what he'd be studying.

They'd sat there waiting for what everyone knew was coming. He'd measured his breathing, slowed his pulse. The principal sat like some ancient monolith behind his desk. James had had a hard time not laughing at the comical picture the man made, neck choked by a starched collar and tie, veins throbbing. Face flushed—expectant. It was then James realized the man wanted him to plead not to be let go. The silence built. James focused on the path his breath took from intake to exhalation, feeling his rib cage expand and contract. Faint noises from the outer room were discernible, since the secretary and clerk sat on the opposite side of the wall. There came the monotonous clack of a typewriter, the ringing of phones, all adding to the weight of the silence.

Finally, looking at his watch importantly, clearing his throat, the union rep exhaled. James stared ahead, past the balding head that nodded for the process to begin. The rep opened his mouth but no sound came out. The principal again cleared his throat.

Disgust pinned James to his chair, where he sat with hands clasped right over left. The principal fixed his gaze on James and scowled. But when James refused to play the game the man stood, pushed back his chair, and walked out, leaving the rep and him alone.

James, for some reason, remembers he'd recalled an incident then from when he was around seventeen and had gone to Holland. His memory of the smells from fish-smoking houses in those clean northern cities cooled the stifling room, thinned the air dense with a cologne the principal always applied too liberally.

Gulping in a quick gasp of air, the union rep took out an official-looking paper. "This," he said, waving it at eye level, "is a document of severance I was able to work out for you. And, I might add," he said, pausing for effect, "while you are relieved of your duties here, it does not prohibit you from seeking employment at any other school."

James did not respond.

"And," the rep rushed on, "I was able to get a commitment of continued assistance for your studies. Though your final semester will be on your own if you aren't hired by another school." He stopped, licked his lips. Catching James' eye, he quickly looked down at the white page filled with black print, typed in triplicate by the woman sitting outside and typing now. Perhaps another such letter for someone else.

"You'll receive your salary up until the end of the school year and any remaining vacation time as well." He frowned, and jerked as if about to sneeze, but only made some faint squeaking noises more akin to flatulence. "Now, I know you have strong opinions which clash with the federal and municipal rulings. But you've been an effective teacher. All the more reason he," and the man nodded towards the door, "wanted you out. But I told him the union stands behind our members. I fought hard for this agreement." By now he was almost pleading, as if desperate to be understood. "I know you want to go back to your class but, well, quite frankly, the principal says you can't have any more contact with the students."

They're afraid of me, James thought, amazed.

Silently he took his copy, reached in his pocket, took out the fountain pen his parents had given him for graduation, and signed. When he handed it back, the union man's relief was so obvious James felt pity. He'd gotten up to go.

"Your things! I mean, we cleared out your locker and desk. Here!" The rep fumbled under his chair and drew out two cardboard boxes, then pushed another form at him. "Just to say that you got all your stuff."

James looked down at the open boxes, which held his notebook where he'd recorded comments on each child. A few books he'd loaned out piled inside. A sweater his mother had knitted. His nameplate. A wooden frame his sister gave him when he'd first started teaching peeped out from under a photo album amassed of children taught during his years at the school. He took the second form silently, too, and signed it, then gathered up the boxes. The union man extended a hand but it was impossible for James to shake it. His hand remained on the boxes, in testimony of the betrayal done to a worker.

He'd then walked out the door as the principal stood staring. The secretary stopped typing. Her hand had crept toward the phone. He'd said nothing. Just walked on past them and out into the corridor. The boxes were so light; they felt so insignificant compared to the importance he'd always attached to his work.

As he neared the exit two former students came into the hall from the long second-floor stairwell where his classes were held.

"Mr. Coles, Mr. Coles, you're back! Come on, I'll help you carry that," said the older boy. Their pre-pubescent voices echoed shrilly in the hall.

The Administration door opened and the principal rushed out. "Boys!" he bellowed. "What're you doing out of class? Go back to your rooms immediately."

They spun to look from one face to the other. Finally comprehension flushed their cheeks. "So it's true? He fired you," the other boy said, looking accusingly at the principal.

"That's enough! Go to class. Your teacher will wonder where you are."

The smaller boy held up a pass, the wooden block children were required to take when leaving their classrooms. "We were sent here to pick up forms from the office."

The principal backed away from the door. "Well, go quickly then, and get them."

The boys glanced again at James and then went inside.

The principal closed the door. "Now you see why you can't remain here? You have a negative influence on the children. It's my responsibility to prevent such bad influences. It was my duty to let you go."

James looked at the man standing in front of him. He knew, as did everyone on the staff, that the principal was hoping to become a district supervisor. He seemed to have no compassion for students, little appreciation for teachers, and mostly disdain for parents. As if reading James' opinion in his eyes, the man turned on his heels and vanished back inside the door. Its frosted glass said, in bold letters, OFFICE OF THE PRINCIPAL.

Now, three and a half years later, James has completed his course work, is writing his dissertation and teaching at two different colleges part time. He's involved in the underground network of pacifist and draft resisters en route to Canada and elsewhere, and without a significant other. His 'woman-friend' as Noreene had always termed herself—discovering she was living with a man with great potential yet no job and dwindling resources—had left him.

So, unencumbered by romantic distractions, James huddles in the hall of his building trying to decide on the best route. Two hours remain to get to their contact uptown. He slowly descends the stairs, again conscious of the unusual quiet. These streets have seldom been without noise; something has to be up. The stalwart junkies who stand guard on either side of East 10th Street and Avenue C shuffle silently about. Their drug-raddled bodies hunch right and left, ears cocked, waiting to hear something, but what? An overacted nonchalance that warns off the usual hustlers. "It's hot, and smells of pigs!" That's what the street hears.

James and the evader trek down the stairs with two heavy bags. The younger man, who could've been his son, moves slowly. They step over the loudmouth slats and see no one, fortunately. James leads him to the basement. Once, when they had had a series of robberies in the building and no one could figure out the thief's escape route, James had followed their then-super. He'd seen him go down the cellar steps. About fifteen minutes later he'd come back in through the front door. After that the super had been fired, James went down there and discovered a bolted door leading out to the back yard. Now here he is in it himself, hoping darkness will cover them in the event there are spotters on the rooftops.

He eases the door open, waits about five minutes, and then walks out hugging the walls. James has done this a few times before so he knows about the little cave-in a dozen paces to the left. Once they get there, a large tree will hide them from view. They can jump down into the next yard and between buildings. There, on the right of it and the decaying wall of a burnt-out shell, is an opening that lets out onto 9th Street. Petty thieves use it to duck the police. He prays the feds, who have people all spooked up and staying indoors, won't be waiting on the other side.

He takes the young man's sweating hand and leads him slowly, pointing to holes in the ground lest he stumble. James tries to picture this scared kid carrying a gun, crouching behind a tree in Viet Nam. He can smell the rancid, metallic odor of fear emanating from his body. A guy James knows who's been to 'the Nam' always walks around looking right, left, over his shoulders every few minutes. He runs for cover if a truck backfires, at the wail of sirens. Fire trucks send him scurrying into the nearest doorway. People in the area all know him. Sometimes kids taunt him but, for the most part, everyone understands. He's a metaphor for the war.

James hurries on, sure-footed, listening for any sound that might signal unwanted company. None comes and, in the open, the young man's rank, fearful smell is frozen in the cold night air, mingled with the everyday scents of the Lower East Side.

Not until they arrive at the George Washington Bridge does James ease up a bit. Until the 'station master' from this newly reconstructed Underground network greets them and he recognizes the man and his wife does he feel it's safe to turn him over to them. There's little more he can do. Making sure the young man has memorized his telephone number, James gives him a hug and then walks away without looking back. Once he's crossed the overpass and stands waiting on the New York side, he dares to look back. He sees only an empty space. Stepping back into the shadows, he scans the opposite side, as he waits for the bus. After about fifteen minutes two black women walk up together. He fantasizes that they are maids to suburban women, on their way home after a hard day's work. Home to wash, cook, and clean for their own families after having washed and cleaned for others. Their presence is reassuring, because they will know the schedule, and that a bus will soon come.

Down a V-shaped abyss, twin lights separate the dark into round glowing balls speeding towards them. James steps back as the two women board the bus. He quickly eyes the passengers. Two men sleeping, one with mouth slightly ajar. In the seats behind him, two Asian women in nurse's uniforms are speaking a language he cannot understand. The bus heads for the open expanse of the bridge. It's a clear night; below them lies New York, a scattering of diamonds in the distance.

A few men who obviously have nowhere to go shuffle from one side of the station to the other. A well-dressed drunk lurches onward to a bus, attaché case in hand, yelling, "Hold that bus! Hold that bus!"

One of the station-cleaners mutters, "There goes Mr. Brady." Laughter accompanies this announcement.

James walks the long corridor to the train. A lone policeman patrols the platform. James is careful not to look at him; he stands near the wall waiting for the train. Willing his body to be still, to expend no energy. Just wait, silent and calm.

An hour later he exits the subway at East 14th Street and 1st Avenue. Huddled against the biting cold he trudges towards East 10th Street. But as he passes Stanley's bar, the fogged windows invite him inside. He decides to go in for a late beer, not wanting to be alone just now. Nusa has her son and studies; besides, it's too late to disturb her.

Four men sit at the bar drinking and smoking, trying to be noticed by a couple of women at the other end of the wooden rail. Coughing on the smoke-thick air, James continues to the back, where he sees some people he recognizes. A poet, a musician, and an actor he recently saw in a play, sitting at two tables pushed together.

"Welcome!" Bill, the actor, greets him, with a voice that fills the room.

James smiles, squeezes between tables toward one end, and sits. The air is less thick back here. He sits, silent, just listening to the men expound on current issues: race, revolution, The War, The Movement. It's warm back here too, so he opens his coat and drapes it over the back of the chair. Looking around at the ensemble he wonders what they'd say if they knew of his activities over the past few hours. Bill might understand. He's been in the military; he's older than the others. He'd once said the army was horrible but that he'd managed to have a good time because there was no fighting in Germany while he was stationed there and, anyhow, he'd been assigned to an office. Still, racism dogged him. The sergeants and others had resented his college education, that he could write and express himself in a sophisticated manner. Most of all, though, they hated the way some German women gravitated to him.

James steals a look at the actor's handsome profile, thinking he could be the proud African prince of poets of old, or maybe DuBois. Strange, why should that name pop into his mind? True he was one of his heroes. James had been introduced to his writings by his father, years ago. Still he wonders what the association is to the current situation.

Tim is speaking now. "Man, I'm telling you, I'd never get close to that woman. She smells like an unclean person. My mama always told me, 'Son, if you can smell it with the clothes on, you don't want to uncover it.'"

Most of the men laugh but James doesn't understand why. He shrugs.

Then Charlie shares a joke at the expense of his boss's son. James has seen that young man; actually he might be his age or a little older. "So there I am in the toilet and this fool comes up behind me. Leans over my shoulder and says, '*That's* what all the fuss is about?' Man, I almost swung at him 'cause he shook me up sneaking around on like that."

Bill adds, "Seems to be an old problem, the size of our members. In Europe, white soldiers told the women to run when they saw us because we had big, long penises, and they wouldn't be able to stand it. That we were, in fact, animals."

James just listens. Jean-Pierre comments on the eerie silence earlier in the evening.

Tim nods. "Yes, I felt it too. Anyone know what was going on?"

No one has an answer. "Probably some narcs fishing around for a big drop," Fred speculates.

A couple of the men at the table share a look. Word on the streets is, Fred's on the needle. Bill says, "If someone wants to poison himself, let him go ahead and kill himself."

Fred shifts uncomfortably. "Sometimes people get into situations beyond their control."

James keeps his face blank, though he knows it was 'Them.' The agents who follow young men desperately trying to escape the clutches of the military draft board. 'They' might not have known that he, James, was their man. But somehow they knew about the young man.

His full name is Joshua McCabe. He likes to be called Josh. It hurts James to think of people spying, plotting to get Josh caught. To have him turned into a killing machine. To destroy the soft light of passion in his eyes when he speaks of music and books. James sighs. His is a gentle soul; he prays Josh reaches safety and finds a companion to complete his life. Speaking of which, James could use that, himself. Certainly there are lots of attractive women around. Often he's joined in all-night discussions. These women hold their own. But none has touched that deeper place in him; none ignited a spark.

So now he sits listening, occasionally commenting, waiting for one of his friends to leave, so he can walk out with him, together, as if he's been here all evening. He hopes the agents have gone. But then that would mean they're off tracking someone else.

"Say, man, where are you?" Bill's voice interrupts these thoughts. James laughs it off without giving an answer. He can't very well blurt out, "Oh, well, I'm part of a group illegally ferrying people out of the country." He especially can't say, "You know, men who are avoiding the draft and military service."

Instead he merely shrugs. "I'm here. It's just, you know, female troubles."

All the men hasten to offer advice then, or a story about the latest betrayal, or a failure to land the desired one.

Fred is the first to stand. "Got to head in. I have an early appointment in the morning." They watch as he leaves. Before he gets to the door, Jean-Pierre quips, "Huh. Guess he has to see his pusher."

Bill frowns and jumps to defend Fred. "You know, I met him when he first came here from the South. Young, impressionable, very sure of himself. A few months of no work and he began to change. Then he worked with Jim. He was straight then. Maybe a couple of beers, but nothing heavy. When that group broke up he had fewer and fewer gigs. So he worked anywhere he could for money, like all of us, to survive. But not playing, not being able to do music the way he wanted and needed…it got him down. So his dabbling turned to a real chippie."

"Hell, I don't think it's that anymore," Tim contradicts. "He's got a jones now. Steals to support his habit." Tim scowls with disgust. Takes a pull on his cigarette and blows out a long plume of smoke.

James sits quietly, not joining in either camp. But tension gradually travels down his neck, and as it does a different weight descends to sit on his shoulders, pushing him further down in his seat. It's an effort to rise up and put on his coat. The heaviness almost disables him. But he feels an increasing need to be alone now, so when the others protest, he begs off.

Out on the street the cold night air slaps his face. He pulls the cap lower over his ears and stuffs fingers into pockets. The coat is a few years old. He'd bought it when he met Noreene, along with a suit and a pair of dark brown trousers and a Harris Tweed jacket. It's just right for tonight because it hides him and keeps out the cold. Walking in long strides, looking down at the pavement, stepping over a pile of dog droppings, James weaves to avoid ripped, spilled bags of garbage. At the corner of Avenue B and East 10th, he ploughs ahead, his body curling into itself to fend off the whistling wind.

He visualizes the East River's mounds of frozen water. The moon and surrounding buildings and occasional barges filigree its icy surface. While that way will be even colder and windier than Avenue B, the cold beauty on such a night calls to mind a time when he'd thought to be a poet. Surely these are poetic elements: a late winter night, an empty pair of arms, a young healthy body aching with need of a warm, passionate woman.

James sighs. He looks up to see an unfamiliar corner store and realizes he's walked three blocks past his street. He needs to urinate badly, so he rushes on, feeling his bladder throb with two bottles of beer. No wonder; it's been four hours since the last time he emptied it. He turns at 7th Street and Avenue C and makes a left. It's then he notices a car continuing slowly south on Avenue B. Nerves at the back of his neck begin to tingle. Braving possible frostbite, he unzips and watches steam rise as he urinates against a wall. Keeping his coat pulled around to shield his sensitive member from the shock of cold, he sighs and lets it all out. When there's no more left, he shakes off and straightens his clothes, using the left hand as he remembers his friend Ahmed from West Africa always did. Ahmed explained that a man should always use the left hand when touching his private parts, his right for greeting people and for eating.

James turns up his collar, pulling it as high as possible, and crosses East 8th Street. As he turns East on 10th, Avenue C has never looked so welcoming. He twists slightly to each side but sees no one following; no cars passing. He takes the stairs two at a time making soft thuds on the steps. When he reaches his floor the dirty windows are brightening; a rising sun announcing the dawn. Pausing to listen for any noises, hearing none, he fumbles out his keys and lets himself in the apartment. All appears as he left it seven hours ago. He hangs up the heavy coat and stuffs his cap in one deep pocket. At first it seems warm but when he touches it the radiator is actually cold. He makes some tea and then undresses. Puts on pajamas, splashes water on his face, then rubs lotion on the dry chapped skin of face and hands. Never mind being born in Wisconsin, where it's much colder than New York; here he has to guard against windburn and cracked lips. He coats them with Vaseline and lies down on his bed.

Thinking of Josh, he sends good wishes that he reach Canada safely. And please, God, end this war.

BLOOD ON EAST 5th STREET

There is blood on the street. A trail of it from the saw-dusted floors of a smoky jazz club. Soaked red clumps of him and his trumpet shining on the floor in death-like patterns. Drip. Drip. The piercing sirens of an ambulance and police cars break the silence of cold February streets. In such weather there are no children running around, no mothers screaming and chasing them. Just icy fingers of lonely winter wind whipping out from the East River to slap the faces of those who do venture out.

Here there are many frozen faces staring in disbelief. Their eyes witness a scene they scarce can believe. Less than five minutes ago they'd all thrilled to the beauty and brilliance of a young musician and a horn, as sweat poured in rivulets down his dark brown skin. His eyes squeezed tight, shutting them all out. His eyebrows rose like the notes soaring from his trumpet. All his cohorts, straining, pulled along with him in that maelstrom of musical fire; ah, the agony, the exquisite agony of it all.

Then it ended and he'd stood for a few moments silent, reining in the vibrations sent out among them by his sounds. No one moved at first. The audience just stared as the drummer signaled the end, *finis*. That's all. A tremor rippled through him ever so slightly. His long fingers reached inside his jacket and found a stark white handkerchief. He mopped his face, delicately touched neck, front and back, and then his ears. The lights glistened on slicked-back hair. He shook himself and then bowed.

"Thank you, thank you very much," he rasped. "Let me introduce my partners, Billy Higgins on drums, George Merritt on bass, Gilly Collins on piano and Booker Little on sax. And me..." He'd paused, giving them a mischievous grin. His name drowned in a swell of applause and smoke. Finally, a changing of the guards. Waiters rushed to collect tabs, to clear empty tables. Those who could afford it and who really couldn't bear to leave remained in their seats. A few get up, some go to the tiny toilets in the back, between the makeshift stage and kitchen entrance.

The musical partners shook hands, patted each other on the back. Pulled towels from bags stashed behind the drummer. The bass player, who'd kept his next to the stool, wiped down while still sitting, then gently lowered his wooden instrument to the floor. The piano player collected sheet music and put it in a flat leather briefcase. He too wiped his face and stretched long arms overhead, flexing the fingers.

The horn player looked right and left, turned back to give some last words to his fellow musicians. They huddled smiling, nodding in agreement. It was a real conspiracy, the coming and final set. New music—pieces never exposed before. They'd be launching into new artistic territory. Someone had taped the two earlier sets, but this next one—ah, *that* would be the one.

He took a long pull on his cigarette and turned. The house lights came up a bit. A cool draft blew in the open door as some patrons left. A woman stood there waiting to be joined by her escort. Smoke rushed out into the cold, and for a brief while the air was clear.

He walked over to the bar and ordered.

"Hey man, you cats were smoking!" said the bartender.

He smiled and accepted the proffered drink, the sting of whiskey floating down his throat, opening his sinuses, making his eyes water. Then took a frosted glass of water and gulped three times. Put it back on the counter. Feeling a presence at his back, he glanced around, eyes alert and shrewd.

There she was: a discordant pitch in a red, too-tight sheath, staring at him, looking more than unappreciative. She had demands. A last-night kiss. There'd been a missed meal two weeks ago. An empty bed.

None of his answers sufficed. Placation had never been one of his strengths. And in any case, the time for thinking, for making excuses had already passed. The present dangers of that moment were real and standing close, right on his toes. But his head was still revolving around the last note of a song composed two days ago. He was unable to comprehend her questions: *Who? What? Where? Why?*

So he'd shrugged and taken another pull on his cigarette.

But atonality would not be denied. Even if her voice was lost in the cacophony, a discarded tune, thrown onto a pile of old songs and charts no longer played.

The urgency to plug his ears felt overwhelming. He made a move to go. Took one step—stopped— and fell.

His blood splashed her face. Only then, with that sacrifice, was her own blood cooled. She'd stood before him feeling the orgiastic explosion of her own rage. And then the slow subsiding ooze calmed her. Though there was something sticking to her hands; her fingers were glued to it. She looked down and saw him sprawled at her feet. The blood pooling there, soaked up by the dry sawdust on the floor. The bar stool and counter were smeared with it.

Her scream came at a pitch to shatter ear drums, to crack a heart. She fell on his dying form and buried her face in his chest. Cradling his head, she called his name, tears mixing with his blood.

A rough pair of hands snatched her up. She clawed the air until a slap across the face made her nose bleed. Then her blood dripped onto the man at her feet. Snot and red streaks marred her face. Another slap, and she sank to her knees.

The front door was still wide open. Cold air met unbearable, angry heat. His partners rushed out from behind the stage, staring, aghast. At his always-immaculate shirt, soaked and discolored. Members of the audience lifted him onto a stretcher, an inadequate palanquin. A tourniquet, tied on too late, could not staunch the ebb of his life force. A tablecloth was draped over his body, and the procession exited the club.

The blood that flows out the door to East 5th Street freezes immediately. Some curious souls stand by, watching, cloaked in a quickly-donned motley of coats, caps, shawls. Shivering and questioning each other: *What? Who? Where? Why?* They stand staring, and the wind bites their faces.

Then, more spectacle: the killer, disheveled and staring, stumbles out. The coat thrown over her dress is redly glued to a voluptuous body. She recoils from the lash of a brutal gust on exposed arms. Her face a smear of heavy make-up and congealed blood and mucous. Embraced now by the arms of the law, she walks by on elegant, hand-sewn boots, her purse carried by a beefy officer bringing up the rear.

The crowd sucks in a breath, heads in ensemble moving back and forth. Not knowing what to do next or where best to look, they turn to watch the fading lights of the two police cars strobe away, trailing a wailing ambulance. Eastwards to the Drive, and then over north to Bellevue. Ah, the irony of words.

Inside the bartender is still frozen behind the counter, framed by bottles and glasses. The musician's partners stand stunned over the last remnant of him: a pool of cooling blood on the floor. And then the rest come back in through the gaping doors: patrons waiting for the next set, sitting again, unsure whether to stay or leave.

His blood trickles across the sidewalk and into the gutter. People walk around it on the way home, back to their beds. Heads shake. Shoulders shrug. Briefly, all ponder the meaning of life and its sickly partner, death. How, in the blink of an eye, thirty-four years end and no one can bring back the smile, the body, the sound of a horn pressed to the mouth of a man reaching deep for the next note.

MARY

Mary steams along St. Mark's Place. Her anger is radiating and so people give her space, plenty of it. Her face heats as blood races under her light skin. Her sculpted Afro is more a study in coiffed electricity. She gulps air; her chest heaves like that of a runner striving to make the last few yards. The wild, abstract design of her dashiki, an optical wonder perhaps woven to drive less brave souls mad, seems to flash a warning: *Get out of my way!*

It isn't as if she started out this way. Coming here was the last thing on her mind. A visit to Khadijah, that's all she'd intended. Sometimes when she needs to be reminded of herself, an African woman born in America, she comes to see her friend. Khadijah's originally from Pittsburgh. The small apartment where she and her two children live is very convenient, because her clothes shop is just below. So she can work and sell her African wares at all hours. The shop is two steps down from the sidewalk, set in a row of five storefronts that offer all kinds of things.

Mary was turned on to the shop by a man she chatted up at one of the bars on Avenue B. Lots of black folks shop there when they want to look 'real.' Khadijah buys her fabrics from a French Jew, who gets them from 'sources' in Africa. He'd fled Algeria when the French were kicked out, he and his parents running with only as much as they could carry. Although there are still some strong elements of anti-Semitism in France, they settled in the 'Mother Country' and established a small import-export business. Jean-Marc is a jazz fanatic; he hangs out with black musicians, mostly. He comes over two or three times a year. With each visit he replenishes Khadijah's stock, so she's always *au courant*.

Mary needs the comfort; she needs the wise words of her friend. Of all the black women on the lower East Side, Khadijah is the most down to earth. There's a strength, a gentle shyness in her that few really appreciate. Most of all, Mary loves the way she interacts with her children. They clearly love their mother and she them, but her firm hand still keeps them in check.

Mary wants to bury her bushy head on her friend's shoulder and let Khadijah hold her in her arms. To tell her all about the past year, and especially about last night. Mary wants to let her know that, although she may have behaved a bit out of character from the way she was brought up, it was in her opinion appropriate.

Last night she and Jerry had a major argument. He's the professor she's been seeing for over a year, who teaches at Howard University. He became so annoyed with her over something she'd said, he left in the middle of dinner and stayed out all night. Mary got up after too little sleep and tried to keep to her usual weekend routine. She never intended to cause any trouble.

Now she wants to tell her story to someone. Or rather, only to Khadijah. To tell her, "I got up and showered and dressed and went to St. Mark's diner for breakfast. The thought of having coffee in my lovely kitchen did not appeal. You know how it is when the Devil's at work? Well, I knew the minute I walked in something was not quite right. Isaac came over as usual and took me to the other side of the room. I said, 'This is not where I normally sit.' He told me they were unusually busy, that there was a big party of smokers and, since I didn't smoke, it would be nicer on this side. But you see, after tossing and turning all night, I decided to sit myself down and just eat."

Images of that scene obsess Mary as she stumbles on toward her friend's shop. In the middle of coffee, she happened to glance up and catch two of the waiters looking at her, shaking their heads as they met her eyes. When she let her gaze travel over to her old, usual spot, the cup slipped from her hand, but she caught it quickly before it spilled. There was Jerry, sitting in a very intimate fashion, a silly grin pasted on as he stared adoringly into the eyes of some blonde woman she didn't recognize.

Mary's face burned with anger. He would sit at her old table with another woman? She had introduced him to the place!

"And then, Khadijah," she would tell her friend, "I set the money for my bill on the table. I remember that much. The rest I'm not too sure of. I guess I didn't carry on too badly, since no one asked me to leave."

She had in fact gotten up and walked slowly to the table, standing there for a few seconds until Jerry noticed. A look of amused shock quickly masked his anger. He introduced the woman as Cindy. Mary said hello. "Khadijah, I turned to him and said, 'Please give me my keys. Call before coming to collect your things.' And then I left."

But when she arrives, the store is dark. The hours posted say it won't open for another two hours. Mary is calmed just by being there, though. Looking in at three batik dresses draped from wire hangers, she smiles. "She's so creative."

Mary turns down 2nd Avenue and heads to her apartment, a space created for herself without the over-bearing presence of her parents. Especially her father. A space now violated by the betrayal of Jerry. He never seemed to appreciate what it meant to her to have gotten the place and furnished it all by herself. To him, she was another 'bougie light-skin spoiled woman.'

Yes, some of that may be true. Her father, Dr. Wentworth, and her mother, Adeline Barnswell, were definitely members of the small black-elite society of Louisville. They were "The Firsts" of everything; first in the Louisville Unitarian Church, first to move into Blue Hills Heights. And her father, the first black doctor to be on staff of a major hospital in Kentucky. *The Sentinel* did a big article on him and the family. Her family had been one of the first of everything, and Mary was the first to break with tradition and leave the state alone and unmarried.

Yes, there is money in the family. Unlike Jerry, she represents the other side of the black experience in America. One of her great-grandmothers, who upon Emancipation left Kentucky and went across the Ohio River, later married a man from Cincinnati. The couple ran a rooming house and a public kitchen. They had a large family and as the children got old enough they too were put to work. By the time her grandfather turned twenty, he was entering a college set up for black students. He became a mortician and soon was one of the wealthiest men in town. When his father suffered a stroke, her grandfather put his eldest son into boarding school, sold his house and business, and relocated to Louisville. Her mother was the first of his daughters born in Louisville. She'd been very frail, but the midwife was determined she should live. So they named her Adeline for the woman who saved her life.

Mary arrives at her building deep in reflection. She climbs the stair and enters her well-appointed place. She sits, still deep in thought. It isn't that she was not proud of them, but Mary has begun to recognize how small her universe, and the limitations of her associates. Days after high school were spent in endless shopping for a new dress or shoes to wear at this or that party. Unimportant phone calls, night and day, relaying intrigues: who was sneaking around with this one's boyfriend, or that one's wife. She'd gradually grown weary of it all. Now that she's studying Marx and other socialist scholars, she realizes she had class and coloration problems. She smiles at the thought, remembering a certain sorority she'd barely managed to get into because she was not lighter and because, despite his prominence, her father was too dark by their standards.

But here, in her apartment, paid for with the money she earns from her job as Rural Development Coordinator for the Episcopal Church, she's happy in spite of Jerry. She doesn't wish to call her parents and cry on their shoulders long distance. Her eyes enjoy each inch of the space. One of the women in the office had mentioned there was an apartment in this building a year and a half ago, so she'd hurried over after work one day. She'd found the super and told him she was very interested in the place. He took her to look at two apartments. Somehow, even then, she'd had the vision of what it could be like with the two apartments joined. So she'd told him she wanted both. When she left that day, after having given him fifty dollars, she had secured the two spaces.

Next she'd called her parents from the Y, where she was staying, to tell them about the deal and ask for advice. Her father suggested she get a contractor and cut a door in the wall adjoining, and that is what she'd done. Now, sitting in a comfortable chair in her living room, listening to a Clifford Brown record, sipping ginger ale, she's again grateful for the money her parents sent to help pay for the renovation costs. She allows herself the luxury of a few more minutes, until the A side finishes. Then she'll hit the books.

Long after she goes to bed, the telephone rings. Mary answers without thinking of him. Her first thought was of her parents. But it was Jerry, wanting to know if he can come by. She almost agrees, then thinks again. "No, Jerry. It's too late. You can come in the morning. Say, seven or so."

She hangs up, his hiss of shock audible. Immediately he dials two consecutive times, so at last she removes the receiver from the hook and buries it under two pillows and a towel.

Monday morning comes in quietly. Mary opens her eyes and stares at the ceiling, planning her day. She gets up, goes to the toilet; does all her early-morning-with-no classes things. She makes coffee, takes out a muffin bought from one of the bread ladies on Avenue C, and puts on a Miles record. Someone turned her on to "It Never Entered My Mind." Now she can't stop playing it. As the muted tones fill the room another, discordant sound peals: her doorbell, breaking the spell.

Jerry stands in the doorway, looking from her to the boxes. "I am astonished!" He explodes. He stands looking down at his things, all stacked neatly outside her door. "This is like some bizarre scene from a cheap melodrama."

Mary remains quiet but meets his disapproving stare and holds her ground. His attempt to push past, inside to her personal space, she counters with, "I'm tired of your shit."

She does not further capitulate, cuss, or shout.

Faced with the immovable force of this new Mary, Jerry changes tactics immediately. "Look, let's go inside and discuss this like adults, please."

She gives him another head-to-toe final glance and steps back enough for him to enter.

Once inside Jerry heads for 'his' chair but she's already changed the arrangement of furniture while packing his things. He stops, disoriented by the new position of the beige club chair, its removal from the central spot in her living room. Mary walks on, not paying any attention to him, and sits. Secure in the knowledge that her crowning bouffant frames a calm face, light skin, smooth shoulders accented by the wildly orange, yellow, and green patterns of her African dress.

Jerry gazes at the rise and fall of her large breasts. Dark splotches of color rise in his face.

Mary notices the shift of power and it straightens her spine. Her back remembers the many slaps from her grandmother; attempts to get her to 'sit like a princess.' Now, well-schooled, it is an imperial

Mary who looks down on Jerry, her subject, commanding him to speak. Also imposing a brief time frame, since she has a lot more important work to do. Her demeanor lets him know how inconvenient it is for him to interfere with her schedule of school work. A knowing smile plays across her face as she observes his stalling antics, an attempt to gain time as he plans his next move. She says nothing. Lets him get himself a glass of water. Watches quietly as he sits and crosses long legs to better show off the elegant cut of the trousers that drape his limbs.

"So what is this, your new persona?" He's obviously trying to bait her.

Mary shrugs one lovely shoulder.

"I mean, I've always thought of you as a refined young woman. One of your many attributes I've admired and which drew me to you. But this," he gestures at the still-open doorway. "I find this, and the embarrassment of yesterday, quite tasteless. Tossing my things outside like a common fishwife is an unforgivable humiliation." He pauses for effect.

She sits on her hands, concentrating on the discomfort of their clenched, imprisoned fingers to keep her tongue still.

"I'm aware of the game you're playing, or rather trying to play. But I'm a well-bred, proud black man. I deplore ghetto behavior. It's demeaning to both of us. We've had these discussions many times, so I thought you were different from other black women…the hot grits, the lye-throwing. But apparently you aren't. So—" He splays long, well-tended fingers.

Mary, in control of herself now, finally speaks. "So?"

He flushes and squints until his eyes are mere slits of steel. "You bitch," he shouts. Then stands, goes to the kitchen, and proceeds to make coffee. All the while keeping his back to her.

Mary does not move or speak, thinking, This is my place. He's not going to be here much longer. I don't have to do anything I don't want to do.

When the coffee is ready, he gets out the cup he'd claimed as his. Takes milk from the refrigerator, stirs in some sugar and then slowly, in what Mary assumes he feels is authoritative posture, returns to the chair he's been relegated to. He takes three sips and gently sets the cup down on the little table at his right elbow. "So let's try, if possible, to discuss this episode rationally."

Mary looks him right in the eyes. "Yes. Let's."

Well, the 'discussion' lasted for almost three hours. During that time Jerry expounded on the million and one failures of Black Women, starting with, "Typically, you got this all wrong. In spite of your education, assuming the worst of me. Coming to the wrong conclusion and then lowering and shaming yourself in front of an innocent person. Had you taken time to think, you'd have asked before distorting the situation."

Mary almost laughs at the abundance of negatives he heaps onto her. Instead she gazes at him, simply waiting.

He clears his throat. "I was in a state of confusion after our argument. Just walking around trying to figure out what was going on, when I ran into Cindy. She invited me to a party she was on her way to, and I went. It was late when we left, so of course I walked her home. She asked me up for coffee. I accepted. I'd had such a nice time, and didn't know which of your many personas I might face if I slept on her couch until morning. I took her to breakfast at that place because it was one of the few in this area where I felt comfortable eating with a white woman. My intention was to come here afterwards to try to talk some sense—but you preempted that plan. And now, you've gone too far. I cannot excuse your actions."

He stops, swallows some tea, and then for added drama takes a deep breath. "I think it's fair to say we've reached an impasse."

Mary snorts. "Oh, is that what you call it? Well, I say fine. Take your things and leave. I wouldn't want you to be saddled with this persona which distorts, comes to wrong conclusions, and is stereotypically a Ghetto Black Woman."

Jerry sputters a bit. So now Mary understands he thought she'd fling herself into his arms and beg his forgiveness. Instead, realizing the game is up, he stands and, with as much dignity as possible, goes to the door. There he pauses to add some really low blows: her inadequacies in bed, his rage against half-white bourgeois black folks and, the grand finale, "castrating Negress." At last he opens the door and gathers his things. But slowly, as if still poised to take her in his arms should she rightfully crumble under the weight of his last salvo.

Instead, imperturbability shrouds her. She is no longer overwhelmed by his years and experience. Her breath comes evenly, her skin is not hot and flushed. Clearly without these indicators he has no way of measuring whether his darts hit their mark. Gathering up his very significant first editions, all autographed with his full name, Jeremiah Matthews III, he huffs importantly. Then counts up the stack to make sure he has them all. The two books Mary bought him when they went to Chicago for the conference where he presented a paper on "The Historical Importance of Dialectics; a meeting with Paul Robeson and George Schuyler" peek out from under a conspicuous Chester Himes.

Ultimately, it takes him two trips to complete the move. All the while Mary stands relaxed in the doorway, observing but saying nothing.

Finally, he is gone!

Three hours later, the neatly stacked blue and green dishes, the glasses gleaming on the shelves of her kitchen create a Mediterranean backdrop for Mary. The décor feels comforting; it mutes Jerry's hate-filled words. She still has the satisfaction of knowing this is her very own place: designed, bought, and fully paid for by her. He didn't contribute a dime to the furnishing or expenses although he often complained, "Why do you want to remain on the Lower East Side?" He complained of the 'locals' and the 'affectations' of some of the people he'd met through her. Mary smiles, remembering his friends she met when she went to visit him in Washington, and their comments. Perhaps she's committed class suicide. The pretentiousness, the showing-off of trivial things, things she'd left behind, back home, no longer impress her. Now she knows that putting on airs runs in all circles, in all cities.

She feels a need for some strong, hot tea. There's an ominous throbbing behind her ears. She puts on a kettle to boil, takes down her pewter pot and rinses it before putting in tea leaves. It was one of her purchases from an antique shop she frequents. Funny, Jerry always labeled these preparations ostentatious. Her two grandmothers, her aunts and mother— in fact, many of the women in her family—showed her how to make a 'real' pot of tea. Coffee is something she's only now getting into. Though she has a nostalgic love of the smell of ground coffee, the sound of percolation, she didn't drink it much back home. Here the literati and pseudo intellectuals drink it black, holding their cups with an ever-present cigarette, while expounding on some obscure subject.

But now the kettle screams; water is ready. She goes to pour it over the tea leaves. But at that moment a violent wrench in her stomach forces her to rush to the bathroom. She vomits, besieged by retching and then dry heaves. Finally she's able to get up and, after splashing cold water on her face and taking a few deep breaths, she walks back to the kitchen. Quickly using a strainer to remove the leaves from the pot so that it won't be bitter, she pours more hot water in the pot, selects a bone-china teacup and saucer, and sits. A fear of having migraines like her mother is ever present. She used to think they were attention-getting mechanisms but knows now they're real. Extreme tension and stress can certainly bring on an attack.

She sips slowly, concentrating on the milky tannin taste, on the warmth of tea sliding down her throat. Once, in a biology class, she'd seen a vivid diagram of the throat and esophagus. An image arises now of the strong, dark-brown liquid lightened by a healthy portion of milk, heading for her stomach. Her breathing slows; Mary focuses on that. The wonder of it all! Her expanding and contracting lungs are incredible mechanical marvels that function with or without her active cooperation. True, she could hold her breath. But eventually she'd have to gasp in air. Beyond her immediate awareness now, a smile emerges on the familiar, remembered face of a young child. But the current person asserts herself, rejecting the statements made by Jerry.

I am my own woman!

Her gaze roams over the room and comes to rest on a photograph bought from one of the many 'cruddy shops,' as she calls them. Jerry called them curios and, with a select few, antique shops. The owner of this particular one is an Eastern European man—Miko, as he instructs everyone to call him. He loves to wear weird combinations of multi-colored scarves with shirts open halfway to his waist. Sometimes he adds a sweater or jacket. His pants are his own design. They billow like floating silk pajamas, usually in black, brown, grey, or navy blue. On his hands, multiple rings, sometimes three per finger, including the thumb. His eyes are heavily outlined, his hair either entwined in a bright cloth or hanging down his back. He has two toy poodles; each has bows on its ears to help designate gender, blue and pink. They are playful little lap pets who, when not in his arms, skitter behind him everywhere.

Such shops hold great fascination; the mystery of their contents always intrigues her. Most of the shopkeepers along East 10th Street and St. Marks Place know her tastes. Often they pull out things and set them aside. Early Saturday mornings are the best times to do her rummaging. That Saturday she'd found two books in almost-new condition: *Oblomov* and *Quiet Flows the Don*. Actually she'd intended to go across 2nd Avenue to get coffee and a bialy, the all-time perfect breakfast for a Southern black girl! But the lure of his shop was too powerful, so she'd ducked in for a quick look before running to get breakfast. A bit of food shopping and then back to the apartment to do some reading.

Miko had on a smug grin. He'd clasped his hands before him, announcing, "A wonderful surprise I have for you." The dogs, his babies, were yapping, standing on miniscule hind legs, held back by a gate across the doorsill. Miko disappeared behind a pile of scarves draped over a chair she'd never seen the bottom of and came back to stand before her with a look of triumph. He took out the photograph and held it up for inspection. The eyes reached hers. The half-smile that plumped the dark cheeks of a woman who could've been Aunt Daisy called to her.

Daisy had been the recipient of all the recessive genes from their African grandmother generations ago who'd so captivated their grandfather he kept her for himself, alongside his white wife. The face seemed to say she'd been through the storm of insanity, the racial and sexual trials so common to many Africans. Mary had to have the photograph. It needed a new frame but the image was the thing.

When she'd handed over the money, Miko told her, "It came in with a batch of things from one of the supers on East 12th Street and Avenue A. An old tenant died and he had to clean out the place for the next occupant. So he bundled whatever he thought he could get a few dollars for, to cover his next fix."

There were boxes of books, a few paintings, a carpet, some clothes and records. Mary promised Miko she'd be back for more. For the moment, she had all she could carry. In fact she'd had to hail a taxi to get home.

Now she sips more tea and thinks about her complicated family history. Not much different from that of millions of Africans who'd been mixed with Indians and White folks. In her family there'd been an acknowledged white great-grandfather who maintained two separate and unequal households. To be fair, as a result her great-grandmother was way up on the economic scale. He'd given her a small farm and about five acres. Built a six-room home with a smokehouse that was always full. There'd been some fruit and nut trees. She'd owned a few head of cattle, two horses, and lots of chickens. Her brother was the only male, black or white, allowed to stay on the farm overnight.

Great-grandfather educated his children so they would be able to make their own way. They could not, nor would they have expected to inherit any of his wealth or, most important, his name. When her little group was reading Franz Fanon this situation was brought up by one or two of the members as a hurdle she and others had to overcome. Mary was encouraged to commit class-suicide. According to Jerry, she'd not made much progress along those lines.

The coloring, or lack thereof, by the time she was born had leveled off. Mary had lighter and darker siblings and relatives. Hair texture, so vital to black people, was indiscriminately distributed amongst males and females. The darkest males often had the 'best' hair. So many tears were shed by the lighter-hued members of the family who didn't have 'good' hair. But various pomades and hot combs altered that. Length and straightness were most desired, and could mitigate darkness. She'd come out somewhere in-between: halfway curly hair, light and soft, but not straight. It was very thick; her mother used to struggle daily to comb and brush and braid it into obedience. Mary wore the traditional three braids most of the time, one up front and two in the back that danced ribbons to the bottom of her shoulder blades. The other style was two up front and two in back, with two ribbons, because the front braids were tucked into the back ones.

Her skin was a bit lighter than many other members of her family. But not enough to make her a member the privileged group with the desired peach-beige skin. She seemed destined to be in the middle all her life. Much smarter than most, but not more so than her brothers. They were doctors now and had always gotten the highest grades in school. Still her father was proud of her achievements, too, and always let her know she was his special daughter. When she made the decision to do a doctorate, there'd been no surprise. Just the question of which university she'd attend. What had made her choose New York? Perhaps that it was the longest distance from them, her parents. So it was fortuitous she'd been hired by the Episcopal Church outreach social programs. They were very involved in what they called 'social justice issues.' Many championed civil rights and religious dialogue on the subject of race. Although clearly disappointed she hadn't selected one of the prestigious black colleges, but still having much to boast about, her parents had let her go.

And now here she is, sitting at her kitchen table, meditating on the picture of the old black woman. Some of Khadijah's words come back to her. They'd been speaking last week when she stopped by the shop, about black men and their shit. Khadijah told the story of her now-estranged husband, and how she'd become a single mother of two. It all had to do with her husband's need to 'disencumber' himself from the comforts of family. "He claimed, in order to pursue the 'true meaning of life and art,'" Khadijah scoffed. This was the last installment of his ever-evolving story, what Khadijah called his abandonment, as he sailed away on a freighter to join his fellow expatriates in Spain. He'd just gotten up one morning, packed a bag, and walked out the door.

That last statement sounded so similar to what Jerry had said.

Mary lets her eyes move to settle on the walls with artwork she'd gotten from up-and-coming painters and photographers. She loves them all, art even though most are by male artists. At present she's saving for a piece from the only black woman sculpture she ever knew. The woman lives about a ten-minute walk away on Avenue C. She's created a workspace in the back yard of her building, reached by stepping out of her window, a makeshift French door. Mary's sandals and a couple of bags come from Tim, a painter who lives on MacDougal Street with a white woman. A tall, very dark-skinned man from Barbados who lives on Avenue A and 9th Street has a little shop where he sells his coats. She bought her winter and spring ones there. And she frequents a little hole-in-the wall take-out stand run by two sisters. All in all, she supports black artists. What more evidence need she offer?

She's hired three black women, two of whom are a little older than she; the other is a young college student. They're the only blacks in the office of church workers. Out of nearly one hundred people, and only four are black. Yes, there are two women and a man who work in custodial along with a staff of eight white workers. When Mary had to let one of the women go because of the poor quality of her work, she then had to endure the gossip that she was prejudiced against dark-skinned blacks. Thinking of it, she sighs. She's looking for a replacement now.

In her classes often she's the only black student. Whenever a racial issue comes up all faces turn in her direction, with questioning eyes, looking for an answer. Now that she's crafting her thesis, she's almost certain it will not be understood. Most of the books she's added to her reading list are of her own choosing. It's taking all her strength not to become doubtful of her abilities and her shortcomings.

She takes a few deep breaths and feels the vise that gripped her head, still reeling from Jerry and his tirade, loosening a bit. Mary gets up and walks barefoot across the room to her record player. She puts on a Miles album to take her all the way to a place where thoughts will float, allowing her to conjure up images and write. Lately she's been thinking about the configuration of class and racial appearances in black culture. Remembering stories she now understands through her contact with African students. She's read two novels by a Nigerian writer who had the courage to say "Things Fall Apart." The society in an Igbo village declines with the oncoming of the white man and his religion and courts. Someone told her about Frank Yerby and she's now reading him. She marvels all he's gotten away with; critiquing the racial and class divide by using the creative process to uncover deeply held but equally hidden secrets.

The music floats and spreads through the air, filling the space. The muted horn opens her up. She breathes in the melody. A piano gently, firmly, undergirds Miles' careful, assertively-tongued notes. Tears stream down her cheeks. Music and art fill her heart, and she inhales.

"All right now, get ready for me!" Mary picks up her pad, and begins to write.

FRED

His name is Fred. Most of the onlookers don't know if there's more to it; whether it's a shortened version of Frederick or not. He's a fixture on the streets of the Lower East Side. On the corner of East 9th Street and Avenue C he stands shivering in the early chill of fall. His dirty clothes hang on him loosely. He clings to the corner of an old tenement where his supplier lives. His body defies gravity, bending, leaning into the grayed brick façade. It's hard to control his knees. They keep folding under him. He knows each crack and crevice beneath his feet. He's lost count of how many days and nights, how much time in between he's spent chasing him. Sometimes he follows the man, begging for credit, begging for stuff. Begging! Begging! He's been doing it so long, so constantly, that "Please" is the first word out of his mouth to almost anyone who has a little money.

He'd said please when he attempted to mug that old white woman. She didn't seem to speak or understand English. Probably a Czech. When he pulled on the purse she'd screamed and clutched it to her bosom. Some people ahead, almost at the corner, turned around. A burly white man ran up the street towards them, voice deep with rage, shouting every racial epithet possible. Fred had panicked and darted across the street, ducking behind a truck. He saw an open door and ran inside a building at the corner of Avenue D and East 10th Street. A long time ago he'd had an apartment there. Behind the stairwell was a door to the cellar. Once in there he could slip out the back way, where clothes, garbage, all the discards of people living in those old buildings were thrown out. He'd managed to escape, though with no money.

Tonight he's trembling. His stomach is rumbling. He feels a warm little ripple, which means he's probably messed his underpants. He wipes his nose on one sleeve and prays the guy shows up soon. "I have your money," he mutters to himself. Running into Jim last night netted him a hundred dollars. He owes the man thirty dollars; he'll keep the rest.

Soon as I cop, he thinks, I'll go to the crib and shoot up. Just to get through the night.

He keeps shifting from foot to foot. His body won't stay still. His eyes are tearing up. The first roll of his gut, calling for stuff, convulses his stomach. What will happen if his pusher doesn't show soon?

He calms himself with the thought that this will be his last night on the street. He's registered at the clinic down the street across Houston. I'm gonna kick you out Miss Jones, he thinks, conjuring a soothing image of being clean, smelling only of fresh-laundered cotton.

"This madness has to stop," Fred mutters.

Going from one fix to another is no way to live. So far he's managed to stay out of jail. Sometimes he hit up one of his old girlfriends for a twenty. A few months he had a gig with a pick-up quartet. It was great to play again. His chops were weak but he got through it and the cat paid him two hundred for two nights, three sets each. He was so glad to play again, and the money helped pay his rent and cop a three-day high. But his business is in the street, so cats don't call unless they're really stuck or want to cheat. Most of the guys he used to play with cut him loose because of H.

But I'm kicking, he reminds himself. I'm cleaning up.

Fred looks up and down the sidewalk but there's still no sign of Jerry. He needs to go to the toilet bad but dare not move. To distract himself he reflects again on his situation. One of the questions the intake person at the clinic asked was, 'How long have you been addicted?' It was still too incredible, almost impossible to claim or even admit to the word. Probably the first time he'd acknowledged he was hooked was the day he pawned his sax. The shopkeeper had peered suspiciously at the extended horn. Their faces elongated, reflected in the shiny surface of his Selmer. A mixture of disgust and pity tempered his pawnbroker's face as he listened to Fred, turning the instrument over, looking for dents. There were none, of course. "I keep Petunia in good shape," Fred had assured him, feeling offended but struggling not to show it. "Ready all the time."

He shifts again as he comes out of a spasm; his body signaling it's now running on empty. "No gas in the tank," Fred riffs. But it was a hard memory to recall. All the silly things; his mouth was running off with him. "Things are a little tight right now," he'd improvised, not meeting the pawnbroker's eye. "I got a couple of gigs at the end of the month. But right now, I got to pay the rent and eat. You know how it is."

The guy had probably heard this line many times before, in a variety of ways. But Fred's mouth wouldn't stop. He just kept on talking, needing to explain to someone, anyone, what it meant to be trading in his horn for H.

"Oh God!" He gags now as a sick wave rides up to his throat. People pass by and shake their heads. He must be a pathetic sight: a frail man with matchstick legs inside thrown-on, too-big clothes.

A couple, young and white, make a big to-do of walking in a wide circle around him.

"I know I stink," Fred mutters.

At last he sees Jerry walking along toward him in that slow, cool-bop strut. "Junkie, listen," he says when he reaches Fred. "I don't want you hanging around where I live. People see you and they know my business."

Fred just pulls out the money. "Here's what I owe, and twenty for this time." He extends the money to Jerry, hands shaking.

Jerry makes an issue of looking all around before he takes the bills. After a quick count, he slips two packets to Fred, who takes off as fast as his condition will allow. Jerry's snicker echoes, following him down the street.

Fred finds his building more by instinct than by motor skills. He doesn't like the place; it's become increasingly filled with junkies. There are four apartments where five and six people double up to save on rent. Some of the women work the streets. They stay to themselves, though, and no one complains because they pay the rent and keep their men supplied. Fred doesn't speak and they ignore him. Fine. He has these social quirks. Can convince himself that he's above them because his current situation is temporary. The club scene is always erratic. Jim, his main source of work, has gotten married to that African lady. Now they live out on Long Island where he has a job teaching and conducts the college orchestra.

Funny how things work out, or not. They'd both met her at the same time. She didn't show any special interest in anyone; just a little country girl. But apparently Jim saw something he didn't. The next thing anyone knew, they were a couple. Then Jim converted and they got married. Well, most of the black cats like him have flirted with Islam. Renouncing Christianity as a part of slavery and white domination, taking on African names. Reclaiming their lost and stolen names and identities. They shunned Western clothes and the look of respectability. Some can expound for hours on end about imperialism, exploitation, racial segregation. In a massive display of solidarity, black musicians refused to play with Jim. Only Mike and him; they were a part of his quartet and sometimes quintet. Jim never said a bad word about them or the whole situation. He liked Mary Jane but drew the line when it came to H. Then he'd just kept on getting up and going home to his African woman.

Fred reaches his door, hand trembling so bad he has to use both to unlock it. Why he bothers locking it at all is something he can't explain. There's nothing left to take: a mattress with a dirty, blood-stained sheet; an old discard of a shaky Formica table; a cardboard box with his charts in it. Even roaches and mice have stopped hanging out in his crib, 'cause there's nothing to eat. Food's better on the third floor. Anyhow, Fred eats at the shelters on the Bowery now. But he always chooses H over food.

Now he shuts the door and locks it. Rushing, rushing against the next wave of nausea, he stumbles on towards the bathroom. He has enough to last until the morning. He'll be able to get something then at the clinic. But he can't make up his mind what to do first. Cook and shoot up? Go to the toilet before he pees himself? Finally he decides to do both. Carefully he mixes and cooks. A string of drool falls from his loose lips onto his arms as he loads the syringe. He dives for the toilet and sits just in time. His bowels unlock and there comes the thud of his insides dropping into the commode just as he ties off.

Deep breath: plunge and pull the needle, in out.

"Yesss!" Then he sits waiting. Waiting for relief.

Fred slowly stands and twists out of his filthy clothes. His underpants are filled with a brown liquid. It's much like changing a diaper. He starts singing himself a lullaby as he shuffles to the sink and turns on the water. Somehow his hands keep missing the soap. The water's cold but he feels so hot. He leaves it running over his soiled clothes and goes to sit in a chair, only then remembering to cut off the water and hang the shorts over the bathtub so they'll be dry in the morning.

Maybe an hour later, he can't really tell, Fred realizes he's standing naked beside the bathtub with his shorts in his hands. He drops them into the tub and crawls to the bed, pulls himself up with great effort, and falls down, down, down.

Slowly the Lower East Side awakens. Bright sun shines in through dirty windows. Fred shifts, a hand creeping down to cover his flaccid penis as he lies curled in a ball on the mattress. Only he isn't a ball. He is . . .what? A junkie, a stinking, poor-butt junkie. This wasn't supposed to happen. Not to him. To Frederick Gadsen, Jr., the son of Reverend and Mrs. Frederick Gadsen Sr. Hadn't he been raised to be the special child, the heir of a great preacher man? Well, he thinks as he tries painfully to uncoil his body; I was the son, the special son of a great man.

His father always loved him and tried to provide everything he wanted. He's a preacher and businessman. He and Fred's brother own a funeral home. His mother is a hairdresser. They have things sewed up. Whatever is needed, they can provide. A widowed sister of his mother lived with them when he was young. Bessie did the cooking in exchange for a home for herself and her young daughter. Fred was always close to his aunt. He spent a lot of time in their little shack, which stood behind his parents' big house.

Fred nods off as he sits, still trying to get up. But he must get up and wash and dress. Going to the clinic, so he has to be clean. He can still remember his aunt's soft hands washing his back, combing his hair. Somehow he gets up and into the bathroom. The sight of himself in the mirror hanging over the sink is shocking. It frightens him to see this old, raddled face. H has destroyed his beautiful teeth. Both his parents were always so proud of his good looks. They made sure his dental appointments were kept and now all their efforts have been for naught. In fact, he's lost two front teeth. They just fell out one day. He can't remember when, precisely, but it must've have been about a year ago.

Fred throws cold water on his face. His hands automatically search for a towel but he can't find one. He goes to his closet and discovers a lone shirt and a single pair of pants neatly hanging. On the floor, a pair of brown shoes with socks rolled inside them. He can't find clean underwear, though. He knows he has some because today is Tuesday, and Bessie does laundry on Monday and ironing on Tuesday. So he should have clean underwear because today is Tuesday, isn't it?

In the bathtub he sees the stained, crumpled heap of his shorts. He picks them up but they are still damp, so he drops them back into the tub. If he has to sit for a long time they might soak through his pants. He paces back to the closet and, miracle of miracles, now he sees an undershirt and shorts are on the hanger next to a coat he got from the Salvation Army. It's an old habit, preparing his things the night before so he'll be ready for a gig. He doesn't know how long these clothes have been waiting for him.

"Guess I have a guardian angel looking out for me."

He holds onto the rickety table, which balks at the pressure of his dead weight. His legs go inside the shorts, and then the pants. Now an undershirt. Next a long-sleeved shirt, to hide the track marks and old sores. It takes a while to get the buttons done but he manages. Even with the shirt stuffed inside the pants, the belt winds loosely around his waist and sags. Last, the socks and shoes. He has to sit on the one chair he possesses when a light-headed feeling rushes over him. Fred takes a deep breath; he must resort to the magic formula that gets him through dressing. "I am the special son of a great preacher man," he whispers. Eventually the socks go on but then he can't manipulate the shoelaces so he decides to go without tying them.

He puts his works in the old refrig and finds his battered wallet, which holds a faded photograph smiling out at him. Who is that boy grinning up? Could it be? God, it feels like an eternity. He gets keys out and the last of the money from Jim. With all the shredded dignity he can muster, Fred opens the door and slowly descends the stairs. He always tries to be as quiet as possible because he never wants 'Them' to approach him. He needs that small remainder of his lost pride, to not be associating with 'those kinds of people.'

They're the real junkies, he reminds himself. I only have a chippie.

Out he goes into the early morning, where a mass exodus of working mothers are struggling with shrilly objecting children who don't want to go to Abuela's, the nursery, or school. Supers drag clanging, overflowing garbage cans and behind their endless complaints about nasty people who live like pigs. Somehow being out with all these folks gives him a boost. Because he isn't running down Avenue D, although he wants to badly. He just keeps saying to himself, "One foot in front of the other," all the way over to Houston and up to Allen Street,

By the time he arrives at the clinic his shirt is wet. The crisp air does nothing to cool him. He gives his name to the woman at the desk.

She tells him to have a seat. "You'll be called next."

Fred sits praying whoever it is will see him soon, before Miss Jones acts up.

The woman behind the drab gray metal desk at last calls his name. Fred jerks his head up with a start. His hand goes to his mouth, self-conscious over the loss of prized teeth, an effort to hide the gap. His legs, unsteady, still manage to hold up and carry him through the door. Inside, a young white man with a long braid of brown hair greets him, his manner very professional, asking, "What are you taking? How much? How often?"

Fred gives minimal responses.

"How do you support your habit? When did you start? How long has it been since you used?"

All the questions Fred answers quickly and quietly and economically.

Rising, the doctor says, "Get undressed. I'll be right back."

There is a short green hospital gown, faded from much laundering, folded at the bottom of a metal cot. Left alone in the very down-to-the basics examining room, now Fred feels scared and alone. His vulnerable state heightened when he sees his bony knees aren't covered by the flimsy material, nor are his exposed arms with the dark track marks running all along their veiny path.

The doctor returns wearing a cotton mask and rubber gloves, a stethoscope around his neck. He listens to Fred's heart.

Inside his head Fred scats, "How High the Moon?" The man's hands feel both firm and soft as they prod and poke all over his body. Fred tries to focus on something else. He sees a stack of magazines piled on a yellow-painted radiator. It seems odd such a bright color would be used on a radiator in a place this.

He fantasizes about the real, crazy dope fiends, the images they conjure up when in the throes of withdrawals. Certainly he himself has felt a thousand centipedes underneath his skin, moving about, while watching his own flesh tremble and sweat. But right now he'd rather think about the yellow radiator because not to do so might cause him to flee his current position. To grab up his clothes and split. Only he does want to quit. He really needs to stop using. His poor abused veins remind him of the rubbers he once found long ago in his brother's drawer. He'd taken one out and filled it with water. Then picking holes in it with a pin, he'd watched the trickles spurt out. What is left in them now, his veins? He's been selling his blood for the past two months to pay rent and to cop. Is there actually any blood left?

H is a vampire, and he is her host.

The doctor's white face looks grim. His thin lips part to say, "You need to stop using, or else you'll be going somewhere to die."

Fred manages to sit up. His stomach is beginning to simmer; he's drenched in sweat. The little gown is sticking to him and he knows he smells. Well, that's why they call it junk, shit, smack. He stinks up the whole room but the doctor gamely keeps on poking and examining him, perhaps until he has satisfied himself that Fred is indeed a male human being. Then he sits back on his little piano stool, facing Fred. "We'll give you something to calm you down. The nurse will be right in. I'm going to take care of the paperwork and meet you outside, in Admissions." He gets up and offers an outstretched hand. "Good luck, man. It's going to be tough. But if you really want to stop this crazy merry-go-round, you'll make it."

They shake hands. The doctor turns away and leaves him alone in the room again.

Merry-go-round, Fred muses. He hasn't thought of that since he was a boy. A carnival had come to town and all the children were excited, begging to go. All the white children were lined up at the entrance, laughing with their parents and each other. All the black children, Fred included, watched from across the street. Their line was as long as the white line but they could not join them. The carnival had posted two days of performances for blacks and five for whites. Rev. Gadsen had already told his congregation that he would not be taking his boys, even though they wanted so badly to go. "I would not let them suffer the shame of having to attend on specific days set aside for them. They have to pay the same prices as the whites and yet, can go only when allowed." He urged his members not to patronize the circus; to try to find black amusement parks for their children. But Fred had wanted to go so badly, he'd hated his father for that, for years afterward.

Military Mary comes in so smartly he almost salutes her.

She says "Good morning," and pulls on rubber gloves.

A mercenary thought crosses his mind. "Maybe I should become a business man like my father. Open a rubber glove factory." Everyone in this place wears them for a few minutes and then discards them, only to take up a new pair and then again discard them.

The nurse is a straight line. Her stiff back shows no indentation where a butt should be. Flat-behind, white-woman shape, he decides. She pulls on a silver chain around her neck with several keys on it. She selects one and goes to a glass and wood cabinet in the back of the room. Unlocks the door and removes a small glass vial. Then goes over to a cart that holds lots of assorted medical supplies. First, though, she locks the little cabinet again, before she leaves it and goes off, saying, "I'll be right back. These careless people, they never remember to set out all the instruments."

Fred knows she's referring to syringes. Staff always hides them from people like him.

During that long 'right back' he finishes dressing. The nurse returns as he is stuffing his shirttail into his pants. Miss Jones is sitting heavy on his shoulders now, her grin a teeth-baring leer. Twitches in his stomach signal the growing crisis. His eyes fix on the nurse's hands. In one she holds a syringe. She inserts the needle into a vial, pulls back the handle to draw up fluid, then pushes so it ejaculates. Fred feels his mouth drop open as he salivates. His breath comes in rasps. When she approaches he offers his arm before she can ask. He's not sure what she'll find there, though. His search last night for a good vein had been extremely difficult. In the end, he'd shot up between the toes on his right foot.

With the practiced touch of a professional, her forefinger traces his thin arm, eyes on the look-out for a spot as she pinches loose flesh. Sparing him further groping, she suddenly plunges the needle into his upper arm. The flesh and muscle there offer no resistance. It will take longer this way than going directly to the blood stream but—sure, OK, this is fine. He breathes deep and slow. Feeling safe, for the moment, in a place not about to be overrun with junkies or raided by the police. He forces himself to concentrate on the growing lightness in his body. No need here to worry about getting caught, or dying from a bad fix. These people are only going to help him, get him clean.

Fred rolls down his sleeve, flexes the arm, and goes out to what is euphemistically called a waiting room. The pleasant-faced receptionist dresses like a nurse too, but doesn't have the bearing. She tells him to have a seat, and brings over some more forms to be filled out. "Would you like some coffee or tea?"

He declines the offer. It takes a while to get his jittering eyes to settle on the words. Whatever he's been given is beginning to have an effect and he's feeling relaxed. The papers keep slipping from his hands, though. Then the pencil falls. His head is spinning. People are moving around him in long, exaggerated steps. The choreography of motion here is a very, very, very slow and sinuous dance.

The doctor passes by and asks, "How're you doing now?"

Fred starts to riff, "If I Were a Bell" but changes his tune. They'd probably think he was crazy. Might ship me off to a nut house instead of the detox unit." When he tries to answer his lips won't cooperate; his voice sounds buried beneath his breath. The words are hanging out somewhere below his stomach and he can't bring them up.

The doctor says something else, and Military Mary comes marching in. She tells him what she's given him, though Fred doesn't catch the name.

"Just take it easy for a few minutes. You've got time to complete the papers. It's a synthetic form of heroin, you see. Your system's reacting to it. You'll be fine." The doctor's eyes are kind and reassuring. Fred feels like a child again, safe in his father's house.

By one-thirty all the forms are completed. The social worker has approved his case. Welfare will pay for his six-week stay. He's going to a private retreat funded by a wealthy white woman whose son died from a heroin overdose. Fred and five others are all waiting, three men and two women. A new guy comes in and goes over to the receptionist. She hands him a stack of folders which he bunches under one arm. He motions for all to follow him.

As Fred leaves, he looks back at the nurse and doctor, waves good-bye, and goes on out to the street.

Outside the little collective of about-to-be-ex junkies are standing around in front of a jeep parked at the curb. Fred comes to the edge of the circle and watches. Two of the men are smoking a shared cigarette. He stopped a while ago because he couldn't afford it. Every penny he could get his hands on went to feed his habit. His luggage sits at his feet, one pathetic cheap suitcase. He'd traded his handmade leather bag bought from the painter, Tim, long ago, because he needed junk. So he traded the nice suitcase for a bag, and this ugly thing. Petunia the sax is still in the pawn shop. He visited her once and gave the owner half the money. Told the guy he was going to clean up and would be back for her. The pawnbroker promised not to sell his horn.

Now he breathes in the cold air deeply, to clear his head. He feels numb, reflexes off from the stuff the nurse shot him up with. He doesn't think he wants any more of it.

"Okay, let's load up," the driver says abruptly, interrupting his meandering. All the junkies grab their belongings and put them in the van. One of the women is dark and shy. She sort of disappears into the seat. The other, the Puerto Rican, seems tough. When one of the men scratches his face near his nose, Fred sees his right hand is discolored; it reminds him of a baseball mitt. Fred steals looks at them all, trying to imagine what kind of music he could compose about them that would fit like a dress, or a pair of pants and a shirt.

He dozes off and on. When awake he stares at the passing scenery. Huge gold trees turning red against the sun as it descends. From the open window fresh, non-city air comes in and he snorts it up in big gulps. Not too much traffic. At times there are no other cars on the road.

The driver says, "About an hour more."

The two women make a fuss, saying they're hungry and need to stop off for some food. One of the men also wants to stop because he's bored. The other needs to stretch his legs. The driver relents; says he'll stop at the next diner for fifteen minutes. The Puerto Rican woman shifts around, fusses with her hair. Fred just stares out the window, taking note of every altered sensation brought on by this new 'medication.'

Ahead a sign announces A GREAT PLACE TO STOP, EAT, AND DRINK.

Applause breaks out. The driver pulls over and finds a parking spot next to a fancy sports car. Fred isn't sure of the make but knows it cost far more than he could ever afford.

When they enter the dark, cavernous space, the thick smells of frying meat, stale cigarettes, and booze ride out on a wave of heat. The smells push back against Fred at the door. The last thing he desires at the moment is food that reeks of oil. He orders ginger ale to settle his stomach.

Forty-five minutes after the stop they all alight from the van and go inside the center quickly, shutting the door behind them. They are leaving their haunted pasts, all their demons and monstrous urges outside, far away back on Avenue C. That's where Fred first shot up. Sitting on a bench in Tompkins Square Park, next to the Arts & Crafts room, the one with filthy male and female toilets on either side. A sculptor who lived down on Avenue C and 5th Street and worked with kids in the neighborhood found him there. One of the boys in her class came in and said, "Miss? A man is dead out there, on the toilet." She probably saved his life. Shelly, the sculptor, made him promise he'd try to stop. It was she who gave him information on the clinic.

After the second day there Fred begins to reorder his list of resolutions. He has to take the new medication because the centipedes under his skin keep crawling around and biting him. He wanted to go cold turkey but that plan failed on the first night. Doubt begins to creep up his skinny back. Now he fears his ability to actually kick the junk. Suppose he can't? The consequences are even more horrible than he can imagine. He tries to shut out these thoughts. One thing is certain; he'd rather die than go back to what he's been doing. You couldn't call that living. Most of the time not eating. The music has flown from his head. His only thought was: Money. How am I gonna come up with cash for the next shot? His life back there revolved around smack and more smack and how to cop.

He's certain no one suspected he was using, though. Fred smiles now, thinking back. He looks around at this bucolic scene; the rolling green hills, huge trees with lush foliage and clear skies. All of this was always available to those with money. He pictures the dead rich white boy ordering his nightly supply the way one calls for his car to brought around by a valet parking attendant. No standing around in freezing cold or on steaming sidewalks waiting for your dealer. "That must've been hip," he mutters. That white boy was able to fool everybody around him, until he died. For a while Fred had done the same.

He has individual sessions with a psychotherapist. Three work at Caleb's House. That was the name of the benefactor's son; he died at the age of twenty-two. ODed in a little flat on East 2nd Street and Avenue B. No one knew until the super recognized the smell of death. When the police came they broke the door in and found him lying on his bed, no sheets or blankets, stiff and cold. His works were on the floor, just below his out-flung hand, his arm which hung off the bed. Fred promises himself this will not be his fate.

The therapist keeps asking a lot of stuff about his childhood. "What was it like being black and young? Do you really like who you are—a black male, that is? What's your relation to your parents? Are they married? Do you like your father?" All that unnecessary stuff.

The only thing she seems to want to hear is that he hates being black, so to escape he resorted to drugs. And oh yes, he hates his parents. This conclusion he feels comes from having shared a moment in his early life with his father. One day his dad drove him to school with a note that read, *Don't hit him. We'll take care of that*. Fred understands the unthinking racism of his therapist. So what! What he wants to know is, How do I keep away from drugs? He needs his dignity and the music back in his life. That's why he's here, participating in all of this. He wants to shout, "Please, somebody. God, doctor, nurse, shrink, friend. Help me!"

After the third week Fred begins to notice small changes in his body. His nose stops running. His night sweats have tapered off almost to nothing. A dentist comes twice a week. Tooth loss is but one of the hazards of heroin usage, the drug most of those in detox are addicted to. The dentist checks Fred's teeth and says, "I'll issue you a partial, because two other teeth need to be removed."

Fred feels better now knowing he'll have some teeth to grip his mouth piece when he gets back to the city and brings Petunia home. He'll be able to resume playing after a few months of practice scales and other exercises. Oh yes, he'll burn the scene up with all the music pent up inside him, til now hidden from the curious ears and eyes of those who openly envied him and voiced displeasure with his musical direction.

By the sixth week a few people have been disciplined. Two were found in beds together, and two somehow sneaked drugs into the house. Everyone expects them to be expelled because of the seriousness of these infractions. At group session one of the members attacks the transgressors. Surprising everyone, the tough, aggressive woman breaks into tears, begging forgiveness, to be allowed to continue in the program. The leader looks around and asks what the word is. Perhaps due to the shock of her tears, her extravagant contrition, everyone agrees to impose a two-week strict probation with great restrictions on personal privileges. No expulsion.

On the eve of his release, Fred walks around the woods. The peace at this time of day settles on his shoulders around the same place where tension, and the fear of returning tomorrow, have knotted up under his shirt and thick sweater. The setting sun gilds the hills orange-gold. Birds are zeroing in on night perches in trees. They are quite noisy, clattering and shrieking overhead, their plumage contrasting against the vast manicured space of Caleb House grounds.

He walks, listening to leaves and twigs crackle underfoot. The colors around him are so much more real now than the drab asphalt grays and faded brick of the Lower East Side streets. A heavy ball of fear settles in his gut. He is afraid of them, those streets, the availability of junk. His dealer will follow him down them, trying to get him back in his clutches. His stomach turns, His palms sweat at the thought of anything and everything; of both using and of not using.

He calls Jim to ask if he can stay at his old studio for a few months to get himself together. The therapist told Fred he would have to sever and disconnect from all former places and people. His social worker's gotten him a job that's about a ten-minute walk from his old place. Some community organizations are renovating three buildings off the corner of East 9th Street. They don't have an apartment yet for him, but if he works out there they promise one as part of his payment for being a junior janitor. Jim agreed that he can stay for about five months. Fred hopes to have his own place by then. The clinic staff is satisfied with his housing plans.

Fred has applied to every college and special program he can think of, any and all recommended. So far none have called. He's been writing tunes and reviving his piano skills during these three months at Caleb's House. He was only supposed to be there for six weeks but the doctor let him stay on to work as an assistant to the music therapist. His sax lip is slowly healing; he practices muscle-building exercises. The deep shadows that underlined his eyes are gone now. The gashes that made deep parenthesis around his mouth have filled in with regular meals of good food. He's been walking about five miles a day from the house to the highway and back, or up to the top of a nearby knoll.

The centipedes beneath his skin have gone. The dermatologist gave him some cream to put on his arms to heal the sores. A health-food nut at the house, the cook, turned him on to vitamin E and Fred puts it on his arms too. He rubs the dark spots that still mark him. The tell-tale tracks of a five-year habit now blend in with his natural skin tone. Maybe by spring he'll able to go home to see his folks. He wrote and told them about his drug habit and his attempt to stop. His mother wrote back, saying they were praying for him. He answered with a long letter, now that he's leaving Caleb House.

Dear Folks,
Well, the day has finally arrived. I'm leaving here tomorrow. I don't mind telling you I'm scared. Not because I want to go back to drugs, because I don't. But the pull of it is so strong. I heard one

of the men who came up here with me plotting his first hit as soon as he gets back. He only wanted to lower his usage, not quit. I don't want to go back to the stuff ever.

I've tried and tried to figure how I got strung out in the first place and can't seem to find a plausible answer. At first I was just fooling around, along with a couple of the guys in the group. All heavy users but fine musicians. Maybe I believed that if I did what they did, I might be as good. And though the first months feel like pure joy this stuff is highly addictive. It imparts a euphoric sense of living, of yourself and all around you. And then one day you wake up with chills and sweat pouring out like you have some sort of fever. Your head pounds. Every nerve in your body is clanging against the walls of your skin. At first you don't know what's wrong. I didn't; just thought I was coming down with a bad cold because I was sneezing and my nose was running. I went to play that night all bundled up because of the chills and hot flashes. One of the older men noticed and explained what was happening. I denied it, and wouldn't shoot up with them to prove they were wrong. Somehow I got through that night. The next day, I felt like I was going to die. A sick feeling rolled over my entire body. I walked the streets desperately searching for a drug user or seller. One of the women I was dating at the time fooled around with heroin, and she introduced me to her pusher. I went through three or four of them. Each time the men are younger and younger.

I've gotten medical help, too, since coming here. My teeth are in now, lower and upper partials. My diet's changed. I get lots of exercise; five mile walks every day. I practice piano two hours a day. When I leave I'll be staying at a friend's studio, a musician I used to play with. There's a piano so I'll continue writing music. I composed a piece for you and hope sometime soon you can hear it. Oh, and the social worker has gotten me a job. I'll be able to save money because my friend isn't charging me.

I know you pray for me all the time, but I really need it now. It's going to take all my strength. Nothing like a fall on the behind to shake your faith. I remind myself of who I am, of where I come from. With all your prayers and a few from myself, I shall be fine. So don't worry.

I love you all. One day soon I will redeem myself in your eyes.

Your loving son,

Frederick Gadsen, Jr.

Packing is emotional. His clothes are neatly piled on the bed. With the money he's earned as assistant music instructor Fred has now an actual wardrobe again: a couple heavy shirts, some sweaters, three pairs of corduroy pants. A counselor took the residents to a local thrift shop and he found some wonderful things. With this new wardrobe he's ready to walk the streets of New York. He places the clothes in his old suitcase and puts his boots and two pairs of shoes in the duffle bag. The director gave it to him, seeing how inadequate the suitcase was. His compositions lie on top of the clothes. Bottles of vitamins are wrapped in his new underwear and socks. After closing the case, and tying the bag, Fred takes a last look around at his home for the past three months. When he arrived it was fall. Now it's mid-winter. He gazes at the view from his little window, where snow paints the trees and hills and roads. No tracks mar the expanse of white. The bare branches of a leafless tree frame a pair of cardinals. He sighs and makes a final search for any missing items or papers. Then lifts the bag over one shoulder, picks up his suitcase, and walks out of the room.

The driver steers the van carefully as they move from the unpaved lane onto the highway and head south. It's very cold but soon the heat kicks in and the riders are warming up. Everyone is quiet, and Fred is grateful for that. He's having leave-adjustment problems. The serenity of the countryside helps but the twitters in his stomach attest to his anxiety.

A little later he wakes up with a jerk. The Puerto Rican woman is speaking to one of the men. They have asked the driver to make a stop, so he's pulling up to a rest area. He gets out and stretches. Two of the men get out to smoke. Fred walks past them.

"Hey man, you ready for the City?" one asks.

Fred shrugs. "I don't know, man. I'm just gonna take it slow."

The other man nods. "That's it, man, slow. I tell you what, I'm scared. This is my third time. I just don't want to do this back-and-forth anymore. My son wants me home with him. He needs me. But, I don't know how to avoid H."

Fred listens and nods. "This is my first time. I hope my last. I want to get my life back together with my music." Then his words dry up. He drifts away, into the diner, to use the toilet and get some hot chocolate.

Everyone climbs back in the van. Closer to the city they encounter more cars and noise. The quiet is displaced with chatter and nervous giggles. The women exchange addresses. They promise to meet next week at group therapy. Fred keeps his eyes closed so it will appear he's asleep. He has no intention of hanging out with any of them.

The driver turns off the FDR onto Avenue D and the Lower East Side. It's early evening and the streets are thick with bodies in heavy coats, pulled-up collars and snugged caps. They pass Jerry's building and Fred recognizes the young woman standing in the doorway, waiting for him to show. It's then he realizes he's crying, so he takes out his handkerchief to fake a cough and blow his nose

The van pulls into the clinic, where the Puerto Rican woman sees someone waiting for her. "It's my mother with my daughter. God help me." She smiles, crosses herself, clambers out and steps into the waiting arms of her tearful mother and daughter. They embrace and cry. Fred is glad his parents aren't there. He doesn't want them to see him yet. He takes his things out and looks around for a cab.

The van driver says, "I'll be heading over to the garage on West 23rd. I can give you a lift to a subway stop."

Fred smiles. "I'm going to West 17th Street."

"Okay, stick around. Leave your things inside. I'll be out in five minutes."

Fred waits outside the van and watches the street transactions. One of the men from Caleb's House dashes across the street to cop. The other is headed to Harlem, to his family.

"Good luck, man," he calls to Fred, his smile deep and sad.

"The same to you."

Jim is waiting when they pull up in front of his building. Funny, Fred thinks, I used to make fun of him. He wondered how this white boy from Canada could be so hip, could love the music so much. He tried hard to make it as a jazz musician, and he was good. But it was his arrangements that were the best. Fred used to be jealous of him, but not anymore. The music he started up at Caleb House has good, tight structure, solid chord changes.

"Hello, Fred! Welcome." Jim holds out a hand.

Fred takes it and smiles back. "Jim, man, I don't know how to thank you."

Jim helps him unload. He calls good night to the driver and follows Jim inside the building.

"You look good."

"I got my teeth in."

Jim laughs and shakes his head as they get inside the elevator. "Each floor has its own key. Otherwise you can't get to your place. The stairs are only for emergencies."

Jim puts the key in the fifth floor slot. The doors close and they go up, by-passing all the other floors. At the fifth the door opens and there's another door. Jim unlocks it and they enter the studio. He sets the suitcase and duffle bag near the door.

"Let's go get something to eat. Then I have to get the train home," Jim tells him.

"Sounds good to me. But I don't have a lot of money so make it someplace easy on the pocket."

Jim shakes his head. "This is a celebration, so it's my treat."

The diner is nice and basic. Jim, now a Muslim, is very particular about his diet. Fred chooses soup and gets them to make a vegetable plate for him. Jim orders fish and baked potato. "So, how you feeling?"

Fred looks around at the diners before answering. "Good, scared, hopeful." He sighs. "Bursting with music." He's quiet a moment. "It'll take a couple of pay checks to get my axe out of the pawn shop. But I've been writing a lot. I'll keep doing that and practicing the piano." Fred sighs again, contemplating the arduous road ahead.

"Look, I can get you a little gig at the university. And advance you the money so you'll be able to get your horn out," Jim says softly, looking him straight in the face.

Fred's eyes water. He's overwhelmed by Jim's generosity. "I'll pay you back, man. You know I got a job as a janitor. Some new buildings over on Avenue A. But I—" He stops short. "I never taught in a college before. Though I assisted the music director at Caleb House. He wasn't really a musician, just coordinated programs. Hope I don't mess up."

Jim nods. "So get settled and set up your schedule. What I'll do is organize a workshop, maybe two classes and a private class. When you come out you can stay with us overnight."

Fred shakes his head because he doesn't trust his voice.

"You only have about three weeks before the semester starts."

"I should be able to do it. The janitor job is part–time. I report Monday," Fred says. "Maybe I can work through Wednesday and then come out early Thursday, do Fridays and Saturdays."

Jim shakes his head. "That sounds good. Maybe a private class Thursday night, a class Friday and a workshop that evening. Or a private session and a workshop on Saturday. We'll figure it out."

Back at the studio, Fred takes his shoes off and walks softly on the wooden floors. His fingers move on his imaginary sax; a new tune he's been working on runs through his head. It's quiet there he's afraid of playing the piano. He doesn't want to cause any trouble with the neighbors for Jim. There's a radio next to the bed. He turns it on. Miles' muted horn floats across the space. Fred opens the suitcase and takes out his things. Puts the music on the piano and hangs his clothes in the closet. Happiness bubbles up suddenly. He leaps and twirls about the large studio. It's great to move so freely with no one around. After half an hour or so he winds down, goes over and turns off the lights, and sits in the middle of room.

Fred does his breathing exercises. Inhale to the count of ten, exhale to ten. He extends his right arm over to the left side, reverses and lies flat on the floor. Pulls his legs up, right and then left, knees to his chin. He does this for an hour, then goes to the bathroom and showers, puts pajamas on and gets under the cool sheets and quilt. The city noise is muffled by the walls. Fred relaxes, lulled to sleep.

In the middle of the night Fred wakes up, disoriented, and panicked. Until at last he recognizes his surroundings and relaxes. He lies back and whispers, "Five years lost is five years too many. God help me. Help me." He stretches out then, humming his new tune, and soon falls asleep.

EAST 10th STREET

Nusa awakens suddenly to silence. Absent is the voice of her son from his room. She begins to get up, to look in on him, but is unable to move. There's a body on top of her, a strong vise that encircles and pins her dark brown arms. Panic floods her and she stiffens. The body reacts, arms tightening. Lips at her ear whisper, "Shh, I'm here." Another heart beats against her naked chest. Her hands move along slender hips—a male body, the rounded knoll of taut buttocks. And inside her most private space, the secret cave of her female person, there is —

Bill moans as he wakes atop Nusa. She's small and strong, her passionate strength matching his. Her celibacy ended the night before in pain and fear, and the joy of sexual release. And he is the one who ended it! The denial of her physical needs, in an emotional surrender that engulfed both and brought tears of pleasure and sadness. Age and experience collided in a climax that shocked and moved them. That deep release led them into a deep sleep.

Now Nusa looks up into his face, searching the contours of his cheeks, the shape of his mouth. But it is the eyes, his eyes—their gentle fire smolders, contrasting with the tightening of his arms, the insistence of his maleness inside her. And her body, responding to both their needs, moves involuntarily.

"Nusa, Nusa," his low voice rasps against her ear. She tries to roll him off, a last-minute attempt to deny the previous night's journey. But Bill kisses her, remaining firmly in her, unmoving—just *there*. His breath mingles with hers. Her lungs fill with his scent and she exhales away her apprehensions.

Finally after the panting subsides, the fevered grips slacken, she feels his sweat trickling onto her belly, mixing with hers. The sheets are damp, twisted about their ankles. Bill's long legs hang over the end of the couch-bed. Coming back to herself she hears the morning mid-summer sounds of a Sunday. The bells from St. Brigit's encouraging the faithful to her doors and candle-lit aisles. Voices rise in conversation or argument. A single blast of music starts the weekend cycle of one person trying to overpower another's radio or record player. She wants to close the windows to block out those sounds—to imprison the quietude and holiness of this time, the memories of their Saturday night.

Bill moves first, long body sluggishly rolling off hers. Nusa stays in the same position a few moments. The air on her skin maps the geography of his just-departed form. His hand caresses her hair and he rises up on one elbow, brushes her cheek with his lips. "Whew, I'm too old for this."

Nusa sits up slowly and leans over him. "Good morning." It's all she can think to say. Almost four years since she's been with a man, and things come back slowly. Her body feels so uncovered. Self-conscious, she looks around for something to cover up with. How can she just get up—naked? Then she remembers the night in all its detail and is embarrassed anew.

Bill, watching her face, reaches up and pulls it down to his. He kisses her with authority, declaring his rights, opening enough to show his vulnerability, her power over him. "Nusa, Nusa, thank you." He kisses her again. His grip tightens.

"Ah-ah, I must get up." She shakes her head. "We need to bathe and eat. Then I must go get Moussa."

Bill corrects her. "We'll go get him."

She gives him a searching look and then a slow smile, a nod, and says, "Yes, we will get him. Now, I'll bathe. Then run a tub for you."

Unable to find anything handy to pull on, she gets up and crosses the great distance of about ten or so steps, to the kitchen. Takes off all the dishes and cooking things, removes the white enamel covering the tub, and runs water from the tap. She turns to go to the closet and finds Bill there, staring boldly, taking in her entire body. Her arms hang limp at her sides. She inhales and mentally shakes herself. Quickly opens the door, selects a green print skirt, a blouse she hand-sewed. Next she bends to take underwear from the bottom drawer. "Oh," she remembers then. Her knickers lie somewhere under the bed covers. She must wash them. "A respectable woman does not leave her intimate garments lying about," her aunt had once said, at Nusa's initiation. "Not even for her husband's eyes." Such was one of the major instructions she had received then.

"But he is not my husband. I have no husband." Imagine saying that in reply!

The truths of her acts nag even as the afterglow of making love still envelopes her body. She sinks into the cool water, ducks her head and soaps her arms. Stands abruptly as the water gurgles down the drain. She fills a little calabash, one she made from a halved coconut, with water, and pours it over her head. Then again down her front, refilling, now the back, once on each side—finished, out.

She wraps up in a terry robe, washes out the tub, and runs Bill's bath. When it's half full, she shuts off the water, takes her clothes into the back room and lays them out on her son's bed. Back in the living room Bill's staring at the ceiling, hands under his head.

She comes to stand near the foldout bed. "Your bath is ready."

He pulls her down to sit next to him, penetrating the layers of her skin, muscles, organs, heart and head with his gaze. What is he looking for? she worries.

"Nusa, last night—this…" He sighs. "This isn't something I take lightly." Another piercing gaze. "I'm not after a one-night stand. Remember, I'm quite a few years older, and not looking for a girl to give me back my youth. I want more than that. So you should decide how and where we go from here."

Leaning over, she kisses him softly. "Come, take your bath." She lays a towel and face cloth on a chair and goes off to dress.

When she comes out Bill is standing there, drying off. He catches her eye, as if to deliberately make her witness him, uncovered.

She swallows hard and smiles timidly. "You like coffee or tea?"

A grin breaks across his face. The fearful tension of the moment eases. "Coffee, tea, and thee, my fair one." With an elaborate bow, he grandly tosses the towel to the floor.

Nusa claps and laughs.

"Hmm, that sounds marvelous, your laughter." He touches his heart. "Thanks."

She curtsies. "*C'est rien.*"

"*Touché.*" Bill responds and lets out a big belly laugh.

How strange there is now male laughter in the apartment. Hamid had only spent three nights here, during which time there was little if any laughing. Emotionally, it is so long ago. She remembers her husband's smile, though, whenever their son gives her a half smile or raises an eyebrow. Now another face is threatening to imprint the canvas of her memory, painted in deep brown with maroon overtones. Or...rosewood, that's the image. Bill is a rosewood composition in the center of the frame.

Nusa serves him coffee because she loves the smell. She has an old Moulinex; the plunger holds down the ground coffee. There's heated milk and she's found two croissants. He lets her pour his cup. When she sets a slice of cantaloupe in front of him, he circles her waist and buries his face in her midriff. She eases away and sits opposite.

He frowns.

"Is all well?"

Bill shrugs. "I just observed you have only two chairs."

She smiles. "There's another in Moussa's room. But because usually it's only the two of us, there is no need for an extra."

He nods but says nothing. At last he gets up. "When do you want to pick up the boy?" She checks the time. "Very soon."

He says, "Look, I'm gonna mush home and change clothes. Meet you downstairs in half an hour."

Nusa nods. "I will be there."

He kisses her lightly and leaves.

She closes the door and looks around at the place. Then clears the table, washes the dishes and stacks them to dry. While changing bed linen she finds her knickers in a heap under the couch and runs a hand over her head, face hot. The tell-tale evidence of last night. She puts clean sheets and a cover on the mattress and closes the couch up. With pillows rearranged the room looks orderly and familiar again. She rushes to make *wudu* and says her prayers, asking forgiveness for her sins. Then, closing the windows, she hurries out, taking her purse along to pay Mrs. Ruiz.

Bill shows up shortly after she gets down to the front door. He's wearing a brown-and-white checked shirt. The short sleeves show off muscular arms and smooth skin. His tan trousers and sandals, along with a straw hat, give him a debonair look. "Ready, *madame?*" He bows.

"*Oui, monsieur.*" She steps out onto the street, walking at his side.

It's fairly early for the Lower East Side. Most of the people they pass along Avenue C are older, or couples with children, either on their way to or from church services. They walk south, on the shaded side of the street, to Mrs. Ruiz's apartment. She's the widow of Nusa's former super, and still lives on the first floor. The couple once had that entire floor, five little rooms, a railroad flat. All their children were raised in that space. Mrs. Ruiz crossed herself when she told Nusa about it. "All my little ones grown now, with families of their own. Professional, all of them have some profession. My middle boy, he go back to Puerto Rico because his wife family and him go into business together." So now she keeps children to add a little income, but mostly to help the local mothers who depend on her for an occasional overnight or in-a-pinch day, week, or sometimes even month-long sittings.

When they arrive one of the Ruiz grandsons is sweeping the front walk. He's going to college and is working in his grandfather's old position because he can get a free room in the unused portion of the old apartment. He throws a bucket of water over the stoop, and it's not pitch-black filthy as would be the case with the super in her building. "Morning," he says, and moves aside to let them enter.

Garlic and olive oil scent the halls; early-morning Sunday cooking for the big family meal later. Children's laughter rings out from behind the door. Nusa recognizes her son's voice, its rhythmic peal of "Hah-hah, hah-hah." Mrs. Ruiz answers her knock and three little faces poke out to greet her. Moussa, who's chasing a boy about his age, stops when he sees her and comes running into her arms.

"*Salaam*, my darling." Nusa kisses his cheek and holds his body against hers. He's getting tall; his long legs make him look gangly. New teeth are growing in nice and straight, and his smile is open and warm. "Mama, you came early," he says, glancing over at the remaining children.

"You wish to stay longer?"

He looks from her to his friends. Before he can answer, Bill greets him. "Hey Moussa, how are you?"

Her son goes over and shakes his hand. "Good day, *monsieur* Bill."

Nusa goes over to Mrs. Ruiz to pay her, then busies herself collecting Moussa's clothes, a container that held his food, and a few toys. Moussa is under clear instructions about eating with people who are not Muslim.

A little girl with sandy hair rushes over. She appears younger than Moussa. "Are you his mama?" she asks in a squeaky voice.

"Yes I am." Nusa turns to face her. The girl needs her hair combed and brushed badly. Clearly mixed-race. Nusa surmises her mother is white and perhaps doesn't know what's best to do about that cloud of hair, so she does nothing. Just lets it be—natural.

The little girl now approaches Bill. "Are you his papa?"

Without hesitation he says, "Almost."

The girl ponders this answer, then in a very grown-up tone says, "Oh, you going to get married soon, right?"

Bill smiles. "Right."

Moussa is standing by listening but doesn't comment. Nusa tells him, "Say goodbye to everyone, darling, so we can leave." He runs down the narrow, winding hall.

Mrs. Ruiz is smiling at all 'her babies' like a proud grandmother. "Thank you very much, Mrs. Ruiz," says Nusa.

The old woman, a knowing sparkle in her eyes, asks, "You have a good time? I hope so. You are a beautiful young woman. Too much study and work. Life is short. Have fun while you can enjoy it. Now, me." She looks down at her swollen feet and rubs an arthritic knee. "When my Pedro and me were your age, hah. Every Saturday night we go to parties, to dance. We were the best dancers. Boleros, everything." She shakes her shoulders and sighs.

Nusa can easily imagine her on the dance floor. But she lowers her eyes, remembering last night—after the party, after the dancing. Alone, with Bill. He says nothing, only smiles at Mrs. Ruiz. A knowing look seems to pass between them and the old woman sighs, nods.

Moussa comes back, followed by another child. "Always, the mother comes late. He likes me but he don't want to play alone with an old lady." Mrs. Ruiz sighs. "Bye-bye, Moussa. I see you next time, okay?" Bending stiffly to the boy, she glances up, locking eyes with Bill and Nusa. "Next time, okay."

Moussa kisses her cheek. "Good bye, *Senora*."

She gives Bill her hand. "Take care. These are my children. Very nice and good."

He understands. "Yes, they're nice and good. I'll take excellent care of them."

A child in the back is crying as they leave.

Moussa skips in and out and around them, avoiding the scattered trash littering the streets. Avenue C is always the second-to-last street cleaned, and the city baskets at the corners are overflowing. New York pigeons and Bowery Street scavengers haven't gotten over this far, yet.

"Mama, can we go to the park for a while?"

Before she can answer, Bill suggests, "I have an idea. Let's take a walk along the river. There's a park there."

Moussa jumps up and down in front of her. "Oh, oh, that's a great idea. Okay, Mama?"

Nusa ignores the inner voice reminding her of the corrections needed on her third chapter before she meets with Prof. Herberts. "That sounds fine. But we must come back early so I can cook, and—" She stops, struck by the sadness in his eyes. "Right. Let's go!"

When they reach their building Nusa runs up to drop off Moussa's bags. Hurrying down again she finds him and Bill playing and laughing. She tries not to say anything else to spoil the boy's happiness as he basks in the glow of male attention.

The laughing clusters of children in the playgrounds of the housing projects, the sun beaming like a fat smile. It all pushes away the foreboding thoughts that often come and keep her from going out, or allowing people to get too close. She almost pulls back when Bill reaches for her hand, then relents. Moussa is clearly so very happy to be outdoors and with them.

There are a few cyclists riding on the path, but for the most part they have the East River walkway to themselves. They walk all the way to the end and back. Bill says, "Let's find a bench in the park. Give the boy a chance to play a little. Besides, after last night, I need a rest."

She notes the teasing in his voice, so she ducks her head as if to admit she's a bit slower, too. "Fine."

They sit. Moussa tries all the slides and climbs the jungle-gym. "Come push me, somebody!"

Bill goes to the swings and Moussa squeals with each push. Nusa thinks about Hamid. How is it he can remain wherever he is without contacting them, all these years? They could be dead for all he knows. Do we mean so little to you that you are not curious about us?

Bill's laughter rouses her from these dark thoughts. To onlookers, they must appear father and son. Funny, he has a daughter that his ex-wife keeps from him. She has a son whose father stays away. And now, she's gone to bed with a man who is not her husband, to whom she is not married. One older and... "Allah, forgive me please," she whispers. "Where is my life heading?"

Later that evening Bill and Moussa entertain each other while she cooks supper. Bill's using the boy to rehearse a new scene. Hollis, one of her floormates, stops by to say he'll be away for a few days. Will she water his plants and feed his cat? He knows Bill; they chat briefly about the possibility of doing a short film together. But now dinner is ready and she worries Bill will miss having his usual glass of wine before and after the meal. She sighs. So many differences. "Yah, Allah, help me," she mutters, and then calls out, "Hear Ye, one and all! Dinner is served."

"Come, young man," says Bill. "Methinks we are summoned to sup."

Moussa giggles loudly. They make a big to-do of coming to the table. Then, remembering, march out the door to the toilet to wash up before filing back inside to sit. "My dearest lady, thou hast o'er taken thyself beyond all boundaries." Oh, how Bill hams it up.

Moussa claps. "My Mama cooks the bestest ever. I love it."

She smiles and decides to ignore grammar for once. His intent warms her heart. "My lord dost honor me," she murmurs. "Pray, I beg, betake thyself of our humble offerings."

After the dishes are washed and put away, the three of them sit in the living room. It's approaching *Mahgrib* and Nusa wants to prepare. She is adding to her son's religious instruction by saying prayers together and helping him memorize *ayats*. His Quranic vocabulary is increasing as a result. "Moussa, it's time for Mahgrib. See, the sun has almost set. We must make *wudu*."

He looks from her to Bill. "Yes, Mama. But what about Uncle? He—"

Nusa interrupts, "Well, Uncle has not made *Shahadah* yet." Deliberately not looking at Bill, still she doesn't want to make him feel left out.

"Oh, but we can teach him. I know lots of *ayats*," Moussa says, looking at Bill and then at her.

Bill seems to feel the shift, but clearly doesn't understand the subtleties. "What is it Nusa?"

She turns to him with lowered eyes. "It's time for the fourth prayer of the day. Moussa wants to know if you're going to join us. I've explained you have not taken *Shahadah*, it's—um." She searches for a translation. "Witness of Islam. Pronouncement of faith, as a Muslim. I mean you have not accepted Islam and so are absolved from prayers."

He looks at her, probably searching for signs of fanaticism. The boy is staring at him. "You're right. I haven't. In fact, I hardly ever pray. I was brought up Christian. Went to church every Sunday and on special days, but..." He shrugs. "I left all of that sometime ago, when I saw the other side of religion. How it can twist a person's thinking and turn God into a vengeful tyrant. My mother always made me feel He was a friend but, well—we can talk about this later." He glances at the boy, who's listening intently. "Moussa, will you do me a favor? Pray for me, please?"

Her son smiles, and gets up to go wash. "No worry. I will make a strong *du'a* for you, Bill."

Nusa puts a small rug on the floor. She covers her head and drapes the shawl around her shoulders. Moussa wears a little white cap. They stand close together, facing the East River. They cup their ears with each hand, fold their hands one across the other at their chests, then bow their heads. Muslims all over the world are doing the same. When they finish and come from Moussa's room, they each greet Bill, "*As-salaamu ala manit-taba al huda.* Peace be upon those who follow the right path."

"And what should I say?"

Moussa tells him. "*Wa alaiykum salaam.*"

Nusa translates, "Peace to you, meaning us."

Bill repeats the phrase, adding, "And I really pray there will be peace to you. To us."

She lowers her head but does not answer.

After she gets Moussa to bed, two hours past the normal time, she comes to join Bill in the living room. He's reading the manuscript of an article she's writing. "This is fascinating. So little is really understood about Islam and African culture. You should send this to a magazine, for publication."

She sits next to him. "My thesis advisor is doing a book on culture around the world. He's going to publish it."

"Hey, congratulations!"

The Lower East Side quiets. Radios are mercifully turned down inside apartments. On Nusa's, Sarah Vaughn's voice sashays into the room. When she comes back to the couch she takes some knitting from a basket at her feet. *Lullaby of Birdland* is syncopated to the click of her needles on the purl side of a sweater for Moussa.

Bill's voice breaks in. "Nusa, I'm leaving this Friday, I think, for Japan. I'll be gone for three weeks."

For a few beats the rhythmic ticking of her needles falters and halts.

"I'm going to do an introductory course in the Noh technique," he explains, "As part of an exchange program."

"But this is wonderful news." She resumes knitting and the tick-tick continues to the armhole of one sleeve.

"Look, I know we're just getting started, but...would you let Mrs. Ruiz keep Moussa a few days while we take a day or so away? I've got friends who have a little cabin upstate. We could go up, say, Tuesday and come back Thursday."

She does not answer just yet, but knits away furiously. The beat is off, and she avoids looking at him. She's thinking about it all: the sin, the boy, what she's feeling. How will Moussa react when this man leaves? He clearly likes Bill, even though she hasn't encouraged it. Surely he still misses his father. Bill has been very attentive, even before. That is, one of the very few black men here who've taken any notice of the boy.

She wants to go away and be with him. This is something she could never have imagined or admitted to a few weeks ago. Wanting a man other than Hamid. But they are not together. He left her, and she divorced him three years ago. The Imam said she'd waited too long, but granted the release, the end of their years together. Nusa trembles, thinking about love and desertion. About abandonment and anger and, most of all, her faith.

Bill continues talking. "Now, I don't have a problem taking Moussa along. That's not it. I'm not even sure if you've said anything about me. About us."

She continues knitting, not looking up. "I am unsure what to say to him, about you and me," she finally admits. Her body sinks lower on the pillows. She feels one tear, then another slide down her cheek.

Never let people see your tears. Her grandmother's words echo in her ears. The old lady, long gone, comes to her at difficult times. Sits on her shoulder, speaks in her ear, both warning and encouraging. Sometimes she appears in a dream; at others in water, or on the faces of older black women she passes on the street, in the subway or on a bus. Nusa shakes her head slightly, breathing deeply, trying to figure a way of wiping the tears without him spotting them.

Bill says in a low, calm voice, "Look at me, Nusa. Don't turn away."

Slowly she lifts her head. Tears are now streaming down her face and there's nothing she can do about it.

He pulls her to him and kisses her mouth, those wet cheeks, and then takes out a handkerchief and dries her face. "Now, tell me. What's all the water about?"

She searches for the right words. "Bill. We, you and me—we're so different." And then she cries more.

He takes her chin and lifts her face so that her eyes are forced to gaze into his. "We are male and female, and both of African parentage."

She shakes her head. "Yes, you are right."

He adds, "I am Christian, older, an actor. I plan to remain in the theater, working as long as I can." She gives him a weak smile. "You are young, Muslim, and finishing graduate school. I have been married and am the father of a daughter I've not seen in close to fifteen years. In fact, she's not a lot younger than you. You've been married and have a son who's almost nine."

She blows her nose. "Yes, all this is true. But…"

"And." He pressed a finger to her lips. "I'm thirty-nine, soon to be forty. How old are you?"

"I am almost twenty-five."

"Is that our problem, then, age and religion?"

She wants to reassure him. "No, it's just that our ways more than our ages are so…"

"Different," he finishes for her. "But I'm not so sure they are. When you get right down to it, language and timing notwithstanding, we're much the same."

She leans against him for strength and feels his fast-beating heart against her back. "In our religion and customs, sex is forbidden outside of marriage. I had a hard time shortly after Hamid left us, getting used to being alone—without him. You see, we met when I was fifteen, and married a year later. I'd not had experience. I mean, with other men." She stops, unable to go on. Explanations are so inadequate, and she is confused. How does one talk with an American man? His African heritage is clear in his face and body. But how to explain Islamic dictates and prohibitions that make it impossible for her to 'hang out' with the young people of the Lower East Side? It has put a stamp on her forehead: DIFFERENT. A social obstacle that now sits in their midst.

His deep voice interrupts her thoughts. "Nusa, I wasn't planning on this." He strokes her head and cheek, sending a current through her. "You, the boy… I won't lie. I've known many women. After a very troubled, unhappy marriage, the last thing I wanted was to get caught up in an emotional tangle." He takes a long breath and falls quiet a moment. "I've dated many, many women. Sometimes for a night. Other times a few weeks or months. But always thinking it was a temporary situation."

He rubs one cheek against hers. "I've made a commitment to my work that I'll never allow anyone to use it to either bash me or inflate me. It's who and what I am." He tilts her face again to look her in the eyes. "Do you understand what I'm saying?"

She shakes her head but looks steadily at him, not daring to speak because it feels like such a dangerous moment. She sees the throb of blood vessels at his temples; notes the few grey hairs that distinguish themselves there. He is strong at this moment. He is fragile in his vulnerability. She nestles closer to encourage him, and his grip tightens.

"To be brutally honest, it's been convenient to have my physical needs met while being free for my art. I can come home, stay up all night reading, rehearse lines or write—and there's no one to interfere. No one to say: Stop and come to bed. Pay attention to me. You've been at it too long."

Nusa understands that pleasure; reading all night, writing from notes jotted down during the day. The quiet of late night has always been special for her. After Moussa has been bathed, in bed and is asleep, with the rest of the night ahead, she claims it. Often reading until the wee hours. If she is writing only the sound of the garbage trucks tells her the time. Sometimes she writes four or five hours straight, until her fingers ache. How very satisfied she feels then. A little voice urges her to respond to him. *Say it! Say it!*

Just as she is about to, Bill kisses her on the neck. "Okay lady, I got to go. If I stay we'll end up in bed. Not that I don't want that. I'm just not sure if Moussa is ready to find me there with his mother yet." He lets go, slowly rising.

Nusa looks up at the body she now knows intimately. Takes his outstretched hands and allows him to pull her to her feet.

"Goodnight, sweetheart, I got lots to do tomorrow," he adds. "The visa hasn't arrived, so I have to stop by the Japanese Consulate. They're very polite, even ceremonial. But whether they understand urgency is another thing. The Arts Abroad Office is keeping our tickets until we meet at the airport." He moves to the door, picking up his bag, setting it next to his shoes. "Then there's a meeting to plot out our participation. And, I do need some sleep."

Nusa stands by, willing her body to be still. Bill continues speaking as he puts on his shoes. He has large but well-shaped feet. Tim's handmade sandals look especially nice on them. Finally he stands, and embraces her again. "Nusa, last night was the best ever."

She trembles, recalling everything.

"I really do respect and hear what you were saying. About customs and things. But I don't want to go away. I want to stay awhile. I don't want you to hide from me."

Those probing eyes beam on her gently, as if penetrating each layer of protection she's built up over the years. His hands cup her face.

"I won't run and hide." She whispers a prayer.

"Good, I'll call around six to see what you want to do for dinner. I'll be over on the Westside, so we could meet at Mother Hubbard's. I know Moussa likes that place."

Yes, Nusa knows it too. "That's fine for me as well. I must go see my advisor. He's bringing someone to meet with regarding my thesis being published. And some future work." She feels his lips lightly but firmly on hers as he whispers "Good night."

She sits listening to Bill's receding footsteps, music from a radio, and a woman's voice calling out in pain; "Jose, enough!"

She inhales, thinking again about the past night. "I'm a divorced woman now." With a sigh she gets up. Does her late-night toilette and says her prayers. She begs forgiveness and prepares the living room, transforming it into her bedroom. How empty it feels now without him. She stretches out in the middle of the bed, trying to concentrate on herself and the next day. She must get Moussa's lunch, take him to Tompkins Square Park for the summer arts camp. Bring the consent slip with her for Tuesday's trip to the Brooklyn Museum. Meet Prof. Herberts with her resume. Her packet is ready with writing samples; the paper on oral literature and snippets of the stories, the first chapter of her thesis for the book Dr. Herberts is doing. "Yah Allah, be with me."

The next day she arrives at Prof. Herberts' office ten minutes early. His secretary looks at her with obvious dislike. Though Nusa suspects racism, she prays for the annoyance she feels toward the woman to dissolve.

"Good morning Mrs. Martinson," she says simply, without an excess of smiles and fawning. "I have an appointment with Prof. Herberts."

The secretary stares at her briefly and then with a dismissive wave indicates a chair. "Good morning," she mutters. "Prof. Herberts is in conference. Please take a seat."

The click-clack of metal on metal. Someone is hammering nails into the wall separating them; the secretary is typing, referring to a document propped on her paper stand. Nusa sits musing on the history of this university. Wondering how Dr. DuBois withstood the racism and class that must've been so blatant at the beginning, in the early 1920's.

'Good morning, my dear! Nice and early, good," Prof. Herberts announces, his rotund body bouncing into the little waiting room. His pleasant face a sharp contrast to Mrs. Martinson's. His grey eyes sparkling and clear. Though when he lectures, in class, on the social justice and class oppression, they darken. Then he vibrates passion, with a certainty of the impending victory of workers uniting and throwing off the fetters of ignorance and separation. His skin radiates joy. His voice trembles as he connects past triumphs of the people in overthrowing tyrants. The Crusades and the Inquisition. The various slave trades. And most especially, The Atlantic Slave Trade. All equal evils, like the bestiality of war. But, he always points out, "Art, intelligence, work and kindness will save humanity, if people can be convinced to work together." All his lectures seem to end with this phrase.

"Come in." He leads the way past Mrs. Martinson who interrupts her rhythmic assault long enough to cast a scowl in their direction. She's an attractive woman, a widow with two grown children. If asked about them, in a voice that carries through the cluster of faculty offices in Liberal Arts and Comparative Studies, she usually announces, "Both doing very well professionally. My son is with a well-respected law firm. My daughter is a pediatric nurse at Women's Hospital. They're always after me to stay home like my friends. But I say hard work never killed anyone."

Nusa isn't too sure of this, recalling female relatives back home who struggle to provide modest shelter and a comfortable life for their children. But she never mentions it because she already knows how the one-way conversation always ends. "Besides, I'm not the stay-home type. Of course, when the kids were young, my husband insisted a mother's place was with her children. So, I stopped teaching. When they were in high school I started here. Now that he's gone, there's nothing to do at home. So I work."

Nusa has heard the story so often she has it memorized. Mrs. Martinson never strays from her script. While it may all be true, it feels like simply another way of letting Nusa know her place. Often when she comes to see Prof. Herberts, Mrs. Martinson makes her wait. During this time, in the guise of making light talk, she asks very personal questions. "Are you married?" At the time, she was. "Where's your husband?" Nusa wondered what this had to do with her enrollment at the university. Sometimes she's asked about the content of her classes with certain faculty, including Dr. Herberts. It made her so uncomfortable she confided in her thesis advisor. He said he'd speak with Mrs. Martinson, but the woman continued her queries. A graduate assistant once said, "Mrs. Martinson is a spy. And very prejudiced. When she doesn't like people she calls them 'Pinkos.'"

But now, with just two weeks until graduation, her thesis bound and signed, Nusa feels more confident of the future. She's had two offers from black colleges in the South. But with Bill in her life, as uncertain as that feels, she isn't ready to leave the city. Not just yet.

A woman enters Prof. Herberts' office, preceded by the administrative assistant. She's tall and thin, her dress as severe as her hairstyle: brown suit and white blouse, no-nonsense low-heeled shoes, plain leather shoulder bag and briefcase, the professional model at her best.

Prof. Herberts stands. "Ah, Dr. Cooper! Come in. Won't you sit down, please?" They shake hands and he turns to Nusa. "This is the young lady of whom I spoke. One of my most outstanding pupils." At this introduction, Mrs. Martinson turns away on the black leather shoes she's told Nusa more than once were custom made, "Because I have such small, delicate feet."

Prof. Herberts' delight is showing, because his German accent is affecting his pronunciation. "Dr. Cooper, may I present Nusa Rasak?"

She extends a hand and Dr. Cooper clasps it firmly. Hazel green eyes pierce her.

They each say, "Good morning," simultaneously and sit.

Dr. Cooper begins. "Prof. Herberts has indeed told me wonderful things about you. He's extremely proud of your ability to work under pressure, to keep to deadlines."

Nusa smiles and nods in appreciation to Herberts and Cooper, but says nothing.

Dr. Cooper adds, "I'm the academic dean of a small but progressive women's college, Chadwick. Some alums are in top positions in leading companies, or in universities here and abroad. We're interested in having you join our faculty because not only of your achievements but because you're African born and fluent in many languages. And because of your interest in the preservation of women's oral literature."

She pauses, and Nusa nods but does not yet comment. "My focus is naturally on gender," Dr. Cooper adds. "I'm extremely interested in your "Tales of My Grandmother's Mother." Such a rich oral tradition that's barely been explored. I hope you'll accept our offer and develop a curriculum of research for our students and courses that look at women, black and white." Dr. Cooper sits back and looks at her expectantly.

Nusa sees clearly the passion of Dr. Cooper. But she does want to do research into oral literature and record and analyze the stories and their meanings. And how will the white students take to her; African, Muslim, dark-skinned, talking about Africa and its peoples around the world. She takes a deep breath to calm herself.

"First, I must thank Dr. Herberts for his concern and guidance. And of course you, Dr. Cooper, for this opportunity. I'm very grateful to be considered. My interest in oral literature is thanks to my grandparents, who told me stories every night. I recalled them in the text as a way of teaching my son his heritage and so he might know his great-grandparents, who died when I was young. It was Prof. Herberts who encouraged me to continue, to expose and remember these tales. My concerns lie with how your students might react to me as an instructor."

Dr. Cooper bends towards her earnestly. "There'll be one semester of preparation and training in methodology and collecting and one in selected reading. You'll create reading lists and organize your materials so the students will be ready for a summer of six to eight weeks of study abroad under your supervision. So you must work closely with them, helping with the shaping of their senior theses. One year you'll do oral literature, the next standard literature. You know; writing, critique, perhaps rhetoric. Your classes will be small. Young women carefully chosen for their academic rigor." She pauses. "Of course you'll be expected to continue your own research and publication. We operate on a two-semester, two-term year. You'll have both terms off from teaching to do your research and papers during these intervals."

Nusa wants to say yes. To shout for joy that she's offered such a position, one that will allow her to do what she wants and provide for her boy. But the school is outside of the city, at least an hour away by train. How will she manage? She doesn't want to move.

What she really means is, what about Bill? Maybe she'll discuss it with him when they meet for dinner. But what will she tell Dr. Cooper right now?

The dean casts a quick look at Prof. Herberts. He's remained quiet during her pitch and does not comment now. She seems sensitive to Nusa's hesitation, though, and smiles. "I know I came off as trying to recruit you on the spot. Obviously this is a big step for you and for Chadwick. We're both stepping onto uncharted roads." She turns to the professor again. "Your confidence has been rightly placed, Dr. Herberts." Her gaze fixes again on Nusa. "You'll need time to think over such a major decision."

Nusa continues to gaze at this confident white woman, clearly on a mission to get an African faculty member for the college. She concentrates on breathing, afraid of making a hasty commitment. "Yes, thank you."

"Do you think you can let me know within two weeks? It's just, I've so wanted to bring in more black women. But the old guard on the Board have resisted the idea. They fear change."

"Yes," Nusa repeats, softly but with more certainty, "Two weeks will be fine. You see, well, this sounds like what I want to do. The intellectual and personal possibilities. But the logistics, travel and time. There is my young son to be considered. He's been in school here for the past three years. If I leave him there, it means hiring someone to get him...I don't know if the class times will work for our current schedule." She appeals to Prof. Herberts with a look but he just smiles.

She stops with a sigh. Maybe this would be a good way to get away from Bill and all the temptation he poses.

Dr. Cooper stands and gathers her things. She opens the briefcase and takes out some papers. "These are employment forms and a brochure on the college, as well as travel information. Before you make your decision, call me. I can arrange a little tour of the campus and town."

Nusa takes the papers and the card pressed into her hand.

"If you have further questions please call my home or office number. Oh, and the salary listed is not the one we're prepared to offer. Ours is a fairly well-endowed school. The students come from wealthy professional families. Our salaries are quite competitive. We're willing and able to pay for the quality of teachers we want." With that, she shakes hands and leaves.

Nusa turns to Prof. Herberts. His kind face is too much to bear. She bows her head and cries softly. Then, drying her eyes, says, "I cannot tell you how much this means. Your trust, the job offer—all of it. I just need to think carefully. My son and I...we have an order in our lives that will be drastically altered. He'll be in fifth grade come September, at a new school. I'd need to find a reliable person to look after him. I need..."

The old professor raises a hand. "My dear, yours is one of the most brilliant minds it's ever been my pleasure to challenge. Take your time. If you don't choose this one there will be other offers. Now, go and have a great day. See you at graduation." He stands and offers a warm smile.

"Good day, sir. And, thank you again." she says as she takes his hand.

She replays the morning's events as she walks along 2nd Avenue, thinking about Dr. Cooper and what she proposed. Passing the diner at the corner of 10th Street, Nusa realizes she hasn't eaten lunch so she enters, takes a seat and orders an egg salad sandwich on pumpernickel. Also a vanilla egg cream. Her usual waiter, Mr. Jacob, beams when he sees her.

"Where's the boy?" he asks.

"He's at day camp."

"Good! You know, I have a customer who runs a camp in Vermont. Maybe I talk to her. You send him there for the summer?"

Nusa smiles and thanks him. She isn't too sure about sending Moussa away from her yet. But she says nothing. After lunch she walks over to Ratner's to buy a treat for her son. It's too early to pick him up so she heads for the apartment to say her prayers. She needs guidance in making the right decision.

It's very hot up in the three rooms. Full sun radiates from the windows facing hers. She draws the curtains to block some of the heat and opens the windows at the top. Moussa's room always seems cooler because it's shaded by the building opposite and the shaft between forces up cool air. When she opens the door a cross breeze rushes in from the dark hallway. She feels comfortable since the former super has been fired. She isn't afraid to keep the door ajar. After washing and making her prayers, she looks around for a pencil and paper. An idea's running around in her head. She sits and writes for half an hour. Then heads out to get her son. Time enough to bring him home, bathe, and change before meeting Bill for dinner.

He's already there when they arrive. Moussa spots him first and runs past the waiter. Bill jumps up and embraces the boy. "*Salaam*, young man."

Moussa smiles. "*Wa alaiykum salaam.*"

Bill leans down and brushes her lips. She isn't accustomed to public shows of affection. She's always thought that not well-bred. But now, in the swirl of new romance, she only blushes, liking the warmth of his body, his face next to hers. "*Salaam.*"

They sit, Moussa in between, and pick up menus. Moussa looks from one to the other, clearly thinking of something mischievous. A Hamid expression paints his face.

"So, did you get all your errands done?" Nusa asks Bill.

He nods. "Everything but the visa. It'll be ready Wednesday. There's been a change in the itinerary. So we leave two days after we'd planned, stopping in Holland first. Meet with another group, stay four days, then on to South Korea for a week."

Moussa interrupts, "Mama, am I allowed to have fried chicken?"

Nusa gives him all her attention. "Well yes, I suppose so. We'll find out what kind of oil they use first."

He nods and continues to study the menu.

"When do you get to Japan?" she asks.

He makes a wry face. "Well, that is the question. It seems the army heard about our trip and they want us to give a few shows on the bases. I was in Korea during the war. A communication specialist."

Nusa stares. There is so much she doesn't know about him.

The waiter comes to take their order. Bill asks, "What do you fry the chicken in?"

A blank look, then vague panic. The young man promises to run back to the kitchen and check. As he scurries away, Moussa observes, "Mama, he looks frightened."

They laugh. The waiter soon returns, looking more composed and knowledgeable. "We use olive oil mixed with corn oil."

Moussa cheers. "Hooray! I'll have fried chicken with spinach and mashed potatoes." He glances quickly at his mother for final approval.

Nusa nods, then blushes as Bill asks, "What'll you have, dear?" She studies the menu closely, as if it's a linguistics text, needing a moment to get her breath to slow down. "I'd like grilled salmon and, um, salad, please."

She listens as Bill gives his order: steak medium well. He starts to ask for a glass of wine, then with a quick glance at Moussa instead asks for two lemonades. She has water with a piece of lemon, no ice.

Afterward, they walk back to the Lower East Side, bodies weighted down by the big dinner. Moussa slips in between, holding Bill's and his mother's hands. Washington Square Park glows under the street and park lights. Benches are full of friends, lovers, young and old, all seeking a cool breeze and social contact. As they pass the fountain Bill dips a hand in the water and splashes Moussa. The boy shrieks and darts his head back, giggling.

Tompkins Square Park is open but not so many people are inside. Police patrol it for pot smokers, search for junkies and winos to lock up. Bill walks them home. Moussa says he has to go to the toilet, "Quickly." Nusa unlocks the door and Bill waits with him. By the time they come inside she's opened all the windows, watching as they shed shoes and sandals.

She knows Moussa wants to have Bill all to himself in his room, to play with his toys. Over the last few years she's gotten him a collection of wooden toys and a train set. A bit costly; second-hand Lionel tracks and three cars. When Moussa got bronchitis two winters ago, Ahmed, a Turkish man she'd met at the mosque, bought the start-up car for him. He said he missed his two sons back home and offered it as a gift at Eid ul Fitr. She'd made a big to-do when Moussa completed his first try at fasting during Ramadan, two consecutive days at the weekend.

In an old dusty shop with faded pictures and broken dolls hanging on the walls, Nusa has become a frequent visitor. Mr. Rosenblum, the owner, is nothing like his name. Tall but with hunched shoulders that make him appear inches shorter. His face is clouded, his eyes sad. Sallow skin loosely covers craggy cheeks and neck. Leopard-spots dot hands and long fingers. After the initial visit with Ahmed, Nusa stops by at intervals to buy additions to the set. She got a two pound net bag of wooden 'people' made in Holland. With these figures Moussa conjures elaborate stories to enact for her.

Now he was showing all of this to Bill, who promises to make a table to lay out the tracks, village and station on. Hollis bought him a puppet when he and Priscilla went to Mexico. James, her other floormate, built a little stage with Moussa's help and he now wants to do a show for them.

"Yes, you may, but remember, day-camp begins at ten in the morning, and it's nine o'clock now. So you need to be in bed by ten." He looks at Bill, who refuses to intervene. "Yes, Mama," he mumbles, clearly not happy.

How similar events can feel! Watching this interaction with Bill is so much like that last week with Hamid, a few years ago. Moussa performs his show, which takes place in California. A mysterious reference point for him, the last known place his father went to live. They applaud at the end as he bows. Then he carefully takes his puppet and places it on the shelf. Bill helps disassemble the Lionel train set.

When all the toys are put away and he's had his bath, Moussa asks to be read to. She and Bill take turns; she reads the Jesse B. Semple stories, then there's a spontaneous offering by Bill. Finally, he allows them to leave his door ajar. "Good night Mama, good night Uncle."

They sit in the living room on pillows, her knees drawn up under her long skirt. She shares the job-offer news with Bill, who listens quietly. "What are you going to do?" he asks.

"I'm not quite sure yet. I'll think and pray for the right way."

He thinks for a moment. "Will this mean you must move?"

It's a question that's been running through her head all day. She avoids his gaze. "I'm not sure about that, either. Dr. Cooper asked me to come up with Moussa. To meet the faculty and see the town. I've never been to Poughkeepsie. Have you?"

He shakes his head. "No, but I've been in that area. We played at one of those rich all-girls colleges, Catholic, I believe. They treated us nice. But then we were only there a few days. It's beautiful and all, but very, very white. I didn't even see a black porter or maid."

She sighs. "I don't think I want to move up there. Moussa is settled here." She pauses, not knowing quite how to voice her feelings. "He's going to weekend classes at the mosque. It will be a big disruption to re-locate." She sighs again.

Bill breaks the silence softly. "And what about us? Because there is an 'us' now." He reaches over to lift her chin and force her to meet his gaze.

She says slowly, "Yes, there is an 'us'. But truthfully, I don't know what to do about it."

His arms are comforting, holding her firmly but not constricting. "Do what you feel in your heart. What your body and mind tell you to do."

Nusa shakes her head. "I—when do you leave?"

"Monday night."

She takes a deep breath. "Would you..." She falters. "I'd like you to come to prayers Friday, if you can. That way you can see a most important part of my life."

Bill stiffens a bit. "You know how I feel about church, religion—any of them."

Nusa pulls back from him, inside, but he seems to feel it. "No, no, don't shut me out. Look, I'll go."

"I'm not asking you to become a Muslim. Just to see and have an experience that may be different from church."

He sighs. "Fine, what do I have to do?"

"Make sure you've bathed. Be prepared to take off your shoes. There are places for you to sit and observe. Afterwards I shall introduce you to the imam. He's from Afghanistan, around your age."

"Hmm, he's old then. Is he married?"

A joke. She relaxes a bit. "Yes, he has a wife and three children, all girls."

Another silence, but it's quiet, easy between them. Bill shifts. "I think I'll go now." But he shows her the need in his eyes, the pressure of his body next to hers.

She has to admit, she wants it too. "I've asked about Wednesday and Mrs. Ruiz said fine. That's my free day. Usually I get Moussa early and we do something. A movie or a bus ride, shopping for a book or toy."

"Two nights, Nusa. Tuesday and Wednesday. Okay?"

At last she nods.

He stands. "Good. Guess I can wait two days more." He looks thoughtful. "You know, Poughkeepsie is less than two hours away by train."

"Dr. Cooper said I can have a three-day week."

At the door she watches him put on his sandals. He pulls her to him for a good-night embrace, then strikes a pose. "Goodnight, fair one. Just think of all the wonders to come." He makes a face and they part, laughing.

Thursday, after she leaves Moussa at day camp, Nusa takes a long walk along the East River. She talks to the trees and asks the angels for help. Her body trembles each time she thinks of her night with Bill. His hands, his tongue, the sound of his voice calling her name. Even now it makes her shiver. The things he shared about his first marriage. She thinks about Hamid; his total absence, his rejection. They could be dead, back home, anywhere in the world or out of it for all he knows. There is no anger anymore, though, just sadness. Before Bill, she still felt angry.

Hamid will never know her body again or hear her love song. He will miss the joy of his son's growth. She walks on until the tennis court comes into view. Checking her watch, she decides to go back, to wash and say her prayers before she has to get Moussa. She'll take him to Essex Street Market because she needs to look at yarn. Time to start winter knitting. If she takes the position at Chadwick, she could get lots of work done in the nine hours a week traveling back and forth.

She breathes a sigh of relief. Yes, she will accept the job. If they're not too bothered by her being African—well, she can try not to mind them being white Americans. "*Yah Allahu,*" she whispers. "Forgive my sins, *Amina Rashada.*"

ANOTHER SATURDAY NIGHT FISH FRY

Around the corner on East 9th Street and Avenue B there's a building that houses a group of black writers—all men. They found their way to the Lower East Side from Harlem, Brooklyn, and points beyond. In the turbulent Sixties they enjoy the relative acceptance of the white artists, musicians, and intellectuals living there; people willing to engage in heavy discussions. They take over park benches and street corners, parties and bars. And so they stay, living in small, cramped apartments with all their equipment; easels, musical instruments, books, makeshift sculpture gardens in cleaned-out backyards which are really just the spaces between buildings at the backs of tenements. Everyone is serious, dedicated to the word and page, writing daily and on into the evening. But late nights find them at Stanley's on East 13th and Avenue B, or other bars along Avenue A. In the back of Stanley's sit a couple tables where the 'real' artists, anarchists, intellectuals hold court. After heated discussions and several rounds of whatever one can afford, the unattached depart with a bed partner drawn from whoever remains in the wee hours. Those in steady relationships have predetermined escorts at the ready.

When economics reach a critical point, these men take employment as waiters, the job favored by actors. They say it helps with memory building. For those with degrees, there's substitute teaching, being shop instructors or music teachers. For those with families, there's the post office. Occasionally, someone actually sells a piece of work or an article or story. The musicians may get a tour, or at least gigs at local clubs. Sometimes even studio work. Lots of them write charts for pitch-deaf singers who can afford personal arrangements. Money, or rather the lack thereof, is a badge of honor. Proof of not having sold out, of being true to one's art. Those who actually have cash, or parents with funds, must pretend to struggle in order to be taken seriously.

Cecelia still isn't sure how she fits into this environment. One of the men living on the third floor is an old friend from Cleveland. She'd never imagined him as a writer. They kind of lost touch after leaving for college. Henry wasn't a boyfriend, just someone familiar from home. When she decided to go to graduate school in New York, her parents were very reluctant to allow her to leave. Her mother is friends with Henry's mom; it's she who put them back in touch. Henry promised to look for a place for her to stay, and it turned out to be in his building.

Her mother and father were glad. "At least he's a man. He'll be able to protect you from those Big City wolves."

Cecelia always smiles when she thinks about their old-fashioned language and ideas. She doesn't need protection from anyone.

She likes the area and all the people. "It sure is different from Cleveland," she tells her mother during the weekly call, and her mother responds, "Mrs. Alice's oldest boy was always a fine young man."

Well, now he's just another black man in New York trying to become a writer. And she, just another black woman going to graduate school for a masters in social work. Very safe, very female. What she's also doing, which no one else knows about, is taking writing classes. She's always kept a journal, writing the occasional poem and or essay. But lately she's started to fantasize about actually becoming a writer. Of course she'll continue the degree as a fallback. In fact, no one's ever seen any of her writings, because she's never shown these scribbles. She just keeps on writing and writing, then putting them into a wicker basket, out of sight.

She was a voracious reader as a child and teenager. At first her parents were glad she was serious about studying, though they'd also wanted her to be a bit more outgoing. But she preferred the worlds of fiction, even the ones she wasn't so fond of. Now her reading list has grown, listing books she's seen in the shops on Broadway and 4th Avenue. It's one of her great pleasures to roam the three or four blocks of old wooden shops filled with millions of books. Dusty, creaky stairs and warped floors, she knows them all well. On payday she always holds back a few dollars for a new acquisition.

One of the best places lies up a long flight of stairs, or a ride on the freight elevator; Universal Books. It's owned by an old man with a heavy German accent, Mr. Weinstein. He's Jewish but not religious. In fact, he claims to be a communist. It's the first time she's ever met one. He talks about class and oppression, and has read almost every book one can think of. She has only to mention an author or quote a phrase, and he'll tell her all she needs to know about the writer, the work, and the value—or lack of it.

One day she hesitantly mentioned, "I would like to write."

"It's a noble desire," he'd said solemnly, though his eyes were dancing. "Writers, whether journalists or novelists, whatever genre. Also artists, painters, musicians. They are the ones who inspire human beings with a mission. And," he said, smiling sadly, "they're usually the first to face the firing squad."

Cecelia always gets the strangest sensation when she talks with him. Or maybe that's just how inspiration feels.

Sometimes she takes time off from syllabus reading, term papers, and such, and goes to Stanley's to have a beer with the little group of male writers. Henry sits in the back, and this gives her entrée to the inner sanctum. Mostly she enjoys listening to the various modes of expression, of passion, and intelligence of the mostly men there. Henry seems well respected. He introduces her as his 'Home Girl from Cleveland.' No one bothers to ask if she does anything beyond school, and she gives out no information. Rather, she listens to Henry make sad situations funny. To him, using irony, to be technical about it.

The man she really likes lives on the fifth floor. At first he too seemed interested. They'd talked on the stairwell, and when she saw him at the bar or ran into him on the street, he'd chat, flashing that sweet, heart-breaking smile. It tickled her soft spot. Made her count the months since she'd last been with a man. So far no one else has stirred her heart. After the disastrous affair with Will she was glad to leave Cleveland and all the sad memories behind. He'd been her first. High school sweethearts; everyone had expected them to marry. But he had different ideas. He'd just stopped: no calls, no visits. And then left town—with another man's wife. Cecelia shudders, remembering.

But now she's living in New York City, eating lasagna, pierogies, and lots of hamburgers with French fries. Not that Fairfax had such limited cuisine; there were even some Hungarians and she ate goulash there, too. But somehow it tastes better, more exotic in New York. So with money from her job at a group home, and what her parents send, she's able to taste new foods, mostly from Eastern Europe. She justifies the extravagance because her schedule is grueling, her work laden with the stress of teenage angst.

Recently she's also become more aware of the things and people around her. The last few months, she's been buying bread and cheese from an elderly Ukrainian couple and their unmarried daughter. The young woman's going to Hunter College. "She wants to be a ladies' doctor," her mother announces. The family's been in America for almost thirty years.

"We come with nothing but my sons Lubomir and Pytor, and my daughter Katya. My Verushka and Tatiana born here," Madam Obchenkov tells Cecelia over and over again, embellishing the story differently each time, as if to commit all possible details to memory lest it be forgot.

Today Cecelia looks around at the clean black and white tiles, the sparkling glass containers and showcase. She wonders who keeps their shop so spotless. She's never seen a maid, or at least a woman she'd assume to be one. There's never even been another black woman in the store when she's there. Buying her food stuffs here makes her feel very cosmopolitan. Cleveland wasn't the backwoods by any stretch, but these kinds of shops were usually in white areas and her mother preferred stores near the house.

Over on St. Marks Place, Cecelia thinks of stopping by the little dress store but decides against it. The bags are heavy and she's tired. Two chapters of reading await her. And she must finish up a paper, "Early Detection of Child Abuse in Religious Households." She walks through the park and crosses Avenue B. Children are dragging at their elders' hands, complaining about having to go home so early. The Social Services Building stands guard across from the park and her building. The strong sense of home is reassuring. In the hall she stops at the wall slots and collects her mail. Three letters, one from her parents—written by her mom, of course—-and one from Madeline Rogers. Or rather, Maddie

Rogers, the last name now decorated with a French accent. And there's one from her aunt in San Francisco.

She trudges up to the top. Along the way various sounds and smells greet her. The man on the second floor is a musician who plays saxophone and piano. Late at night, when she's sometimes restless and goes onto the roof to smoke a joint, she hears him playing. It's so beautiful to sit under the sky with music unspooling below. She forgets how tired or lonely she is—it's just the music—her and the music.

Hey, that's a nice thought, she decides. Maybe I'll write something tonight.

She repeats the phrase aloud so she won't forget before reaching her door. She puts her bags down, fumbles for the keys, and enters. Then rushes back out to the hall toilet. She still hasn't gotten used to going outside her apartment to the toilet but rather likes the bathtub in the kitchen. It's so cozy in the winter to jump right into the warm water and then go off to bed.

Inside her three room apartment she jots down the inspired sentence, adds a bit more, and then puts away the groceries. She opens the windows so early evening breezes can cool her place. Henry's warned her about leaving them open when not at home. "Junkies do all kinds of crazy stuff when their Jones hits. Climb up fire escapes like nothing, steal everything and anything they get their hands on." But now that she's home, and will be up for some time, she opens all the windows and lets the gauze curtains ripple and dance.

She checks behind the stove to see if the little mouse she spotted last week has been caught. A cat would fix his tail, but she doesn't want a pet—too much trouble. Kitty litter and bad smells. "You could put the box in the bathroom or on the fire escape," a voice inside her head argues. Well, she'll give it more thought later.

Just as she begins to wash dishes the telephone rings. She hasn't made many friends yet. There's so little time for fun; it's all work and school, school and work. So the sound makes her a bit anxious. The black phone is insistent, though.

At last she picks up the receiver.

"Hey, CeeCee."

She recognizes the voice. "Hey back, Henry."

"Just called to invite you to a fish fry tomorrow."

"Really?"

"Now, before you say no 'cause you got a paper due and forty chapters to read, it's gonna be right below, on the 5th floor."

"Oh, you mean at Jake's?"

"Yeah. Says he's gonna fry up some fish and, you know, have some folks by, blah blah blah."

Cecelia considers. "What time?"

"Around nine."

Oh, why not? "Sounds good. I'll be there. Thanks, Henry."

"Good," he sings, "'CeeCee Rider'."

"Oh Lord! Hang up the phone. You're a writer, not a singer."

The next night she listens to the growing swell of voices and judges the apartment to be overflowing. She opens her door but no cooking smells rise up the stairwell, so she toys with the idea of waiting a bit longer. But no, she doesn't want to be the last to arrive. Giving her 'Fro another fluff and pat, she goes down one flight to Jake's apartment. Sure enough, the place is packed. The lucky ones, probably the first to arrive, are sunk comfortably into his one couch. A few sit on a window sill. All the windows are open; two fans do their best to keep it cool. But there are just too many bodies. The promised fish-fry is nowhere in sight.

Cecelia checks her watch. It's ten-thirty, over an hour after the party started, and still no food? No one else seems bothered, though. A few dancers move in a tight spot, hot bodies sweating, trying to obey the command, "Do the Watusi!" Black men with white women must be the requirement tonight, because there are very few black women present. Cecelia recognizes some of the men. The women change so often it's difficult to keep track.

Henry greets her with a great show of brotherly love. "Hey Sister Cleveland."

"Hey back, Brother Cleveland."

At that moment Jake comes out of the kitchen and joins them. "Henry, man, I don't know how to cook that fish and my sister can't come." He pouts like a disappointed little boy.

Cecelia feels sorry for him, "Maybe I can help."

Jake jumps to. "Oh Cecelia, would you try?"

She smiles and goes off to the kitchen, where a bowl piled with raw fish sits on a cluttered table. Dishes fill the sink. Jake has the same layout as she, with bathtub acting as drain board. So she attacks the sink first. Next, she washes the fish and looks around for lemons.

A burst of music blasts away her concentration. Jake pokes his head around the partition he'd built. "How's it going, sis?"

"I need some lemons."

"Oh-oh, I don't think I have any."

She shrugs. "That's okay, I have a couple. I'll go get them." She pauses. "On second thought, why don't I take the fish upstairs and fry it, then bring it all down." She has good utensils and knows her space is clean. Looking around, she spots cooking oil. "Bring the oil and that bag of flour." Unopened, so it's probably okay.

On their way upstairs the redhead from New Jersey runs straight into Jake, placing herself between him and Cecelia. Cecelia says nothing but understands what she's doing. Jake is obviously enjoying the attention of all these young and willing pretty girls. Hah!

Jake explains to the redhead, "Sorry, baby, but we're on a mission and can't be stopped. There's fish to fry."

The redhead purses her lips. "Ooh, can we come up with you?" Cecelia notices, as she starts up the stairs again, that they do not ask her. And it's my place, she thinks darkly.

"Yes," says a brunette, rubbing up against Jake. "We want to learn how to make fried fish."

Fortunately Jake hasn't lost all his good sense. "Not now, sweeties. Go back and keep people entertained until we get the fish fried." The girls make a big show of departing, kisses all around, loud smacking sounds and lascivious laughs intended to leave him panting in wild expectation of things to come.

At the top of the stairs Cecelia turns back and fixes a look on all of them, eviscerating the whole bunch with her cut-eye. Quickly they retreat, in step, disappearing back inside his apartment.

Cecelia is all sweated up by the time she finishes the last batch of fish. She looks at her dishes, trying to decide what to use. She'll need at least two platters. Her gaze falls on identical white ones. She takes these down from the shelf and rinses them, then arranges the nicely-browned crisp fish onto the smooth white china. Standing back for a minute, she admires her handiwork. "Oh! I know." Going to the refrigerator, she finds parsley, takes a sprig and tucks pieces all around the fish and, in one corner, slices of lemon. Next she mixes hot sauce in a glass and puts it on the plate.

"Good," she pronounces, about to head back down to the waiting crowd. Then reconsiders: Oh no, CeeCee, you need to wash and change. So she puts the fish in a warm oven and does a quick bath, changes into an African gown with matching head wrap. "The queen of Ghana has arrived," she murmurs at the mirror, applying a little lipstick on full lips and drawing a thin line around her eyes. She stands back to admire herself. "Okay, queen, get them vittles downstairs. It's almost midnight!"

She's very careful going down the stairs in the long gown, but almost has an accident as Henry and a couple silly white girls doing some no-dance jerking bump into her. Jake's in the center of a whole group, mostly blondes, with the redhead wound like a snake around his long torso. One girl towers over the others. But Jake, who actually played basketball for his college and still has an athletic build, is taller than anyone there. He looks over their heads, sees her, and disentangles himself from the clinging vines and honeysuckles.

"Wow, CeeCee, this is great!" He clears a space for the platter. "I'll get the salad and French fries from the kitchen. There's some cheese, too."

So she goes along to get the rest of the feast and slices bread to bring to the table. She sets the cutting board next to the hot fish. Jake takes paper plates from their cellophane wrapping and dumps boxes of plastic forks right onto the table.

Suddenly a white arm, its dark hairs wet with perspiration, darts in to hover over her platter of fish. "What! What're you doing?" She grips the offending limb before it lands.

"Oh God, I'm starving," whines redhead number one, defending her lack of etiquette.

"Then go wash your hands," CeeCee scolds. "You don't just grab food like that when everybody else has to eat as well."

Jake comes over. "Sorry, baby. Black folks got rules about good table manners. Now go on and wash your little hands. We'll be ready soon." The girl slinks off, clearly not pleased to be lectured on her shortcomings.

Jake uses his height and deep baritone to get everyone's attention. "All right folks, sorry for the delay but, here it is. Just line up over here. Take a plate and get your fresh-cooked fish. But first, we got to thank Cecelia for saving the day—or night, as it were."

A cheer rises. People clap and form a line, coming to the table like penitents to the Host. Cecelia portions out the salad and fish, allowing them to take bread at will. The first platter is soon almost empty but everyone has been served. Little groups of eaters all over the rooms are picking the bones for a last morsel, licking their fingers for a final taste. Jake brings out some beer and lemonade. "She made fresh lemonade, too."

A cackle disrupts the mood. "Oh, sorry. It's a private joke," Redhead number two says, with a sneering smile at Cecelia.

"Well then, share it, baby," Jake insists.

"Oh, we were just saying we could understand why Aunt Jemima was so fat. She had to taste everything she made, and that's what did it. I mean, there's fish and then lemonade. You people really have a whole cuisine all to yourselves."

Jake stands awkwardly, mouth half open, innocent face clouded with pain. Cecelia realizes he must be seeing his mother back in her 'white folks' kitchen, the times he went along with his big sister to help her. He doesn't respond, though, just shrugs and sits again. Clearly this is not the response the girl had hoped to provoke, but at least she has enough wisdom to say no more.

"Jake, I'll go up and get the rest of the fish and let folks help themselves to seconds. But I don't have any more lemonade."

"Thanks, CeeCee. Don't know what I would've done without you." He gives her a quick kiss on the cheek.

One of his admirers steps between them. "Come on, Jakey. Let's dance."

Cecelia gets up, goes to the table for her empty platter. All the bread is gone. "Hm, I thought he said there was more," she mutters. In the kitchen she finds two loaves in white wrapping paper. So she'll get the rest of the fish and then cut them up.

After all the fish and bread have been eaten people start to get really loose. Wine, beer, and joints flow hand to hand. Around two A.M. the crowd has thinned quite a bit. Across the small space, the heavy smokers are in a corner by the window. The door is propped open because Jake's floormates are sitting on the floor of his apartment.

Cecelia clears away dishes, then pushes the table against the wall in the kitchen. Tim is in a corner sketching. Pedro's taking pictures of the night revelers. Melvin and Susan are on the floor engaged in serious foreplay. Her face is flushed; Melvin's sweating profusely.

Cecelia takes an empty chair because its previous occupants, Pete and Sophie, are now out on the fire escape sharing a joint. A couple men argue about 'the situation' in Greensboro. Charlie, who's now been designated an Author, believes he can make pronouncements. That people should listen to his every word. Actually his first novel is due out mid-September, thanks to Mary-Mary. No kidding, that's what she said to call her although behind her back most people call her M&M. Her daddy is a big financier, close to the publisher. Everyone says the novel is okay, but that without M&M, it would've gone the way of many-a-good-work: the reject bin.

Cecelia doesn't feel comfortable saying negative things about him or his writing. After all, her stuff is still in the basket. No one's seen it but herself and that doesn't count because she's the writer. But she does think here and there are some wonderful pages.

"Look, I'm not saying they're wrong," Charlie opines with authority. "Just that when something comes out of the blue to challenge a way of thinking, threaten a way of life, and from those you never believed would do so, you get scared and react accordingly."

Isaiah, a young man just up from Mississippi, asks shyly, "So you think the white folks are acting this way because they afraid and…and shocked?"

Charlie casts a quick glance across to a couple men as if for support. But Mel's too involved with Susan's lips and Jake's being fed some peanuts, one by one, by a girl he called 'Miss New Jersey,' since apparently he can't remember her name. Tim is sketching. Cal has gone silent. Jean-Pierre looks far too high to comprehend anything.

Charlie takes the plunge. "What I'm saying is, I understand why those white folks are acting the way they are."

At this, Cal rouses himself. "You do? Good. Explain it to me, then, 'cause I really don't understand setting dogs on women and children."

"No, that's not what I mean."

Isaiah adds, "I can tell you those white women are the worst. When I tried to go to one of their schools, just five minutes from our house, it was the women who threw shoes and bricks at our car. A white woman came up to my mother, spat in her face, and tried to slap me. My mama stood in front of her and said, with that woman's saliva sliding down her face, 'This is a child, and I'm a mother just like you. Now, I'm committed to nonviolence. But if you raise your hand again to my child, God give me strength, I'll knock your lights out.'"

Cecelia applauds. The white women in the room recoil into the waiting arms of black males. A couple white guys make appropriate angry comments. It's the crazy combination of male and female, black and white, that forms the greatest resistance. She doesn't understand why, not yet. But she's been learning, listening carefully, trying to hear the nuances of certain phrases and words.

Jake steers clear of this discussion, maybe because he was born and raised in Brooklyn and never experienced the overt forms of racism practiced in some areas of the country. Josh and Heather, an interracial couple, are very political. Some say they're communists. Heather is heavy with their first child. Cecelia feels if anyone has a chance with this marriage thing, they do. There is only one black couple, Bill and Nusa. She isn't quite sure what's going on there. Nusa has a son and is divorced. Her husband left her a few years ago. Bill's a bit older than she, a fairly successful actor and director. Very attentive to her and she seems to be what Cecelia's mother would call 'very respectful.' Yes, that's it, respect without servility. Maybe that's the way they train them over there, in Africa. But either Jake doesn't know any black women, or they don't want to be with him in this environment. "Well, whatever the reason, they're sure not here," she mutters to herself.

She notes that Cindie, a beautiful black woman from Philadelphia—Charlie's ex—is nursing a bottle of beer. Her sharp eyes are focused on him and Mary-Mary. They seem happy, oblivious to the anger contorting Cindie's face. They laugh over something private, quietly, and the sound spreads across the room, highlighting the silence surrounding a lonely women with a half-empty beer bottle.

Cecelia feels Cindie prepare to launch her attack.

All the men dancing have white partners. The few single women are hovering around Jake, forming a circle, as if he's a maypole, the center of "Ring around the rosy." As in her childhood, when someone was 'It,' surrounded by shouting children.

But there's no happy chorus clapping and singing here; just sweating bodies rubbing against one another, adding to the stifling heat. Cecelia wants to walk over to her and say, "Look, it's all right. I'm alone too."

But before she can get up, Cindie explodes.

She jumps up and shouts, "You black men make me sick. Always sitting around with your arm draped over something like what a cat drug in. Drinking sauterne like you some French bohemian telling me how black women don't understand 'their men.' How they not ready for the intellectual revolution. Hah! A damn insult. Like most a' you'd never be caught in your former domiciles drinking wine, good or bad. Smoking all that dope. You know good black folks don't dig winos and junkies. All that crap about emasculating you, man, that's what happen every time you enter a white woman."

Coming out of nowhere, her words penetrate every inch of space, every nook and corner, each head and heart, black and white. They float out to the fire escape and glide up to the roof. The music stops but no one moves to put on a new forty-five. Caresses halt mid-air. Unfinished sentences sit parked in the middle of Jake's apartment. No one dares speak or move.

Cecelia turns to her and says softly, "Tell them, Cindie. Tell them all." Because she's lonely and only wants to dance, but not one man has asked her. And she knows she's fine. Clean, her dress proper without being prissy. So why won't one of them dance with me? I know all the steps and can move. Those white girls look like they're having fits, jerking about the place.

The room is holding its breath, but Cindie's not finished. The pent-up rage from Charlie's defection, his flaunting M&M in her face, the insults black women have suffered over the centuries, it all wells up in her. She had told Cecelia that his words had cut deep into her, when he left, flinging out in his wake, "She got me a contract. That's what my white woman did for me!" Implying the only good thing Cindie could do for him was to step aside from the path leading to that white woman, and stay the hell away. And now she is staring him and said woman right in the face.

"It's always black women. White men in slavery taking us any time, any way they wanted. Black men doing pretty much the same. White women treating us like dirt. Now, we're s'posed to be free and equal. Equal to what? I got an education. Got a job. I work hard but you know what? A white woman just got hired, not even finished with one degree, and now she my boss and don't even know the job. Asks me to do her work and mine too, making twice my salary. And I got two degrees! Now I'm emasculating and unsophisticated? Hell, no, I'm just an angry black woman, tired of being disrespected by my own men. So you know what? Go start your revolution without this black woman and see how far down the road you get. And this time when they send the dogs after you—don't look to hide in my house." She stood, steadied herself, and left.

White girls shift to watch her well-shaped head and full body stride away. The faint scent of wild roses mingles with all the other smells inhaled by the crowd. She was just here. Now only the fading click of her heels on the stairs remains as testimony of her presence.

Cecelia wants to run out behind her, to embrace her and say, "My dear hurting sister, I don't understand the whole world, but I know some things. One is that you are beautiful." But she doesn't get up; the chair holds her firm. Instead she lifts her head and looks across the room, out towards the fire escape. One by one, the redheads, the blondes and brunettes all lower their gazes. One blonde, a silly girl who giggles all the time, is still wrapped around Jake. Her friend pokes her in the side and she gulps, peeling herself off.

Charlie and M&M release their clinch and walk over to the couch. Squeezing close together, they sit. A couple comes down from the roof. "What's happening?" asks the man. "Why's everyone so quiet?"

"Yeah," mumbles a glassy-eyed woman who looks like a strong wind would knock her down. "Thought you'd closed down the party."

No one speaks for a few moments. Jake changes the tune, playing something mellow. But the smell of cigarette smoke and Tabu still binds them.

Suddenly a heavy older white woman named Leah jumps up. Turns right and left, but no one meets her eyes. At last she sets her beam on Cecelia. "Oh God, now is not the time for you to be jugging with me."

Cecelia steels herself as Leah bounds over. No doubt the woman would've preferred Cindie to spar with, but Cecelia is black and still present, so she'll have to do.

Leah is red-face and trembling. Her chin fuzzed with a growth almost thick as a man's. It suggests she hasn't been with anyone for a while. Cecelia sees this, trying to quickly decide whether Leah is upset over Cindie's outburst or her own lack of man-woman status.

Before she can make up her mind, Leah's up in her face, stabbing the air, the stubby finger dangerously close to Cecelia's nose. Her first inclination is to punch the mess out of her attacker. She steps back to put a little distance between them. The startled room is hushed, tense. Waiting to see who will move first. Cecelia recalls the one other time in her life that she almost had a fist fight. With Hazel, whom she'd hated. Thinking too, Hey, maybe I am a writer. Listen to that alliteration. But this is New York and right now this old sex-starved fool is yapping in her face and she wants to wipe the floor up with her.

Cecelia finds her voice. "First of all, you better get that finger out of my face." She raises a hand and slaps it down.

"Oh," gasps Leah's red-red lipsticked mouth, the sound maybe a cross between shock and fear. "I just can't understand you people. After all, we have so much in common. You've suffered. My people have..." Leah stops mid sentence, maybe because of the look on Cecelia's face.

Cecelia's breathing heavily now. "Know what? I don't want to hear that stuff. Every time black people talk about their problems, you come back with yours. Well, I don't want to hear about how the Jews suffered. I don't want to hear that you know what discrimination's like, because you too are barred from country clubs, or hotels, or swimming pools for real white people. But I know there are Jews, Italians, Irish and other almost-white people who hate black people and have killed, maimed, and taken advantage of them, too. So get out of my face and go back to your corner. I hope you get lucky tonight, Leah. Maybe you'll be happier tomorrow."

The woman sputters as the words hit between her eyes. She casts a furtive glance around the room. A cute boy just up from the South, the one she's been trying to talk up, is silently watching. No one moves. No one gives any indication of sympathy for Leah. The white women won't look at her. The black men shift about uncomfortably; this show is more than they bargained for. The food was great and Cecelia did a fantastic job. They all like good debates on controversial topics, sprinkled with jargon and ideology. But this is going too far.

"I was attempting to intervene." Leah steps back, smirking. "I'm only trying to speak with you in a mature, adult fashion."

"Look Leah, don't give me that patronizing B.S. Let's put it all out in the open. What Cindie said is true. The black men here are into white women and art, in that order. To justify their choices, they put black women down." Although she didn't turn to face him, Cecelia was speaking to Jake and most of the other men in the room.

Leah touches a mezuzah on a chain around her neck. It hangs down into the heavy valley between her breasts. "I'm sorry if what I said offended you. It's just, I see things from a *class* perspective. Race is a convenience the ruling class uses to keep us apart." She pulls at her dingy Mexican wedding dress, obviously bought years ago when she was wilder, younger, much thinner. And, so Cecelia has heard, the mistress of a great artist. A passionate lover who'd painted her endlessly; in the nude, wearing only a Fedora, poses of her from the shoulders up. But that has been a long time ago.

Cecelia feels the need to explain how a young black woman feels. "Look, I'm just saying it's curious that in this country when acid is poured in a swimming pool to keep black kids from being in the water with white kids, that's not seen as a problem. They all just want to cool off, to swim. Just like the Deep South, Cleveland has its racism, as does New York. So it makes me suspicious when…" She pauses to sweep an arm around the room. "…all of you date, dance, and live with white women only. And then, in the midst of mostly white people," she turns now to look at the men, "you put down black women."

None of the men look directly at her, nor does anyone answer.

"What's your name?" She turns to a white couple nearby.

"I'm Steve, and this is Margo."

Cecelia smiles at them. "When you're discussing issues, I hear you speak about oppression. But I don't hear you criticize white women for being teachers of their white sons, infusing them with superiority and a sense of whiteness."

Steve's face reddens a little at having the spotlight turned on him, but ploughs on. "Well, uh, I happen to believe that if we could address the class issues and stop the ruling classes from oppressing workers and those they consider as lesser, racism would no longer exist. So yes, I do criticize white women. But not all should be condemned. Nor should all black women be characterized as not understanding, and – and the other things you mentioned. A lack of opportunities, education and exposure creates most problems for all of us."

Cecelia nods. There was truth in what he said. She turns to Charlie. "Last week you read a poem, a tribute to your sister. Remember?"

He reluctantly nods.

"An hour or so later you denounced that very sister and all black women, saying we are not supportive of black men. That we insist on them having a steady income, to provide security for the family. But that white women understand the life of an artist is not easy. They have patience and are willing to sacrifice for the sake of their men."

She turns back to Leah. "Perhaps it's a throwback to slavery and Jim Crow. But black women need to feel safe, that their children are protected. You make us sound like a pack of reactionaries. Cal, you said we weren't ready for the revolution. Hank, you said, with your arms around some white chick, that you were tired of the smell of black women. Sick of Dixie Peach spots on your shirts."

Hank sputters on a swallow of wine. His jaws clench, so she knows he's furious. That if they were in a different place, he'd probably cuss her out.

The men she hasn't named yet either sink lower in their seats or duck behind the women close to them.

Henry speaks up. "Aw, CeeCee girl, we just having fun. It don't mean a thing. Away from home, from our parents and we doing all those naughty things they told us not to do. You know we all respect you. I mean, come on, you're my home girl. We both from Cleveland. Both got parents who sent us to college and that's how we got here."

She gives him a hard look. At least he has the decency to lower his eyes. She resents him using a pet name in front of all these people she doesn't really know. It's best not to answer, she thinks.

Leah butts in. "CeeCee, I..."

She cuts a sharp eye at Henry. He opens and then closes his mouth.

"My name is Cecelia Marie Hawthorne," she tells Leah.

"Oh, he said CeeCee, and I thought... I mean, it sounded so cute and friendly." She stops when she glances at Cecelia's face. "I'm sure these men don't mean anything. Some of them call me 'fat' and 'baby snatcher' but I don't let that bother me. You're too sensitive. Like Henry says, life is short. We just like to enjoy ourselves. A little sex, a good M.J from time to time. Music, books, stimulating conversation with friends." She shrugs fat shoulders, upper arms sagging under the gauzy sleeves of her dress. "All I want is to have fun with friends." Leah's hungry eyes seek out Isaiah, but he's no longer sitting there across the room.

Jake eases over and kisses Cecelia's cheek. "I want to thank you again for saving this evening. That fish was a gas."

Bill gets up, and then Nusa. They applaud and give her big smiles. A few of the other black men clap but, aside from Bill and Nusa's thanks, Cecelia is unmoved by the show of appreciation.

Jake glides over and puts on a record. Sonny Rollins. Music again blows all around and through them. Pedro takes Josefina's hand. They plan to get married someday, although they've been together for a few years. She loves his photography.

Heather and Josh cling to each other. She places his hand on her belly. A smile lightens his face; Josh leans over and kisses her tenderly. It's done quickly, discreetly, an intimate moment that makes Cecelia feel like a voyeur, an intruder for noticing. She has a warm place in her heart for them; they actually care for each other. They're recently married. Heather's parents sent them a sizeable check but no invitation home. Josh has just gotten a position at CUNY in the English Department, the first of African descent to be hired as faculty at his alma mater. Heather is still a legal secretary at a prominent law firm. They're currently looking for a larger apartment. Their three rooms will not be big enough when the child arrives.

Cecelia waits but no one asks her to dance. A few come over to say pleasantries; nothing really. Leah is in the corner again working Isaiah, but he's leaning away. Jake and his harem are dancing around the maypole again, giggling and kissing. Pedro and Josefina are on their way out. She picks up her big white platters and catches up with them at the door.

"Hey, CeeCee! You leaving?" Henry calls out.

"Yes," she says, and keeps on walking.

"I'll call you later. Maybe we'll take in a movie or something."

She doesn't look back, just says over one shoulder, "Sure. Good night."

Jake shouts, "Thanks again, CeeCee."

"Oh God," she moans. "Now everyone's going to use that stupid name."

Back upstairs in the little apartment she slips off her shoes and pads around barefoot. "Now I need to wash all that stuff and put it away."

First she makes elaborate preparations: a candle, some bath salts, her special Shea butter soap. After a complete submerging under the cool water, she steps out of the tub and wraps up in a thick towel. Winds another around her head, then goes to the window by the fire escape. She looks down but there's no one sitting below. Music and voices still drift out of Jake's apartment. She lights up a joint and inhales deeply. After a few minutes she tamps it out in a little ashtray and sits there, quiet. An idea is brewing. She imagines writing a play to recap the evening's events. "Writing is a noble passion," Mr. Weinstein said. Except she doesn't yet know how to make noble what she went through back in Jake's apartment. Still…

Maybe it could be produced at Karamu house. Her parents and their friends would come. They'd be shocked by the language. 'Oh, Mrs. Hawthorne, don't get upset. That's just the way the younger generation is these days." Of course, she'll keep out any mention of marijuana. They'd never understand that.

Yawning, she crawls back inside, fits the screen back in the window, blows out the candle. It's hot but not unbearable and so she doesn't turn on the fan. The bedroom is cooler, and the street light blocked by the close wall of the next building. Her textbooks on the pine desk sit closed, a crooked little tower accusing her. She turns her back and gets in bed.

The next day she shuts off the alarm but remains in bed, the light cotton night gown is sticking to her. A few hours later the sun, noisy birds, and a radio blasting the latest Tito Puente hit force her eyes open again. She stretches, groping over the night table next to the bed for her tablet and pen. The idea of a play has blossomed into a title, even a list of characters.

"A Night at Jake's," she whispers.

No, that's no good. Don't use his name. Be more creative. Mysterious.

She tries to come up with something smart. More witty. How do those men do it? She thinks of all the snappy titles she's seen, the ones that tease and conjure up images.

She chews on the pen. "I've got to come up with something better, more hip." She sits still for a moment, and at last it hits her.

"A Fish to Fry."

Yes, that's it. Now for the characters: Mr. Eisenstein: a white man, age fifty, tall and slim. Oh, and he wears thick glasses. Like a combination of her thesis adviser and the owner of her favored bookstore. Then there's Malachi, the son. That's so nondescript. Oh, but she loves the sophisticated sound of that word! "Well, I'll come back to him later." And then Neil, Diana, and Laura, all white and about the same age, in their twenties. Jerome and Theo will be black. Jessie is the only black woman in the cast. And…and…her head feels light, as if it's spinning.

"Aw, it's too early for this." She puts the pad down and gets out of bed.

In the midst of breakfast the phone rings. "Hello? Oh, hello Henry. What? A reading. Hmm, I don't know. I've got so much reading to do. Oh, stop that!"

She laughs as Henry teases her by so accurately saying these lines along with her.

"Okay, when and what time? Saturday at seven, good, I'll be there. But I'm telling you now, I have to leave by nine. Okay, nine-thirty. Fine...bye."

During the week following the fish fry, Cecelia stops by Mzuri barber shop for a trim, shampoo and treatment for her 'Fro. She'd put out two fiery fights between a new girl and an older one at The Group Home. Coleen, a big-boned Irish girl, and May Rose, small and black, had gotten into it. The day counselor reported May Rose as a troublemaker and put her on restriction. Coleen was made to apologize for hitting someone so much smaller, then put on restriction for racist language and threats. Despite the disparity in size and whoever 'started it,' May Rose had apparently beaten Coleen's white butt.

During the long debate over Cecelia's report, two white colleagues were shocked—shocked!—that she'd created such a false racial spin. She and the evening worker spent an hour trying to make the two women see how they were taking sides. But the head refused to have any of the other young residents speak, because it would set the black girls against the white girls. Cecelia had argued, "But Coleen's twice the size of May Rose. And she's been overheard making threats, by staff." Though it was true that several residents had also witnessed her threatening Coleen. Anyhow, getting it all on record was important in case Coleen tried another attack. She got them to lift the restrictions on May Rose but made her apologize to Coleen, to make their punishments equal.

She'd had both girls in session for two hours, draining her last ounce of energy. So now she could only exhale and say, "Thank God for the weekend!"

Stepping into Ratner's, she helps herself to butter-rich pastries; apple turnovers, croissants, and a newly-discovered delight, Linzer tortes; one apricot and one raspberry. She already feels rewarded, her bags bulging with the pastries, plus cheese and a good Beaujolais she can hardly wait to get into. As she adjusts the bags to distribute the weight, she sees Isaiah crossing Avenue B but doesn't call out to him. She wants to get upstairs, drop her heavy purchases, chill the wine a bit, take a bath, and then eat, in that order.

At home, on her second glass of wine, Cecelia begins to feel relaxed. Contented. A wild idea pops into her mind: Suppose I finally meet a man and he wants to stay over—will I be able to give up this peace, quiet moments like this? Then she snorts at her own fantasy. Well, girl, don't fret. From the looks of things you have nothing to worry about. The men down here are not thinking about you.

Finally, she gets up, puts the wine in the refrigerator and goes to her desk. The need to write feels overpowering. She wants to say something to those women counselors and to Coleen and May Rose that would inspire them to respect each other and themselves.

The pad and pencil stare up, daring her to try. Outside the noise of the streets fades, as she squirms in her chair, muttering, "Mr. Weinstein, are you sure about my writing? I mean, if I really have a voice, well, where is it?"

Cecelia sighs in frustration, gets up, shuts off the light, opens the window to sit on the fire escape. She looks around at the back windows of other buildings. Voices blend below. Occasionally a word or two rises clearly over the din: *"Mira, niña!"*

This world continues to fascinate her. In Cleveland, she lived in the comfortable house of her parents. Here, she inhabits a tiny apartment in an old tenement building with the toilet in the hall, the bathtub in the kitchen. Surrounded by Spanish-speaking people who look like her but say they are not black. Two white guys seem to be chasing her. All the black men are chasing white women. No, take that back. Two or three are with black women. Anyhow, there aren't many black women in the immediate area. The ones she knows are alone, divorced, or in strange relationships with black men who come to them between affairs with the preferred blondes.

A white jazz musician from Canada is dating an African woman. All the brothers are outraged that a 'sister from the Motherland' is with him. Yet none of them are going to date her! And then there's Bill. She thinks something's going to happen with him and that sister on Avenue C and 10th Street. Nusa has a little boy. Henry said he'd asked her out once, but she said in her culture when a Muslim woman is divorced it is such a big shame, she couldn't just date the way American women do. "Besides I must finish my PhD, and work, and take care of my son." And yet now...

Cecelia closes her eyes and sighs, imagining herself in cap and gown, graduating with a PhD. "Girl, you haven't even finished your M.A. yet," she scolds herself. Speaking of which, she'd better get to that paper, and read those chapters, before wandering off too far in Dreamland. But it's so nice out here on the fire escape. No one to see or bother her. She leans against the window and dreams. Oh, what the hell. Maybe she'll go back inside and try again. After all, writing is a noble idea.

THE END

About the Author

Rashidah Ismaili is an internationally-known poet, dramatist, and nonfiction writer. Her poetry collections include *Cantata for Jimmy* (2004) and *Missing in Action and Presumed Dead* (1992). Ismaili coedited the anthology *Womanrise* (1978). Her work is included in *The Heinemann Book of African Women's Poetry* (1995). A reading of her play *Rice Keepers* was staged in 2006 at the American Museum. She conducts soirees at her Harlem apartment, Salon d'Afrique, and has taught or presented at St. Peter's College, Rutgers University, Hunter College, Pratt Institute, and Wilkes University in African, African American and African Caribbean Literature and Creative Writing. Ismaili's awards include the Puffin Travel Award, PEN, Dramatist League, Kennedy Center for the Arts, STARS, Miami International Book Fair, Zimbabwe International Book Fair, National Association of Negro Business and Professional Women's Club, Inc., and the Sojourner Truth Meritorious Award.

Northampton House Press

Northampton House LLC publishes carefully selected fiction, as well as lifestyle nonfiction, memoir, and poetry. Our logo represents the muse Polyhymnia. Our mission is to discover great new writers and give them a chance to springboard into fame. Our watchword is quality, not quantity. Watch the Northampton House list at www.northampton-house.com, or Like us on Facebook – "Northampton House Press" – to discover more innovative works from brilliant new writers.

Made in the USA
Middletown, DE
19 March 2015